B-MORE CAREFUL PREQUEL

This is a work of fiction. Names, characters, places, and incidents either are the product of the author's imagination or are used fictitiously. Any resemblance to actual persons, living or dead, events, or locales is entirely coincidental.

B-more Careful Prequel

Published by Shannon Holmes Media
shannonholmesmedia@gmail.com

Facebook : Shannon Holmes
Instagram : @shannonholmesmedia

Published 2019
First edition April 2019
Printed in the United States of America

ISBN 978-0-9814978-9-1

B-MORE CAREFUL PREQUEL

SHANNON HOLMES

ACKNOWLEDGEMENTS

This book is dedicated to the loving memory of

Hesikiah Gidron
Chris Moultrie
Maggie L. Hickson-James
Margaret McGee

Rest In Peace Uncle John Lee Holmes Aunt Jessie Bell Hemmans, Roxanne Chestnut, Brion Sawyer, Jules Jackson Jr aka Half Pint, Dave McGeechi, Mark Coates Ronald Simmons 'aka Rose Gold' Edenwald Projects finest, Ronald Carol Jr. Miss Mary Baker Clemmons, Ms Dianne Lewis, Barbara Eberheart, Audain Williams Vernon Haynes, Doc LaRock, Pam Coleman, Kim Hop , Mildred Dupuy,

RIP Bernard 'Hardest Nard' Tyler, Pretty Black.

RIP HOWARD RICE Derrick Rivers Left hand TY

Special thanks to Roberta James & Frida Hickson

My editor Antrina Richardson

My Daughters Laila & Malaika Holmes

Robert 'Boogaloo' Smoot If it wasn't for you I wouldn't have ever come to Baltimore thus there wouldn't be a B-more Careful. Well at least not written by me.

Lionel "Black Caesar' Cook I never had to question your allegiance or loyalty to me. You were my brother when I had no brothers and I got two brothers.

Franklyn Greenaway you are my brother from another mother. Whenever we see each other it's always love.

Lamont 'Go' Nelson Thanks for everything and I wish you well on your debut novel Kayla.

Shout outs to Darrell and Samantha Greene, Kim and Barry Williams.

Shout out to the Barber Factory, Nestor Lebron & Bernard Rosario, Ricky and Kenny thanks for always holding me down.

Shout outs to Curly Bennett aka Moe dollar, Tina Dupuy, Jerome 'Mac' Mcfadden, Gerard 'Shakim' Emptage,

Cousin Ideania Henderson, BO Collin Watson, Godson Mekhii Watson Floyd 'Pretty Boy' Chenault, Madison Jordan Hill God daughter, Latasha Phillip, My friend to the end Julie Nin, Shelly Brock, Rob Wise, Ronald Boardley, Rodney Mcfadden, Everett 'Evie' Gatling, Juan 'sukkafree_beast' Vaquez, Craig & Wayne Betterson Dawn Montouth, Olga Davis, May Simmons, Miss Priscilla Layer-thanks for always seeing the good in me even when I was doing the wrong thing. Jamia & Samantha Kinnard, Tonya Larry, Toni Johnson, Trisma Layer, Sissy Layer, Bernadean McArthur Larry 'Dunk' Deshields, Mark Deshields, Robert Coleman

Free my guys, David Shuler jr. Shaquan Houston, Doren 'Lil Q' Gaines, Hassan Fitts.

CHAPTER 1

The ambulance darted in and out of traffic, racing through the streets of Baltimore. Bright flashing red lights doused everything in its path, cars, trees, buildings and pedestrians, with the color red. Accompanying the frantic display of lights was a loud, ear-piercing siren that invaded the thin night air. The frantic display of lights alerted anyone within earshot that there was a medical emergency, and to please get out of the way.

Behind the wheel of the ambulance was a young, clean-cut, white male named Brett Anderson. The rush of adrenaline that coursed through his veins, from driving at this high rate of speed caused the Caucasian paramedic to grip the steering wheel so tightly until there was a slight discoloration in his knuckles. He ran every red light and stop sign in route to his destination; maneuvering the large vehicle with the ease that only comes from years of experience. Somehow as an ambulance driver, he had always seemed to find the correct balance of driving recklessly and safely.

Nevertheless, he knew that this was a matter of urgency, one of the highest medical emergencies that he'd dealt with all year. His skillful yet reckless driving reflected that. He knew time was of the essence. Every passing second was crucial. The high speed at which he traveled was a grim indicator that the potential for loss of life was high. Still, if he could help it, this patient wouldn't be Dead on Arrival.

Countless times he had made trips like this to a multitude of hospitals from different neighborhoods in Baltimore city, wherever the need to transport severely injured victims or patients had arisen. He transported people from car accidents, house fires and violent crime scenes. Every call that he responded to was almost always critical in nature. The driver understood that his current trip was always the most important one. He understood that his aggressive driving could possibly save someone's life.

At the moment, the patient's poor condition conveyed the seriousness and the urgency of the situation.

As the paramedic gunned the engine and raced down Eutaw Street toward the emergency room at the University of Maryland Medical Center, everything became a blur. It was as if everything was at a standstill except his vehicle.

Other automobiles moved out of the way, pulling over, allowing him to pass. Those that didn't, he sped around them, weaving in and out of the traffic lanes.

At these high speeds, the driver ceased being able to make out the makes or models of cars, or even see pedestrian faces as he blew past. Instead he was focused on one thing, and one thing only, getting his patient the medical treatment she so desperately needed. The young lady was already on basic life support.

While concentrating on the road, he couldn't help but think of the patient in his ambulance that his partner worked on feverishly, and what terrible condition they had found her in. She was badly beaten and lying in a pool of her own blood when her body was discovered in a downtown hotel.

"Hold on baby," the female paramedic mused as she continued to monitor the patient's vital signs. Her pulse was weak, but in this battered condition, she was fortunate to have one at all. Her vital signs teetered on life and death.

Although she had no previous connection with this stranger, the paramedic was sympathetic toward her grave situation. Her emotional support didn't just stem from them both being of the same race, African American. It was deeper than just that. It was a maternal instinct the paramedic felt toward her and the condition that she was in.

The middle-aged paramedic had a daughter of her own around the patient's age. Maybe, just maybe, this could have been her child. In spite of the fact that this wasn't her own flesh and blood, it was still somebody's daughter; so she was going to care for this young lady to the best of her ability.

In her fifteen years on the job, Pamela Jones struggled with the emotional toll of being a first responder. In her line of work it was hard to cope with the trauma she witnessed on a daily basis, as she watched life and death play out right before her eyes.

Day in and day out, the pressure was on her to perform life saving techniques under some of the most pressure packed situations. She suffered in silence, finding no one, outside of her co-workers, who could identify with the atrocities she had seen, while dealing with every medical condition known to man; heart attacks, strokes and drug overdoses. She also witnessed the aftermath of fatal car crashes and the carnage of murder. On a lower level, she also had to deal with trauma victims, gunshot wounds and victims of stabbings and domestic violence. It never ceased to amaze her what human beings would do to themselves and others.

Years on the job had done nothing to insulate her from the catastrophes she witnessed. Somehow, she had learned to emotionally distance herself from her job.

However, it was when tragedies or accidents afflicted the young that it bothered her the most. She hated to see young lives cut short due to negligence or a violent malicious act.

Currently, she was sick to her stomach. Never in her entire life, on or off the job, had she seen anyone this badly beaten, male or female. That's what disturbed her most about this incident. The paramedic couldn't help but feel like the world had failed this patient in many ways. Least of which it failed to protect her.

I wonder what happened to her, she thought.

Usually, Pam suspected a husband, boyfriend or an ex of this type of brutality. In her mind, this case was no different. Only someone that this young lady was intimately involved with could produce such rage to beat her within inches of her life. Whoever did it really did a number on her, the paramedic concluded.

Why? she wondered.

This badly beaten victim gave new meaning to blunt force trauma. Her face was swollen twice its normal size. There was a large cut on her scalp, trickles of blood leaked from her nose and mouth. The welt marks on various parts on her body, back, chest, arms and buttocks, testified to the severity of the physical attack.

Everyone who had laid eyes on her couldn't help but wonder what kind of animal or psychopath would do this to another human being, let alone a woman. Looking at the injuries inflicted on her patient, she felt justified in labeling the perpetrator by any name she could think of, other than a child of god.

The paramedic wasn't an overly religious woman, yet every time she looked down at her patient, she felt compelled to say a silent prayer.

Lord have Mercy, she thought. *Please don't let this child die. Not like this. Not tonight . Not on my watch!*

Pray as she might, every time she laid eyes on her, the paramedic couldn't help but wince. Netta looked that bad. She had serious doubts about her survival rate in this condition.

"Pamela, how's everything back there?" her partner shouted through the glass partition. "How's the patient holding up?"

The situation looked grim, but the paramedic tried her best to be optimistic, shouting back to him some words of encouragement.

"The patient is holding up just fine. She's one tough cookie, but she'll be even better once we get there," she replied optimistically.

These two knew each other like a book after working together for the last six years. They had built a rapport that extended off the job. They had become trusting friends who truly cared about each other's well-being.

Pam's message to her partner was coded. Brett immediately knew exactly what that meant, *Hurry the hell up*. He gunned the engine even harder, desperate to win his race against time.

In an emergency situation like this, it seemed as if the ambulance was moving slowly, although in real time it was moving at break neck speed. For the paramedic tending to her patient, it felt like it was taking an eternity to reach the safe haven of the hospital.

After checking on the IV in Netta's arm, Pam continued to care for the patient by placing an oxygen mask over her mouth, while simultaneously keeping track of her pulse. The paramedic was sure that she had done everything in her power to stabilize the patient until they arrived at the hospital, where a trauma unit team awaited their arrival.

At best, all they could do now was try to keep the patient's condition stabilized. The paramedic hoped things didn't take a turn for the worst before they reached their destination. Yet, that was wishful thinking to say the least. Netta was severely injured. Anything could happen on the way to the hospital. There was always a chance that she could lose her life. The journey to the hospital was unpredictable, even to a seasoned medical professional such as herself.

Helplessly, Netta looked on, her swollen eyelids staring up at the bright lights inside the ambulance. Pain had consumed her. Tears trickled down her cheeks. It was the first time she had cried from physical pain since she was a kid. Physically, she was in a bad way. Her aura of invincibility was shattered. Netta, the boss bitch of the Pussy Pound clique, was now just another victim of the streets of Baltimore, fighting for her life.

Subconsciously, she began to replay the events that led to her being a passenger in the ambulance. Netta even envisioned her assailant, Black, as he administered the savage beating on her. She felt every blow as he unleashed all his rage and fury on her.

Netta's head was spinning. Her body was swimming in a current of pain. Submerged in the darkness of the hotel room, she never saw the first punch coming. Black, her ex-boyfriend recently released from prison, had ambushed her just as she exited the bathroom and prepared to go home. She knew it was a bad idea to come here with him, especially after what she had done to him, but she felt like she had no other choice.

Although he hadn't forced her or kidnapped her, Netta knew it was come willingly or die. Right there on the spot. She knew Black was a killer many times over. She also knew he wasn't the type to take no for an answer. Especially when she owed him. And especially when she stole from him.

Black savagely pummeled her with punch after punch as she came crashing down on the floor. He straddled her and continued to pound every part of her body with blow after blow, until Netta blacked out from the beating. Another powerful blow from his fists would only serve to bring her back around again.

His steady stream of punches put a quick end to any feeble defense Netta managed to mount. She covered her head only to be beaten in her body. With his bare hands, Black injured her in countless places. Still, it wasn't enough. He wasn't satisfied. Now that vengeance was his, he wanted more. Nothing short of her death would make him happy. This was a day he had longed for while he was in prison.

Black grabbed a handful of her hair and dragged Netta to her feet. He cocked back his fist and cold cocked her over and over again, for good measure. He watched as she crumpled to the floor, blood oozing from her mouth and nose. He stood over her limp body, verbally chastising Netta.

"Bitch, you dead! I'll teach you about tryin' to play me, yo," Black growled while delivering bone-jarring kick after kick to his fallen victim's rib cage. Quickly Netta felt the agonizing pain of bones breaking. As she lay there withering in pain, too badly injured to make an escape attempt, Black prepared himself for the second phase of his attack.

Going into the hotel closet, he retrieved a wire hanger. Black quickly dismantled it and then doubled it, fashioning it into some sort of makeshift weapon.

"Since you wanna be a hoe, I'ma beat you like the hooker you is, yo," Black threatened. "When I'm finished with you, yo...They gonna have to give you a closed casket funeral bitch. Nobody steals from Black and lives!"

Menacingly he stood over Netta. He brought the hanger high over his head, then brought it down hard on her back. Simultaneously, Netta let out a blood-curdling scream. Her screams for mercy only excited him. He repeatedly lashed her until he drew blood. Black beat her unmercifully. He blacked out while dispensing his brand of street justice.

In the back of the ambulance, her recollection of the attack shook Netta to the core. Although she was restrained to the stretcher, Netta began to go into a series of violent convulsions. This caused the paramedic to spring into action.

She tightened the straps on the stretcher so Netta couldn't flail her limbs, thus further injuring herself.

"Calm down baby, everything is going to be all right; we almost there," the paramedic told her, while gently rubbing her forehead.

Softly she spoke to Netta as she waited for the convulsions to subside. Once Netta was in a more stable condition, the paramedic began to look through her personal property that the police had handed over to her. She was curious about the patient's name. The paramedic wanted to be able to check up on her after they dropped her off at the hospital emergency room. She really cared if Netta lived or died. Already she was deeply vetted in Netta's well-being.

"Shanetta Jackson, huh," she said silently as she looked at the Maryland driver's license.

The photo caused the paramedic to do a double take. She looked back and forth at her patient strapped to the stretcher, and the driver's license. She soon realized just how unrecognizable the woman really was. Under normal conditions, she could tell that the young lady was a very attractive dark skin sister. Nothing like the grotesque figure she was currently staring at.

"Shanetta, hold on baby. You're going to make it. You hear me?" the paramedic assured her, while speaking the words of life into existence.

Moved by her own words, the paramedic gently squeezed her hand, like a concerned parent. To her surprise, Netta faintly squeezed her hand in return, applying the minimum amount of pressure. It wasn't much of a response, but a response was a response.

Her reaction bought a smile to the woman's face. In a show of emotion, tears welled up in his her eyes as Netta began to show signs of life for the first time since they found her.

Through swollen eyelids, Netta couldn't quite make out her caretaker's facial features, but she sensed the presence of a loving female paramedic. Barely able to see, the image was dark and shadowy. However, it wasn't anything for her to fear. It wasn't like the evil presence she had encountered in the hotel. She knew this person wouldn't do her any harm.

However, Netta was in so much agonizing pain she began to drift in and out of consciousness. Her life began to flash before her eyes. She looked back on recent and distant memories, the most vivid ones were tragic. All the negative images seemed to flood her mind. Like the brutal murder of her elderly caretaker and grandmother figure, Ms. Mae. The woman was Netta's saving grace. She practically raised Netta, instilling in her morals and what little sense of decency she had.

"Looks are God-given, so be thankful. Praise is man-given, so be humble. Conceit is self-given, so be careful." she remembered Ms. Mae saying. Her words of wisdom seemed to stay with Netta throughout her entire life.

Netta could see the old woman's inviting smile, her head full of gray hair, and rich dark skin. The heavenly image that she saw of the lady she loved so dearly was comforting.

Suddenly, the glimmer of light was gone. Netta breathed deeply as a sense of relief washed over her body.

Her chest cavity expanded and deflated with such regularity that it eased the paramedic's fears. This was a good sign. Now there was hope for Netta, where there once was little or none.

Netta existed in a suspended state, coherent yet incoherent. Every survival instinct inside Netta pleaded with her subconscious to stay awake. However, it was another matter trying to comply with that request. She didn't have an ounce of energy left in her body. The brutal beating she had endured exhausted her, both physically and mentally. She was holding on to life by sheer will power.

Netta had experienced pain in the form of hurt and heartache, more often than she cared to remember in her life. She had suffered through enough hardships to last a lifetime. But this was something totally different. That had been emotional and mental anguish. She had never been physically incapacitated like this before. Her body exploded in pain in places she never knew existed. She was trapped in her own personal hell, which in this case was her body.

Yet, she had the audacity to keep fighting, to believe that everything was going to be all right. Whatever was happening, whatever was causing all this pain throughout her body, she was going to pull through. She visualized her recovery in her mind. Netta always believed in the power of positive thought. She feared that if she thought otherwise, then she was doomed.

Netta was in the fight of her life, for her life. Yet, she was accustomed to fighting in one form or another. She had been fighting all her life. Life had always been a constant struggle. Yet, some how, some way, Netta had always emerged the victor. She was a survivor in every sense of the word.

Try as she might to stay awake, her puffed up eyebrows were becoming extremely heavy. Closing them was too easy. Sleep was slowly overpowering her. Netta desperately needed a release from the pain and slipping into the darkness provided just that.

Once again she began experiencing flashbacks of her life and loved ones. Random images began to flash before her mind's eye. With vivid detail she began to see the most important people in her life, whom had shown her a lot of love at one time or another, people like Ms. Tina, Mimi, even her estranged deceased mother Renee.

These were people near and dear to her heart. People without whom she wouldn't be the person she was today. Netta felt they helped shape her, the good and the bad experiences. So she was thankful to have had them in her life in one form or another.

Then there was her old neighborhood in Baltimore, which she cherished so much. It was a source of pride for her; she always seemed to puff out her chest when she told people she was from Murphy Homes. Yes, thee Murphy Homes, a bleak housing projects on Baltimore's West Side. She loved the crime-ridden place to death, however, what Netta witnessed and experienced while she lived there had harden her. It prepared her for the cold world outside her project apartment door. So she'd always be forever grateful to have been raised there.

The immense pain snapped Netta right back into reality. She wasn't back at any of her old haunts, surrounded by loved ones. She was alone in the back of an ambulance, struggling to make sense of it all.

Just then the ambulance came to a halt. Finally, it had reached its destination. The sudden stop had roused Netta out of her state. She could clearly hear a loud bleeping noise sounded as the ambulance reversed into the emergency room parking bay.

Suddenly, the doors were flung wide open and paramedics rushed Netta's stretcher out of the ambulance. The emergency response workers looked on as they whisked Netta away. They both were thankful to have made it to the hospital with their patient still alive.

Quickly, Netta was thrust into a chaotic environment of the emergency room where a team of doctors, nurses and other medical professionals rushed to take possession of the severely injured patient. The ambulance driver had radioed ahead and requested that the trauma unit be on standby. Now the burden of saving this patient's life rested squarely on their shoulders.

In haste they rushed Netta's badly mangled body down the long, winding corridors and into the operating room. The sterile smell of the hospital invaded Netta's nostrils as the nurses prepared her for surgery. By now she was wide awake, yet she was unable to move. She heard and saw all the preparation the trauma unit team was making for her surgery.

Lying on the operating table, she began to see the build up to this moment, the cause and effect that her decisions and actions had had on her life.

For a long time the street life had been her savior, now suddenly it had become her downfall. Netta's actions had consequences and these were the consequences of her treacherous acts. The street life had cost her dearly.

Suddenly she was filled with deep regret, knowing that this entire situation was all of her own making. Her injuries might as well have been self-inflicted. All the wrongdoing pointed back to her. That thought alone made Netta begin to question herself. Why had she done some of the things she had done? Was money that important? Why had she even crossed Black? At the moment she had more questions than answers. So she forced herself to think about something else. Knowing she was at fault was too great of a burden for her to bear.

Her mind turned to thoughts of New York Tone, her new friend, and the future she'd thought she'd have with him. Netta thought about Tone for good reason, he was the last face that she saw before slipping in and out of consciousness. He also had discovered her body, so essentially, if she pulled through, he would be one of the many people responsible for saving her life. She'd be eternally thankful to him for that.

He was the last thing on her mind, not surgery, not life or death. Just New York Tone.

Netta's oxygen mask was replaced by anesthesia as the nurses continued to prepare her for surgery. Now modern medicine and the grace of God would dictate the outcome of her surgery. From this point on, one way or another, Netta wouldn't feel a thing. Her ill-fated life was now in God's hands.

CHAPTER 2

Wearing a black oversized hoodie pulled low over his head to conceal his facial features, Tone navigated New York City's Port Authority building in search of his bus boarding gate. His oversized apparel had done little to mask his muscular physique. Standing 6'2 with a low cut, Tone struck an imposing figure, the kind that commanded respect wherever he went. However, now was not the time to stand out. It was the time to blend in with the hundreds of other travelers and commuters. Traveling alone, he walked with a calm demeanor that contradicted his inner nervousness. Adrenaline ran through Tone's veins as he strolled through the busy bus terminal, past dozens of travelers at various gates on their way to unknown destinations.

Scanning their unfamiliar faces, Tone tried to decipher who might be law enforcement or who was a legitimate traveler. In New York City one could never be too sure who was who. Tone was street smart enough to know things were never what they appeared to be. The streets had trained him to be suspicious of everything.

Tone continued to wander around in search of his boarding gate. One minute he felt he was going in the right direction and the next minute he felt he wasn't. He may have been lost, but his temporary confusion wasn't enough to make him stop someone and ask for directions. Despite the fact that he was pressed for time, Tone was more inclined to find his own way, just like a typical New Yorker.

The fact that he was traveling light, carrying only a few meager possessions in a small duffle bag, some underwear, socks, and a few white T-shirts, he was inclined to believe that he could break out in a full sprint if need be. That didn't mean that he wanted to. Tone didn't want to draw attention to himself like that.

Besides the duffle bag, Tone clung tightly to the black knapsack slung over his shoulder. The contents of that bag meant more to him than anything in the world right now. It contained a few ounces of cocaine and a nine-millimeter handgun, his currency and insurance policy. These two things were Tone's passport to a new life. Everything else that he forgot or left behind in his haste to flee New York City could be replaced.

He was starting over, far from home. However, he had a plan. In his mind all he had to do was execute the plan and everything else would fall in place. Tone knew he had the right amount of heart and craziness inside to make it happen. What he didn't know was what he would be facing once he arrived at his destination. He knew he had to familiarize himself with this new city, the different culture and the street vernacular. Once he adapted to those things, Tone was sure he would be fine. The streets were pretty much the same wherever you went, he reasoned. Real always recognizes real, and Tone was a real one. He knew how to handle himself.

Sweat trickled down his face as Tone stopped and examined his boarding ticket then looked up and scanned his surroundings. Instantly he realized he was nowhere near the gate he was suppose to be at. Panic began to set in so he swallowed his pride and asked for directions.

"Excuse me, Mister, could you tell me which way is gate 59?" he asked politely.

"You going in the wrong direction young man, it's back dataway. Down the escalator," the terminal employee told him.

"Is it far?" Tone wondered. "I gotta 6:15 bus to catch."

"Nah, it's not too far," the man said, staring at his watch. "But you better put a pep in ya step if you plan on making that bus."

"Thanks," Tone hollered as he reversed his direction.

"You're welcome," the man replied. "Have a safe trip."

"Damn, this fuckin' bus station was bigger than I thought," Tone mused.

With his ticket in hand Tone broke out into a light jog. Every so often he glanced down at the bus ticket to make sure he was on track. At this point he was sure that his bus was probably already beginning to board. He wasn't sure how long they would wait before leaving. He was cutting it close by arriving so late.

Timing was a fact that he couldn't control. Everything was so spur of the moment. Yet Tone knew he couldn't afford to miss this bus. He couldn't afford to stay in New York City another minute. His freedom was at stake.

With the heat on, Tone was heading south until things died down. That was the plan, lay low. If he like it he'd stay, if not he'd leave. When the time was right, he would return back to New York, back to his beloved Edenwald housing project.

Luckily Tone had a girlfriend named Sonya who attended Morgan State University. Once word reached her about the incident involving him, she begged Tone to come stay with her in her off-campus apartment. She feared for his safety, probably more so than Tone did.

At first, Tone wasn't sold on the idea of leaving New York, but once the police raided his mother's apartment, kicking in her door looking for him, it didn't take much convincing thereafter. There was a lot of speculation surrounding him. The streets were talking, there was a high possibility someone might be snitching on him. Knowing that, his hood wasn't the place for him to be. He never thought he would be leaving New York, especially under these circumstances.

New York City was end all, be all to him. It was all that he had ever known and all that he ever wanted to know. To Tone there was no other world outside his city. New York was the capital of the world, to him. It saddened him, having to leave his place of birth. But he had no choice. It was either stay and go to jail, or leave and be free.

As he jogged toward his boarding gate, Tone glanced up at the large digital clock located just above a billboard. It read 6:12 pm. His bus was scheduled to depart at 6:15 pm. Quickly he broke out into a sprint, trying his best to remain discreet.

Slightly winded, Tone arrived at the Peter Pan bus company terminal 59 just in time to board the bus with the last remaining passengers.

"Ticket please," the bus driver stated, standing just outside the bus entrance.

Tone handed over his bus ticket and the bus driver punched a hole into it with a small silver hole puncher before handing it back to him.

"Enjoy your trip, sir," the bus driver commented.

"Thanks," Tone replied.

To him, it was such a relief boarding the bus. It was more than a means of transportation, it was a route to a new life. It might as well have been a portal to a new dimension, especially with the New York City police department looking high and low for him. Just making it this far felt like an accomplishment to Tone. Leaving town, he felt like a great deal of his problems were solved, however temporary that may be.

Tone eased passed the bus driver, up a short flight of steps, heading down the narrow aisle in search of a seat. It was a relief to him that the bus wasn't jammed packed with passengers and he didn't have to sit next to a stranger. He wouldn't be too comfortable with someone sitting beside him for the entirety of the ride. The emptiness of the bus was a blessing, so finding a seat or a row by himself wasn't difficult at all.

Tone took a seat with no other passenger within his eyesight. There was no one sitting directly in front of him, behind him, or across from him. He needed a little privacy to do what he had to do, which was to remove the gun and the drugs from his knapsack and stash them for safekeeping. He looked around carefully before he quickly made his move. In an instant he stuffed the gun into his waistband and then he placed the drugs in his hoodie pouch and headed immediately for the bathroom to stash it in the garbage. In his mind, hindsight was 20/20. It was better to be safe than sorry. He already had a messed up legal situation looming. Tone didn't need to compound that with additional gun and drug possession charges.

Inside the cramped quarters of the bus bathroom, Tone quickly removed the gun and the drugs off his person, stashing them in the garbage then covering it with some trash. When that was done, he returned to his seat, placing his knapsack and his duffle bag in the overhead compartment like every other passenger on the bus.

Next, Tone sat down and immediately removed his hoodie in an attempt to cool himself off. Even as he disrobed, revealing a plain white T-shirt, Tone could feel the deodorant running down his arms. He took his hoodie and wiped away light beads of sweat that had formed on his forehead. Tone felt sticky from the perspiration, but it was nothing a nice hot shower couldn't solve once he arrived at his destination. For now, he'd just have to deal with it.

Tone was still cooling off when a white man suddenly boarded his bus.

"Excuse me, Sir," the stranger suddenly called out.

Although the stranger had grabbed his attention, Tone completely ignored the voice from the front of the bus. He assumed the male voice wasn't referring to him. He couldn't be.

A number of passengers stared at the man; none of which acknowledged him at all.

The man continued, "Hey, you… You in the white t-shirt."

Tone cringed. He couldn't ignore that physical description. The first thing that came to his mind was he was caught.

Tone pointed at himself in disbelief, as if to say me?

"Yes, you," the white man reiterated. "Could you come here for a second?"

Quickly Tone rose from his seat and began to approach the man with an air of confidence that belied his uneasiness.

The closer he came toward the man, the better he was able to size him up. He took a long hard look at him. From his perspective, the man looked like a cop. Truth be told, most white men looked liked cops to kids from the hood. His clean-cut look, freshly shaven, broad shoulders with a navy blue New York Yankee baseball cap. It was the same kind that plain-clothes policemen in New York City loved to wear. He might as well have had the word cop written on his forehead as far as Tone was concerned. The man was giving him a bad vibe.

At this point Tone's mind was racing; the closer he got the faster Tone's heart began to beat. He began scheming on ways to escape. He was just hoping the man would let him get off the bus before he tried to take him into custody. That way, at least he had as good a shot as any to escape. He'd take his chances in a foot race with a cop any day of the week.

"Does this belong to you?" the man asked, holding up an identification card.

Speechless, Tone didn't know what to say. It was obvious that the photo on the identification was indeed him. There was no denying that. But what wasn't so obvious was if the man knew that the identification was fake or not. It was a catch 22, Tone was damned if he did lie and maybe damned if he didn't. Against his best judgment, Tone decided not to lie.

"Yeah, that's mine," he admitted.

"Here you go." The man said, handing over his identification. "I saw you drop it as you ran for your bus. I figured you might need it, wherever you were headed."

"Yeah, thank you." Tone replied. "I sure will."

Inwardly, Tone exhaled. It was a relief to know that the man wasn't a cop. That he was simply a Good Samaritan, returning his lost identification.

"Your welcome buddy," the man spoke.

Tone smiled as he received his identification card. This time he placed it firmly inside his front pants pocket; then he retreated back down the isle. He caught a few suspicious stares from a few nosey passengers. He didn't think too much of it as he returned to his seat.

Quickly, Tone put that incident behind him. Now there was nothing to do but wait for the bus to depart and ponder whatever lay ahead of him in Baltimore.

The Peter Pan bus sped down the long New Jersey Turnpike portion of Interstate 95. Like a child, Tone pressed his face against the dirt stained glass and took in the sights and sounds of the trip. The steady stream of traffic allowed passing vehicles to zip past the slow moving bus on either side. It didn't take long for Tone to realize that the bus window provided no entertainment value whatsoever. Still, the trip was interesting to him just the same. Tone had never been this far south by himself. The farthest he had ever been was to Philadelphia as a child with his mother to visit family.

The traveling experience was new to him. Eagerly he awaited his arrival in Baltimore. Tone knew his girlfriend would be at the bus station to pick him up. He looked forward to seeing her again. He hadn't seen her since the summertime when she was on break from college. The thought of being with her on a daily basis, just like when they were in high school, made him happy. Yet their reunion wasn't the sole purpose of the relocation. It might have been for Sonya, but it wasn't for him. Tone wasn't going to let anything get in his way of making a dollar. Not even his girlfriend.

First and foremost, Tone was coming to Baltimore to make money. The gun and the drugs in his knapsack was proof of that. He had no intentions of cleaning up his act and staying out of trouble once he got to where he was going. On the contrary, it was business as usual.

Have drugs, will travel, might as well have been his motto.

Long before he even thought about coming to Baltimore, his girlfriend had tried to entice him to come down. She had mentioned to him on several occasions how much money was out there in the streets of Baltimore. She even put her male cousin, Stew who was from Baltimore, on the phone to try to convince Tone to come hustle down there. He didn't listen then, but he was all ears now. Tone was going to see for himself just what the streets of Baltimore were hitting for. Was there really money out there? Or was it all a myth. He would soon find out.

As far as he was concerned, Sonya was merely repeating what her cousin Stew had told her. What did she know about the drug game except for what he told her? Or what she saw on television?

She don't know nuttin' about nuttin' except for how to look cute and school books, Tone reasoned.

There wasn't an ounce of street in her. Sonya was a private house chick who lived in the hood. She wasn't in tune with the ways of the streets. She was a good girl who hadn't seen any part of the streets. The closest she had come to illegal activities was watching Tone bag up crack in his bedroom.

Still, one thing Tone knew was, he'd soon find out exactly what was going on in the streets of Baltimore.

The bus ride was long and boring. There was only so long Tone could stare out the window. Before the bus had made it half way down the New Jersey turnpike, he had dozed off with his head leaned against the window. Tone was exhausted. He had an adventurous few days and he had barely slept. Sitting still for this long, it was easy for sleep to overcome him.

In his subconscious as he slept, Tone's mind replayed the violent events that led to his exodus. Words exchanged; guns were drawn; bullets flew. An innocent bystander, an old lady, was shot. A community was outraged. One person was in custody. The other person, him, was on the run.

All for what? A petty dispute over a ten-dollar crack sale.

The shooting had made headlines all across the city. Tone's face had been flashed on the local news channels for a couple of days. An old mug shot of his had even made the *New York Daily News* under the caption, "Bullets fly Granny hit."

Since he'd been on the news and in the paper, Tone had gone into hiding and tried to alter his appearance by cutting his high top fade haircut style in favor of a low Caesar.

His recollection of the incident had been so real, even in his sleep Tone regretted his actions. He wished it hadn't come to that, but when you're young, wild, reckless, and living in the hood, it goes down like that. A moment of indiscretion could lead to a lifetime of regret, or a life sentence. There were plenty of men and women in prison today with lengthy sentences who wished that they could have that one day, that one moment, or that one action, back.

On that note Tone counted himself lucky not to be facing a first-degree murder charge.

Although he wasn't the aggressor in the situation, he knew the law would never see it as such. He would be lumped together with the other assailant and found guilty in the court of public opinion, long before he ever went to court.

Tone didn't regret defending himself, he regretted that an innocent person got shot in the process. In other words, he wasn't mad that someone got shot. It was merely the fact that the wrong person got shot. That lady didn't have anything to do with that situation. She was merely in the wrong place at the wrong time.

The timing of the situation couldn't have been worst. Just as Tone felt like he was about to make a come-up, things were going good with his drug business, then disaster struck. He was beginning to feel like the hood was some sort of elaborate set-up, existing only to supply him, and others like himself, with street dreams, but ultimately resulting in an unending supply of jail, death and disappointment.

The only people Tone ever saw make it out the hood were those who moved away in search of a better life. The same held true for him. He hoped his move to Baltimore would bring about greener pastures. Hopefully the move would turn his fortunes around and revive his street dreams.

Whatever street ambition Tone held for himself, he had to be mindful of his legal situation. The prevailing thought of prison weighed heavily on his mind. The criminal warrant issued for his arrest made him restless. Tone stressed over the possibility of the Baltimore Police department lying in wait to arrest and extradite him back to New York City to face the music. Despite the possibility of being arrested in another state, Tone was already committed to taking his chances in Maryland.

Tone wasn't ready for prison, at least not financially, right now. Part of his plan was to hustle up enough money to hire a good attorney. That way he'd having a better chance at getting a lesser sentence in court, whenever he was picked up on the warrant.

At the moment he was a fugitive from justice; one step ahead of New York City's finest. Armed with a fake ID in his pocket, he planned to stay that way. As far as he was concerned, he wasn't even Anthony Thompson anymore. He was now Jason Jones. At least that's what his identification said. The police would either have to fingerprint or positively identify him to prove otherwise.

The concealment of his true identity gave Tone hope. Once he hit Baltimore he could be whoever he wanted to be and no one would be the wiser.

Tone woke up on the bus in a cold sweat. He had a bad dream about getting arrested. The dream felt so real, he was happy as hell to open his eyes and find out that it wasn't. He was still free.

Tone's anxiety was building. He wouldn't feel completely safe until he reached his girlfriend's apartment. At the moment all he wanted to do was hurry up and get to his destination. In his mind the bus ride was taking forever and a day. He continually grew restless. His only reprieve was to fall back into his seat and try to forget about everything, where he was going and how long it took to get there. He came to the realization that traveling by bus took time and his arrival couldn't be hurried.

Dwelling on the trip wasn't going to make it any shorter. He reverted back to staring out the window, at the never-ending highway and endless amount of cars that had now turned into just a stream of bright headlight and red taillights.

That trick seemed to work. The three plus hour trip didn't take as long as he thought, once he took his mind off it. The sudden change of scenery and reduction in speed as the bus exited the highway alerted Tone to his arrival in downtown Baltimore. As the bus made its way toward the bus station, Tone felt butterflies in the pit of his stomach. Unsure of what to expect, he took a deep breath and exhaled.

As the bus turned off on the exit ramp, Tone began to get his first glimpse of downtown Baltimore. He was unimpressed at the modest skyline that outlined the downtown area. The tallest building in downtown Baltimore didn't even compare with the skyscrapers in New York City. With his face pressed to the window, Tone took it all in.

Then he calmly walked down the aisle to the bathroom to retrieve his drugs and handgun out the garbage. He grabbed his knapsack from the overhead compartment and placed the items back in there.

Shortly, the bus came to a halt. It became evident to Tone that he had reached his destination, finally.

"We've arrived in Baltimore, Maryland," the bus driver spoke into the intercom as the interior lights of the bus came on. "All passengers headed to Washington, DC, Richmond, Virginia, and all points south, please do not exit the bus. For all those passengers who've reached their destination, thank you for choosing Peter Pan."

The driver exited the bus, opened the luggage compartment, and began removing suitcases and baggage. A steady stream of passengers departed the bus to retrieve their belongings. Tone was amongst the handful of other passengers that stood up and grabbed their own possessions that they had brought onboard the bus.

After grabbing his things, Tone navigated his way down the narrow bus aisle to the exit. As he did so, he intently studied the bus station, scanning the terminal for his girlfriend or anyone who may have looked like a policeman. The moment he stepped off the bus, his girlfriend instantly spotted Tone. She stood near the bus station entrance and where the passengers departed their respective buses.

"Hey boo," she excitingly said as she ran over and gave him a big hug and a kiss. "Yo, I'm so glad ya here. I missed you."

Tone had that boyish charm that made Sonya weak every time she saw him.

"I missed you too," Tone responded as he broke the embrace to get a better look at her body.

Inwardly, Tone shook his head. He conceded to himself that Sonya was looking better than ever. Maybe it was because he hadn't seen her in a few months. Whatever the reasons was, Tone definitely liked what he saw.

"God damn. Ya ass is gettin' fatter," he said while taking a long lustful look at his girlfriend. "Who you fuckin' wit' down here? I don't remember ya shit bein' this fat."

Flirting with his girlfriend required little effort on Tone's part because he was genuinely attracted to her. But it wasn't just her sex appeal that made her so enticing. These two had great chemistry. Sonya was looking even better than Tone had remembered. She stood 6'5 and thick in all the right places. Her smooth brown skin and large bubbly light brown eyes seemed to attract him more than anything.

"Tone, if you don't stop fuckin' playin' wit' me," she laughed.

Tone loved the fact that Sonya could take a joke. It was one of the reasons that their relationship was different from all the others he had before. He also loved her affectionate exuberance that she always displayed whenever they were together. These things endeared her to him.

At the moment Tone could care less about his girlfriend's special qualities. He was putting on an act for any prying eyes that might be watching. He was dying to leave the bus station, but not before this warm welcoming scene played itself out.

"Let's get up outta here, Ma. Where you parked at?" Tone asked.

"Out front. My girlfriend is sittin' in the car waiting for us," Sonya explained.

"Let's go. We out," he blurted.

Trying to play it cool, Tone grabbed Sonya's hand walked her through the bus terminal. Playing the role of loving boyfriend, he occasionally made small talk as they walked.

"So, when you gone tell me what happened in New York," Sonya wondered.

"Homegirl, slow down. Now ain't the time or the place to talk about that shit," he informed her. "We'll talk about that later."

Sonya had so many questions she wanted to ask him pertaining to the shooting incident. Who was the other dude Tone was shooting at? Did he think it was his bullet that hit the old lady? But she didn't want to press the issue, at least not now. In her mind Tone would be here for the foreseeable future, so they'd have plenty of time to talk.

The short walk from the bus station to the car went smoothly. Tone finally breathed a sigh of relief when the car pulled away from the curb. He glanced back once or twice to make sure that they weren't being followed. Then a broad smile spread across his face. Now he could relax. The hard part, or so he thought, was over.

Although Tone had arrived safely in Baltimore, his journey was just beginning.

Now it was Baltimore or bust for him. He had to make this move work. Returning home, broke and a wanted man wasn't an option he wanted to exercise.

CHAPTER 3

Tone glanced out the back window of his girlfriend's blue Honda Accord. It finally dawned on him that he had really made it to Baltimore. In the backseat his girlfriend was pressed up against him, her head resting on his chest, her eyes glancing up at him almost in disbelief.

"What you staring at," he gently asked.

"You," Sonya admitted. "I can't believe you're here."

"Believe it or not, here I am," Tone joked.

Sonya continued to stare starry eyed at her boyfriend. Her thoughts were solely on Tone as she romanticized their reunion. Now that they were together, Sonya couldn't imagine it playing out any other way. Something bad happened in New York with the shooting, but something good came out of that, they were together. Sonya prayed

Tone wouldn't get homesick and return back to New York. She feared if that happened she'd lose Tone to the system for a few years or worst. In her mind, that was the only thing that could break them up. So she planned on doing everything in her power to convince him to stay.

The car slowly came to a stop at a red light. This gave Tone the opportunity to do something that should have been done from the moment that they entered the car. Unfortunately, both their minds had been elsewhere. However, now he had the chance to make things right. Tone had been so preoccupied by the thought of being arrested and Sonya had been so infatuated with his physical presence that they both neglected to make a formal introduction.

"Tone," he said, extending his hand toward the driver as they exchanged a formal greeting.

Her first words to him were, "So you're Tone, huh?"

She said it with a hint of seduction in her voice, as if she had heard so much about him. Maybe Tone's reputation may have preceded him. The thought made him smile and wonder what had been said between them. Tone was well aware how spicy females could talk about their boyfriends.

"I didn't wanna say nuttin'.... I was waitin' to see if Sonya would introduce us. But the bitch is so sprung she can't even think straight," she remarked in a northern accent. "Brianna, but people call me Bri."

From the soft grip of her handshake, Tone became aware of femininity. He was staring at a very attractive light skin female with light brown eyes and juicy bubble lips. He held the grip a little bit longer than necessary, as he locked eyes with Bri. It was a covert flirtatious move, done right in front of his girlfriend.

"Aiight bitch, that's enough," Sonya playfully stated. "Let go of my man's hand."

"Bitch please," Bri responded. "Ain't anybody thinkin' bout him except you."

"Yeah, right," Sonya joked. "I gotta keep my eyes on you Morgan State hoes. I know how y'all get down."

As soon as the stoplight turned green, Brianna continued to cruise the streets of downtown Baltimore. As she drove she talked, carrying on a conversation almost exclusively with Tone. She badgered him with silly questions as she drove, as if she'd known him well.

"It feels good to be out of New York right? You like it down here? You happy to see Sonya?"

A couple times Tone had to catch himself. He was on the verge of saying something smart, like shut the fuck up. He knew that wasn't the nice thing to say, so he didn't. He knew it would kill the vibe. But he was growing increasingly annoyed by her questions. For the sake of peace, Tone remained polite and continued to enjoy the ride. Soon he realized it was just talk and Brianna didn't mean anything by it. She was just running her mouth.

"Where you from," Tone wondered, picking up on her accent. "Brooklyn? Queens? You can't be from the Bronx."

"I ain't from the city," she stated strongly as she drove. "Why do people always say that?"

"Then where you from?" Tone reiterated

"The Bricks!" Bri responded.

"Fuck is that?" Tone commented.

"Newark," Sonya interrupted.

"Oh, Jersey. Got you," Tone acknowledged.

"What you know about the Bricks, huh? New York niggas don't come over there for some strange reason. We party in the city, but y'all don't come to Jerz," she stated.

"Pppllleeeeeaaaasssssseeee," Sonya cried. "Don't get this bitch started wit' that geographical nonsense. Okay, okay you from Newark, we get it. You rep ya city hard, we get that too. Let's not turn this into a New York vs. Newark conversation. End of story."

"Ooooohhhh, you so salty," Bri told her. "You hate when I rep my hood."

Sonya replied, "No, I don't. I heard this shit from you so many times… Don't forget we lived together our freshman year of college. This conversation is gettin' old."

"You just mad cause Newark better than New York, that's all," Brianna fired back.

"Just drive bitch!" Sonya joked.

Tone found Sonya and her friend amusing. Underneath the playfulness he could tell that the two were close. In his book Bri was very hittable. So he immediately scratched Bri off his short list of chicks he wanted to fuck in Baltimore. He knew it would kill Sonya if he had sex with her friend.

Eventually the group conversation died down and Tone and Sonya were back in their own little world, communicating without saying a word. There was a touch here and a kiss there. It was the language of love that they were communicating to each other. Sonya was so head over heels in love with Tone. She was lost in his arms. She snuggled close to her man, inhaling his masculine scent.

Meanwhile, Brianna drove around downtown Baltimore aimlessly. She was content with playing the role of chauffeur, despite the fact that the lovey-dovey vibe inside the car was making her feel more than a little uncomfortable.

"Can't y'all wait til y'all get home?" she remarked.

"Just shut up and drive Bri," her friend told her.

Tone ignored the exchange as he busied himself with examining his girlfriend's physical features. It was obvious that he liked what he saw. It was even more obvious that he was into her. Even Bri could see that as she looked at the lovers from time to time through the rearview mirror.

Lots of discreet touching of the private parts was exchanged between the couple in the backseat. They alternated between rubbing, squeezing and caressing each other's private parts. Quickly Tone turned his attention to her breasts while stroking her inner thighs. The more Tone did it, the more sexually aroused Sonya became. In turn she gently rubbed his penis until it was rock hard and bulging out of his jeans. Sonya's touch aroused him, but what really turned him on was that dreamy look in her eyes. The one that seemed to say that she was his for the taking. All of this seemed like foreplay to him, the calm before the storm. He couldn't help but think how bomb the sex would be tonight.

Soon the aroma of food infiltrated the car. The scent reminded Tone just how hungry he was.

"Yo, Bri," he began. "Pull over, I gotta get somethin' to eat. I'm starvin' like Marvin back here."

Bri did as she was told and pulled the car smoothly to the curb. Sonya rose up from the backseat to check on their whereabouts. The neon lights and bright flashing signs advertised illicit businesses, peep shows, bars and strip clubs.

"Where we at?" Sonya wondered.

"The Block," Bri replied. "Baltimore Street. I was tryin' to give Tone a lil tour of the town, but obviously y'all weren't payin' attention. Too busy back there lovey-dovey."

Bri was right, the couple hadn't noticed a thing until now. It didn't matter to them where they were or where they went, as long as they were together.

"Yo, this shit look like 42nd Street Time Square out here. All I see it bright lights, prostitutes, drug dealers, junkies and perverts. It's goin' down out here, huh?" Tone observed.

"You could say that again. But the food spot is right there," Bri pointed. "Crazy John's."

Quickly both Tone and Sonya took note of the yellow restaurant sign and began to exit the car.

"You want somethin' Bri?" Sonya asked before closing the car door.

"Yeah, you can get me a large order of fries," Bri said. "I ate already."

Sonya continued, "That's it? Bitch ya greedy ass don't want nuttin' else?"

"Nah, I'm cool. I got some leftovers in the microwave," she responded. "I'll eat my food at home after y'all drop me off."

After getting her friend's order, Sonya closed the car door. She took hold of her boyfriend's hand and together they walked to the fast food restaurant holding hands. Each time Tone held her hand, images flooded her mind of all the times they went out on dates in high school. Sonya couldn't help but feel safe in Tone's presence.

Men looked lustfully at Sonya as they walked down Baltimore Street. Tone mean mugged a few, those whom he felt stared too hard or too long at his girl. The look on his face said, *she's with me.* One by one they got the message and diverted their stares elsewhere.

They entered Crazy John's and quickly placed their order and paid for it. Then the couple returned to the car with multiple bags of food. After reclaiming their original seats, they began eating. Sonya handed over the fries to her friend. Slowly, Bri pulled the car back into traffic while enjoying her food.

As she nibbled on her French Fries, the scent of fast food begins to fill the car, getting Bri's full attention.

"Damn, that cheeseburger smells good," Bri commented. "Who eatin' that?"

"Me," Tone replied between bites of his burger.

"Don't start that lemme get a bite shit. Ain't nobody eatin' behind ya nasty ass," Sonya commented. "Bri, I asked you what you wanted and you said some fuckin' fries."

"I did," Bri stated. "But that was then. I suddenly changed my mind when I smelt that burger."

"You the worse, Bri, you can never make up ya mind," Sonya added.

"I'll tell you what. I gotta deal for you Bri," Tone announced. "If you show me around the town, not downtown, but the hood, I'll give you one of my burgers. How that sound?"

"That's a bet," Bri assured him. "Gimme my burger."

Tone went in the bag and handed over the cheeseburger, but not before Sonya could interrupt.

"You ain't gotta give that bitch shit," Sonya insisted.

"This an A and B conversation," Bri replied, "C ya way out."

Tone laughed at the childish statement. He hadn't heard that in a while. The rapport between these two was comical, to say the least.

Sonya urged, "Please, Tone don't encourage this heifer. It'll only get worst."

"Ha!" Bri laughed as she took a bite of the burger and drove simultaneously.

"Anyway, can't that shit wait till tomorrow?" Sonya asked. "I'll show you around then."

"Nah, I need to see B-more the hood tonite," Tone insisted. "Need to see what I'm dealin' wit. I wanna see how different this hood is from mine. You know they say if you ever want to really know about a neighborhood, go around there at night. It'll tell you everything that you need to know."

Truth of the matter was Tone was on a scout mission. He was trying to locate a drug block where he could set up shop and sell his product. What he said out loud was misinformation. He knew he had to conceal his true intentions from her. He didn't know if Bri knew he was a drug dealer. In case she didn't know, he wasn't going to tell her. That was none of her business.

"Bust that move, Bri," Tone called out from the backseat. "Take me to the hood."

"This nigga," Sonya complained, rolling her eyes.

"I got you, kid," Bri announced.

Since the city of Baltimore wasn't big, the proximity from downtown to East Baltimore wasn't far. Before Tone knew it the vehicle he was riding in arrived in the hood. The stark contrast between downtown Baltimore and East Baltimore was like night and day. He went from the clean, well-lit avenues of downtown to the dark, rat-infested streets of the hood. On almost every corner, Tone noticed a cut-rate liquor store or a Chinese carry out. It was like if the powers that be couldn't kill black people with one form of poison, then they'd kill them with another.

"Fuck is wit' all these fuckin' cut-rate liquor stores? This how they livin' out here?" he observed.

No one else in the car bothered to answer. If Tone didn't know the level of affliction in Baltimore's inner city, then he was about to see for himself. It was deeper than just liquor stores. Here Heroin was the black peoples' Achilles Heel.

Tone didn't know what to expect when he hit the hood, but this wasn't how he pictured it. The hood was depressing. He had seen bleak and impoverished neighborhoods before in New York, but it seemed like Baltimore had its own monopoly on urban decay.

As the vehicle rode from hood to hood, Tone got a good gauge where the money was, which blocks were popping and which ones were dead. The streets of East Baltimore felt so vibrant to him. North Avenue was like a car show. He saw young dudes such as himself driving expensive foreign cars accompanied by some good-looking women. That sight seemed to repeat itself at every light.

Just a few blocks over on Greenmount Avenue, he had to admit, he never saw such a great disparity of wealth in one place. Tone saw luxury foreign cars parked in front of rundown row houses. Still, he got the idea from the looks of things that there was a lot of money to be made out here.

The tour of the hood continued, taking Tone pass infamous Baltimore housing projects like Latrobe homes and Lafayette Courts. These projects were much smaller than the one's he was use to. But from what Bri was saying, they were no less dangerous. From what he was seeing, Tone couldn't help but think that this might be his kind of town. Danger was like a rush of adrenaline to him. He was far too reckless to be afraid. Tone felt New York City had prepared him for everything and anything. He felt he had seen it all and been through it all.

In comparison to his hometown, physically the landscape was different. In terms of size, one could fit a few Baltimore City's inside New York. Yet the hustle and bustle seemed to be the same. The streets of Baltimore were about a dollar. It just so happened that coke and dope were the main commodities on this market.

Tone's brief tour of East Baltimore sobered him quickly to the harsh realities of the streets of Baltimore. The sights and sounds got his mind where it should be, into a hustler mode. He could envision himself getting money out here.

They drove through a few more crime ridden corridors and hotspots, places like Eager Street, Hoffman and Holbrook, Ashland Avenue. On these blocks Tone got to see large congregations of people and open-air drug markets that ran around the clock. He burned all these locations, streets and avenues into his memory bank. The information might be useful to him at a later date. He vowed to return to these blocks soon, next time without his two chaperons.

Bri continued playing the role of gracious tour guide, driving the vehicle at a moderate enough rate for Tone to scope the scene.

"I usta date a Baltimore guy from around here," she admitted.

"Where's here?" Tone asked, looking around for a street sign. "What's the name of this block?"

"Federal and Chase," she told him. "The nigga was major. One of the biggest d-boys in the city. I don't know where he was gettin' his shit from, but he was gettin' it."

"What happened?" Tone asked.

"What happened to what?… Oh, he got like fifteen or twenty years," she replied nonchalantly. "Feds indicted him. He was under investigation, from what I understand."

"Word?" Tone responded.

"That's how the story goes out here," Sonya hinted, as she looked at Tone. "It ends one of two ways, dead or in jail."

Tone didn't care what Sonya said. He had already sold himself on the idea of hustling drugs on the streets of Baltimore. He knew he was going to take that leap again, and dive head first into the drug game out here. Even if he had to launch a small scale drug operation and go hand to hand himself. So be it.

"Yeah, he got busted wit' a whole lotta dope A couple of kilos if I remember correctly," Bri admitted. "Yo, I'm just glad I didn't get caught in that mess. My parents would have killed me. They didn't send me way down here to school to become a drug dealer's girlfriend. Shit, I could save they ass the tuition and did that shit back home."

"Word," Tone groaned. "I hear you."

Bri continued, "I ain't gonna lie. It really goes down out here. I ain't just talkin' about the drugs. I'm talkin' about the shootings and killings too. These b-more streets are like the wild wild west."

To her the streets were wild. To Tone the streets were typical. He was in his element. This was his domain. He spoke the language of the streets fluently, violence.

"Oh really?" he said aloud. "You think New York is a joke? Ma, it's goin' down everywhere. No disrespect, I ain't worried about none of that shit you talkin'."

Bri replied, "No, its cool. I'm not sayin' you can't hold ya own. I was just tryin' to put a bug in ya ear."

"Good lookin' out," Tone acknowledged her.

Tone tried not to take her comment personally. After all, she didn't know him. Bri didn't know how he got down in the streets. She was just like everyone else, they didn't know what he did until he did it to them. With that thought, he shook off the irritation that the conversation caused him. There was no need to get mad at Bri for her so-called good intentions.

Momentarily, Bri took her eyes off the road and glanced into the rearview mirror. Her eyes met Tone's. He gave her a serious look, which she returned. Neither person said anything. On that subject, what else was there to say?

That's why God made guns, Tone found himself thinking. It was a saying his deceased friend was fond of saying. *God made guns for wild niggas, hot blocks and hostile environments like Baltimore, Maryland.*

He went back to looking out the window and eating his food. Bri's horror story about her boyfriend had done little, if anything, to deter Tone from hustling on the streets. Instead of being scared off by the danger, he thought the fate that befell her ex-boyfriend wouldn't happen to him. Tone focused on all the money he could possibly make. He had a vested interest in making this situation work for him.

"I'm ready to go home now," Sonya stated, interrupting his thoughts.

"Me, too," Tone added. "I seen enough for tonite. Tomorrow's another day."

"Good," Sonya said, clearly frustrated. "Bri, drive to ya house so we can drop you off."

Bri nodded her head in response. The car fell silent for a few minutes as Sonya continued to enjoy Tone's company in the backseat.

"Baltimore, the city that reads," Tone mocked a sign he saw at a nearby bus stop.

"Niggas out here call it, *the city that bleeds,* Bri retorted.

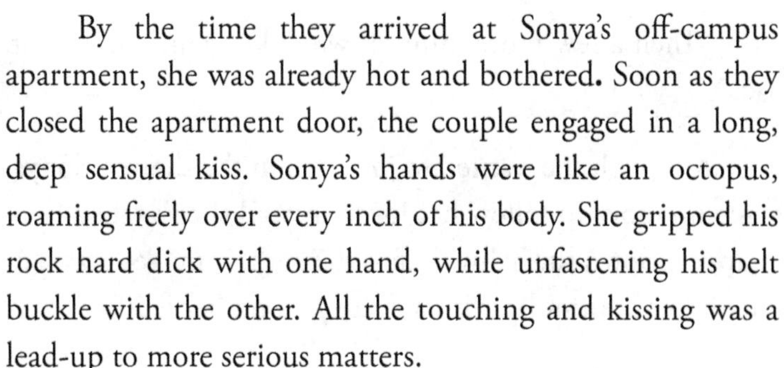

By the time they arrived at Sonya's off-campus apartment, she was already hot and bothered. Soon as they closed the apartment door, the couple engaged in a long, deep sensual kiss. Sonya's hands were like an octopus, roaming freely over every inch of his body. She gripped his rock hard dick with one hand, while unfastening his belt buckle with the other. All the touching and kissing was a lead-up to more serious matters.

"Chill," Tone cautioned his girlfriend as he felt his pants becoming undone. "Yo, I need to hit dat shower real quick. That bus ride got me sticky."

Sonya didn't like the idea of postponing their sex, not even for a few minutes. But since it was a hygiene issue she understood.

"Lemme get you a clean washcloth and a towel," she told him.

She returned quickly with a big, fluffy white towel and a matching washcloth.

"The bathroom is in the back, first door on ya right," she explained, handing the things to Tone.

"Thanks," Tone said, with a devious look in his eyes.

"Don't take long." Sonya warned. "I been waitin' on you all day."

"Then a few more minutes won't kill you," Tone shot back.

Although she wanted to join him in the shower, Sonya made no move to follow her lover, instead she watched him disappear down the hallway, into the bathroom. Seductively, she bit her bottom lip with a nasty grin on her face.

"I won't," Tone promised as he closed the bathroom door.

Sonya entered her bedroom and went to open her top dresser drawer. She put on a t-shirt, minus the bra, and sexy lace hot pink boy shorts on, then returned to the living room and waited for Tone to exit the shower.

"How was ya shower," Sonya asked.

"Good money," he admitted. "A nigga really needed that. Yo, I was sticky as a motherfucka. Word!"

Tone headed straight toward Sonya, bare-chested and naked, except for the white towel that donned his waist. This was the first time today that Sonya could fully admire his chiseled physique. His well-defined upper torso glistened with small beads of water. Walking straight into Sonya's arms, the lovers picked up where they had left off.

Their lips locked in a kiss as their tongues swirled inside each other's mouths. After a few passionate minutes of that, Tone maneuvered his lips from her mouth to her neck area. She trembled as the hot, wet, tingling sensation of his tongue traveled down her spine. Sonya threw her head back, exposing more of her neck. The good feeling was going directly to her head. Her body hadn't felt this aroused in months. All she wanted was for Tone to continue to touch her, keeping up the foreplay. Sexually she was his for the taking.

Tone placed his hand near Sonya's private area. Her legs quickly spread to give him full access to her vagina. He rubbed her clit through the thin material, discovering just how wet Sonya was at the moment. Slowly, Tone began to nibble on her earlobe before shoving his tongue into her ear. He receive his own sense of enjoyment from just the thought of knowing what he was doing was pleasing her.

"Damn, ya pussy is so fuckin' wet," he whispered.

Suddenly Sonya ripped off Tone's towel, flinging it to the floor and grabbed a handful of his manhood. In one motion she pulled away from Tone and dropped to her knees. Sonya began sucking Tone's penis, using both hands. She bobbed her head back and forth with such ferocity

Tone's toes curled. He had to do everything in his power to keep from cummin'. The anticipation was driving him crazy.

"Yyyyeeeeaaaahhhhh…" he moaned. "That's what I'm talkin' bout. Suck that dick like you love me."

Placing his hand on the top of her head, Tone help guide his dick deeper and deeper into her mouth. He forced so much of himself into her mouth that Sonya gagged a few times, forcing her to stop temporarily. He pulled Sonya to her feet and tongue kissed her deeply as he removed her panties, then her t-shirt. After that, Tone dragged her to the living room floor and immediately began eating Sonya's pussy. He had done this a million times, performing oral sex on her wasn't just standard practice, it was mandatory. Sonya really got off that way.

"Oh, you shaved this pussy, huh?" Tone stated as he came up for air.

"Just for you," Sonya confessed.

Like a madman Tone went back to eating Sonya's pussy, with the intent on making her cum. At this pace it didn't take long to make that happen. Sonya's body began to twitch violently as she clamped her legs around his head.

"I'mmmmm ccccuuuuummmiiiinnn'," she cried out.

Hearing those words made Tone go harder. Sonya desperately tried to pry his head from in between her legs as she climaxed. Successful, she moved her vagina away from Tone's mouth as she savored the moment.

"Good, huh," Tone bragged, looking up at her.

"Yyyyyaaaassss!" she raved.

Sonya may have gotten hers, but Tone had yet to get his. Earlier in the car, he had whispered in her ear that he was going to fuck the shit out of her, now he was going to make good on that promise.

Tone got on top of Sonya and slid right inside her. He began fucking her missionary style. As their bodies pressed together, the heat and friction that they were producing caused the couple to sweat profusely. Perspiration came with the territory as they ignored it and continued having sex.

"Turn over!" he commanded her.

Sonya followed his orders and flipped into doggy style position on all fours on the floor. Immediately Tone inserted his penis back inside her vagina and began jamming away. Loud sounds of skin smacking together, combined with the sight of Sonya's round ass, sent Tone into a sexual frenzy. A few seconds later, he busted a nut and collapsed on top of her.

That first night together they had sex all over the house; the living room, bathroom, kitchen, and finally the bedroom. There was no limit on what they did sexually or where they did it.

After taking a shower together, the couple called it a night and went to bed. They were both sexually satisfied and physically exhausted. Sonya lay in the bed underneath the down comforter, spooning with Tone. This was the happiest she had been in a long time. Her mind, body and soul were in a good place. She began to drift off to sleep.

"Yo, what's up with ya cousin Stew?" Tone suddenly inquired. "Wasn't you suppose to call him for me? Huh?"

"Yeah," she mumbled. "I'll call him tomorrow. It's late right now. His ass not home. He probably out runnin' the streets."

He replied, "Yo, I'm really tryin' to see son."

"Tomorrow baby. Tomorrow," she assured him. "When I get up and go to the bathroom in the middle of the night, I'll leave his number on the dresser for you so you can call him as soon as you get up, if I'm not up."

"Aiight, cool," Tone commented, satisfied with that.

Within seconds Sonya was sound asleep. She went to bed with the notion that every inch of Tone belonged to her. On the contrary, Tone fell asleep thinking about the streets of Baltimore and all the promise that it held. Clearly they had two different agendas.

CHAPTER 4

The warm rays of the sun beamed through a gap in the curtains, gently kissing Sonya's partially covered face. The heat was just enough to stir her from her sleep. Even in her sleep, a blissful smile was pasted on her lips. She was engulfed in a euphoric feeling of disbelief. Sonya couldn't believe that the love of her life, Tone, was here in Baltimore and would be for the foreseeable future. It was as if she had suddenly remembered what it was like to have her boyfriend in her everyday life. She loved him deeply, the time she spent away at college had done nothing to diminish that.

With Tone being nearby, she felt whole. She was that girl again. Immediately, she poked out her butt in an attempt to feel for him. She wanted the warmth of his body and his manhood pressed up against her. Sonya scooted her butt over again and again, to no avail. When her actions didn't yield the results she intended it to, she rolled over in the bed to discover that she was alone.

"Tone?" she called out from the bedroom.

No reply came.

"Tone!" she shouted this time, suspecting that her boyfriend was either in the bathroom, the kitchen, or in the living room watching television.

Completely naked, Sonya rose up out of her warm bed in search of Tone. He was nowhere to be found. In his place she found a handwritten note stuck to the apartment door.

Stew came by and scooped me. I'll be right back, the note read.

"Damn!" Sonya cursed herself for being stupid enough to give him her cousin's number. As if Tone wasn't persistent enough to call someone he had only spoken to a time or two on the phone.

Sonya crumpled up the note and threw it on the floor in disgust as she headed back to her bedroom. She thought that Tone should be introduced to the city of Baltimore gradually and carefully. Clearly he had other ideas. Despite Sonya's best intentions, Tone was quickly turning his move to Baltimore into his own personal field trip.

Sonya sighed and decided to go back to bed. Her day had already gotten off to a bad start. Despite the great night she had last night, Sonya was having a rough morning. As she lay in the bed all she could do was replay last night's sexual sequences. Sonya thought she was going to wake up to some morning sex. Obviously, now that wasn't the case. Tone's disappearance frustrated her. He was beginning to flash signs of the old Tone, her high school sweetheart who danced to the beat of his own drum. The person who did what he wanted, when he wanted, no questions asked.

Sonya wasn't in the mood for Tone's thoughtless behavior today. But she wasn't in the mood to argue with him either. With no classes on her schedule for today, she decided to go back to sleep. Sleep usually prevented her from overreacting, saying or doing something she might later regret. It wasn't like she could contact Tone and tell him to bring his ass back home. Neither he nor her cousin Stew had a pager. So there was no way to get in contact with them. They could be anywhere in the city, so Sonya nixed the idea of jumping in her car and riding around looking for them. She was forced to wait for Tone's return, whenever that was.

Hopefully when she woke back up, he'd be home. Then they could go about their day.

The smoke filled burgundy Toyota Cressida maneuvered through the streets of East Baltimore. Stew hit the Philly blunt filled with weed until he had his fair share then offered Tone some. Tone declined the blunt. He wanted to stay focused and analyze everything around him. Getting high might cloud his judgment. Almost from the moment Tone arrived in Baltimore, he was all business. If it wasn't about a dollar it didn't make sense to him.

Riding around East Baltimore smoking weed wasn't Tone's idea of looking for blocks to hustle on. But for the time being he bit his tongue. Because if nothing else, the time he spent with Stew would give him a good idea of what he was all about. Stew could claim he was a hustler all he wanted. However, time would tell. He could show Tone better than he could tell him.

"I gotta make a stop yo," Stew suddenly announced in between tokes.

"No problem," Tone replied. "Do what you gotta do, kid."

Shortly Stew arrived at his destination and parked his car. He tried to pass Tone the blunt, which he declined, having had his fair share of weed.

"You want some pussy, yo?" Stew questioned him. "I'm about to go knock on this broad's door. She gotta sista, you could spit some of that New York game to her and probably fuck shorty."

Because of his statement, Tone immediately became suspicious of Stew. He didn't know if this was a trick question or if his girlfriend was using her cousin to set him up. The fact of the matter was, Tone just met this guy a few hours ago and he didn't know whether to trust him or not. It was a point of principle for Tone not to mix business.

Tone began, "Yo, c'mon man....You know I'm fuckin' wit' ya cousin, right?"

Stew broke out into a grin. There was no clarification needed. Tone wasn't with it and he had to respect that.

Tone wasn't thirsty. He didn't mind passing on a piece of pussy. To him it was a respect thing, *Don't eat where you shit.* Besides, he knew if he got his drug dealing operation off the ground and he did his thing right, pussy wouldn't be a problem. In fact, it comes with the territory. There was a time and a place for everything. Now wasn't the time for this, and it certainly wasn't the place.

"I don't mean you no harm, yo. I know you my cousin's boyfriend. But a man gone be a man. Variety is the spice of life. I just ain't want you to feel left out when I go do my thing," Stew explained.

Tone didn't know it, but at the moment the contrast between the two men was clear. Stew wasn't a go-getter he was more of a skirt chaser. He wasn't who he projected himself to be in the conversation they had over the phone.

All the talk of him being a hustler was starting to look like a façade. Another incident or two and Tone would officially relegate Stew into the category of being a clown who didn't want to make money.

The car came to a stop on Ashland Avenue.

"Let me go handle my business real quick. I'll be right back, yo," Stew announced. "You'll be alright out here right?"

"No question," Tone told him. "I'm good in any hood."

"I know I been bullshittin' all mornin'," Stew insisted as he exited the car. "But when I come back yo, we gone go find you a block to move that shit."

"Word!" Tone remarked. "Now you talkin'."

Tone watched as Stew quickly climbed the steps of a nearby row house and knocked on the door. After a brief pause the door was opened and Stew disappeared inside.

Time went by slowly. Tone sat in the car fiddling with the radio. Stew was taking longer than Tone thought. He grew bored and restless sitting in the car. Finally Tone got out the car and smoked a cigarette. As he did, Tone took notice of what was happening around him. He saw groups of people entering an alleyway, cars constantly pulling up and dropping people off, but no one exiting the alley.

Even from a distance Tone could tell that there was some illegal drug activity going on. On this block, the alleyway seemed to be the center of attention.

With all the people going to and fro, Tone got the sense something major was happening around here. The block had a certain energy about it that he couldn't explain. One that he'd only seen in New York on the first and fifteenth of the month. There was money out here, Tone could sense that much.

He sat on the car, continuing to observe when fate intervened.

"Hey," an older woman said. "You wouldn't happen to have another one of them cigarettes would you yo? I'll buy it off you."

"It's aiight," Tone said. "You good. I gotcha!"

Reaching into his pants pockets, Tone retrieved a pack of Newport cigarettes and handed one over.

"You gotta light, New York?" she asked with the cigarette perched between her dark lips.

For the first time Tone took a good look at her. She was not a bad looking woman, but by her frail weight, Tone could see she had seen better days. Her black cornrowed hair had large traces of gray in it. Her eyelids were so heavy they drooped. It appeared as if she hadn't slept in days. Her forehead was creased with lines etched by years of stress. This woman bore the earmarks of the street life and drug abuse all over her. She was by all accounts a street person.

Tone didn't immediately discount her presence because of that. Her look would only lend to her credibility. He had the unique ability to treat a person like a person regardless to what condition he found them in. In fact, this woman being a street person was a plus. It only meant that he could relate to her in some form or fashion. She could put him down to what was going on around here.

He sensed that there was a wealth of information inside her. Tone knew he couldn't just let her leave his presence without picking her brain about the drug game in the area. He knew he had to hold a conversation with her, so he initiated one. Tone cut straight to the chase.

"What's goin' on out here?" Tone suddenly said.

The woman remarked, "You already know what it is, New York. If you ain't in it, you in the way."

"Word? How can I get some money out here?" Tone asked.

"Easy," she said. "If you got some good product, I can help you move it. Alotta this shit out here stepped on. It's garbage. Junkies can't get high off cut."

Tone was equal parts hustler and equal parts opportunist. The information he was receiving from her was exactly what he wanted to hear. The wheels in his criminal mind began to turn.

"Take a walk wit' me," Tone said as he locked the car doors.

"Where to, New York?" she wondered. Truth be told, she would have followed the stranger to the moon. He was talking her kind of talk.

"To the store," he told her.

As they walked the short distance to the corner store, Tone and the woman conversed as if they had known each other well. The entire time Tone was just observing his surroundings.

"How you know I'm from New York?" he wondered.

"I could smell you New York niggas a mile away, yo. This ain't my first rodeo. I done dealt wit' a few New Yorkers before," she bragged. "I know y'all muthafuckas. It's the way y'all walk, the way y'all talk. It's the accent all y'all have. Y'all just carry yaselves differently, yo."

Tone joked, "So is that a good or a bad thing?"

"Both," the woman snapped. "It could be good if you out here just tryin' to fit in. It could be bad if you comin' out here tryin' to show out, yo. You can't come out here and try to get all the money and fuck all the bitches. That shit right there breeds jealousy. A jealous muthafucka will kill you quicker than a scared muthafucka. It ain't what you do, New York, it's how you do it. Trust me I know. I done seen New Yorkers come and I done seen them go. In this game longevity is key."

The wisdom in her words caught Tone's ear. He could relate to what she was saying. Intelligence was always attractive to him, no matter where it came from. He yearned to hear more from her.

"Word," Tone chimed. "You don't have to worry about me. I ain't on it like that. I don't want no trouble, but I damn sure ain't gone run from none. I'm out here to get this paper first and foremost."

"That's good to know, yo," Shorty assured him. "Because there's money to be made, you just gotta stay focused."

They stopped at the corner store where Tone bought both himself and his companion a soda. As they sipped their individual drinks, they continued to walk. Tone made it a point to walk into the direction of the alleyway where he saw all the foot traffic headed. He remained observant as he continued sipping his soda.

"Yo, what's ya name?" he asked. "I'm been kickin' it wit' you and I don't even know ya name."

"Shorty," she answered.

"Fa real? Yo, how you get that name?" he laughed, admiring her small stature.

"You got jokes, huh? How the hell you think? Look at me," she chuckled. "Now what's ya name, yo?"

The question caught Tone off guard. He knew better than to give her his real name. "Jason," he said with a straight face.

Shorty took a long pull on her cigarette, smirking as she blew the smoke out her nose.

"Jason, huh?" she spat. "Yeah right! That ain't ya damn name. That's a fuckin' alias yo. All you New Yorkers are liars."

Tone couldn't help himself. He doubled over in laughter.

"It's Tone," he admitted, unsure why he had just given her his real name. "But if the police ask its Jason Jones, aiight?"

"Okay, New York Tone," Shorty teased. "Pleased to meet you."

"Yo, I like ya style," Tone commented, taking an instant liking to her. "New York Tone, huh? Got a lil ring to it."

Tone felt like he had met a mover and shaker in the streets. Shorty was someone on the frontline who was very knowledgeable. That he could already see. Already she was his eyes and his ears.

As soon they got to the opening of the alleyway, Tone peered in. There he witnessed a sight he had never seen before. Grown people, addicts, standing in a single file line, silently, like children waiting to receive their bags of dope. The line seemed to stretch from one end of the alley to the next. Unsure of what he was seeing, Tone did a double take and continued walking. Then suddenly he doubled back to get a second look. This only served as confirmation. He had seen what he thought he saw. It all happened so quickly nobody noticed him.

"What's that?" Tone asked.

"Dope," she assured him. "That's a dope line, yo."

Damn! Tone thought. All he saw was dollar signs in his head as he did a quick count of all the customers on line.

"Yo, it's like that out here?" he wondered.

Shorty replied, "It's like that everywhere out here, New York. If you got good product and some hustle in you, you gone make money, yo. Believe me."

"No doubt," Tone added as his mind continued to race.

They walked back to the car with Tone remaining rather quiet as thoughts of money raced through his mind.

Meanwhile, Shorty continued to fill him in on the drug trade in the area and the players involved. She told him who was who and what was what.

"This neighborhood is wide open, yo. Ain't no good quality coke around here since the Feds come through here, yo." Shorty proclaimed. "The game don't stop because a player gets popped."

Shorty told him that there had been a big drug bust a few months before he arrived in Baltimore. A federal indictment had swept the area clean of any major drug organizations that had control of the area. So the neighborhood was basically up for grabs. She explained to him that the time was right for him to come in and do his thing.

"What you got, girl or boy?" Shorty questioned.

"What?" Tone answered, confused.

"Dope or Coke?" she reiterated.

"Coke," Tone replied. "Fishscale."

"Is it raw?" she wondered.

"No question," Tone added, confident in his quality of drugs.

"You got some that shit on you now, yo?" she moaned.

In Baltimore, everyone and their mother was looking for a good New York drug connection. Here it was Shorty, out of all people, had the good fortune of just stumbling across one. Inwardly, she was thanking her lucky stars. She knew their relationship could be mutually beneficial.

He answered. "Nah, I ain't bring none out. I wanted to scope shit out first."

"Damn yo, if you had that shit on you and yo shit as good as you say, we would have made a killin' right now," she said, trying to entice him.

"Shorty, slow ya roll. Tomorrow is another day," Tone stated. "I'm not rushin' into nuttin'. It's better to be safe than sorry."

Shorty replied, "Yeah, you right New York. What time tomorrow we meetin' up?"

"You tell me? What's the best time?" he wondered.

"Mornin'," she assured him. "The junkies cop that boy in the mornin'. If we set up early and put the word out, they'll come cop that girl from us. Once they know it's raw, they'll keep comin' back all day long."

Tone liked the sound of that. From what he had heard, there was a whole lot of money to be made.

By the time Stew finally exited the house, Tone and Shorty had arrived back at the car and had made arrangements to meet up at a prescribed time and place.

"Shorty, what up yo?" Stew greeted her. "You out here hollerin' at my people, huh?"

"Oh, this ya peoples?" she replied. "I was wonderin' who he was waitin' on… New York you should have said somethin'."

"Why?" Tone said. "Did it matter?"

"No, but ya peoples is my peoples. Me and Stew go way back like car seats. Ask him bout me, yo! He'll tell you how thorough I am."

Stew cosigned her street credibility. "Shorty more thorough than most of these niggas out here yo. She's a soldier."

Stew went on to explain how Shorty's name was good as gold in the streets. Shorty was as much of a staple in East Baltimore as any good brand of heroin. When junkies wanted to know who had that good stuff, they sought out Shorty. When drug dealers wanted to spread the word about some good product, they bought a few vials or bags over for her to sample. If she said a dealer had the bomb, then he had it. Shorty was the number one drug runner and tester around.

Tone felt fortunate to run into the right person on his first trip to the hood. That was all Tone needed to hear. He was completely sold.

"Yo, Shorty," Tone announced. "I'll see you later."

"New York, lemme holla at you for a second," Shorty replied before Tone and Stew could drive away.

"Yeah," Tone responded, taking a few steps away from the car.

"Say, New York," Shorty began as humbly as possible. "You wouldn't happen to have a few dollars on you that you could spare. I'm on e right now."

Tone dug into his pockets and handed over the first bill he touched. It was a ten-dollar bill.

Shorty's eyes lit up in anticipation of the bag of dope that she would soon be copping.

"Thanks New York. You alright, yo," Shorty said.

Tone knew in the grand scheme of things, it was a small price to pay in exchange for all the helpful information Shorty had given him. He saw value in Shorty and it was way more than ten dollars. If no one else saw value in her, Tone certainly did.

"You're welcome," Tone told her.

"We gotta go," Stew interrupted as he blew the horn. "Shorty, we'll holla at you later yo."

From the minute Tone hopped in the car and they pulled off, Stew began bragging and boasting about the sex he had just had.

"I tore that pussy up yo," Stew told Tone.

"Yo, take me back to the crib," he interrupted.

"Why?" Stew began. "I'm about to show you the strip. Introduce you to a few of my people so you can do ya thang out here yo."

"We can do that anotha day," he explained. "Yo, just take me back to the crib before ya cousin start buggin'."

"Tone, I know you ain't gone let no pussy get in the way of you getting' some money, yo," Stew told him.

"Nigga, look who talkin'?" Tone said sarcastically. "I'ma tell you what I ain't gone do. Let another nigga fuck up my shit. I do a good job of that myself."

Tone's statement had been an excuse to get away from him. It seemed like he spent the entire day sightseeing, smoking weed or just chilling with Stew. He felt like he had wasted enough time with this dude.

In Tone's book if Stew couldn't be used then he was useless. He served no purpose. Stew acted like he didn't want to make any money, so Tone didn't want to be around him. He didn't want to be sidetracked by Stew's nonsense any more. He wanted to make money so he had to hang around like-minded individuals.

Stew laughed. "Alright Tone, I hear you. I'll drop you off. I'll holler at you tomorrow yo."

Fuck you! Tone thought. Tomorrow he planned on striking out on his own. He felt the urge to make something happen by himself. Stew's heart wasn't into hustling. Tone could tell. A real hustler eats, sleeps and breathes the streets. Hustling was merely something Stew did from time to time. At the moment this was very much Tone's life. Hustling was the only hope he had.

"Yeah, do that," Tone replied.

On the way home Tone couldn't stop thinking about Shorty. He hadn't been this pumped up about a block in awhile. He felt like he had connected with her in a way he might not never have with Stew. He knew sometimes it took a lame person to bring two real people together.

Despite her flaws, her drug habit, Tone felt Shorty was a real one. But only time would tell.

CHAPTER 5

Normally Tone wasn't a morning person at all. However, on this day his body's internal alarm clock had awoken him in more than enough time. He was already dressed by the time his girlfriend woke up. He could hardly contain his excitement, not knowing what today's adventure would hold. Today would be his first taste of the action. Tone would get to see what the hustle was really like in the streets of Baltimore. He wouldn't be observing any more. From here on, he would be a fulltime participant in the drug game.

"Whenever you ready," Tone said through the bathroom. "I'm ready."

"Okay," Sonya replied as she finished brushing her teeth.

Tone walked back into the bedroom and inspected himself in the full-length mirror. He was concerned that his nine-millimeter that he carried in his waistband might be too revealing. He adjusted the weapon until he was completely satisfied the bulge was gone.

The thought of the gun remained with him as Sonya entered the room to grab her book bag. He moved cautiously away from her, not wanting her to have too good of a look.

"I'm ready," she announced, grabbing her books off the floor.

"We out," Tone said.

"You sure about this?" she wondered. "I mean, goin' to a drug block to meet a junkie you just met yesterday? How smart is that?"

"I'm doin' what I gotta do," he replied strongly. "Lemme worry about that."

"I'd feel way more comfortable if my cousin went with you," she stated.

"Nah, Stew good right where he at," he remarked. "I ain't got time for his B.S today. I'm makin' moves."

Although Sonya voiced her concerns she knew she couldn't tell Tone how to move in the streets. Tone was too stubborn to heed her advice or listen to her woman's intuition. Still, his safety was her number one concern.

"If anything happens..." her voice trailed off.

"Yo, stop talkin' like that. I hate when you get like this," he huffed.

Sonya felt bad that Tone was mad at her, but she hated when Tone made her feel guilty about caring so deeply about him. She merely was trying to imply she didn't think it was wise to be making drug related moves on his own, without anyone watching his back. He knew she had a point. He had come to the same conclusion himself. Yet he'd rather not rely on someone so unfocused as her cousin Stew.

"Sorry Tone, that's not what I meant," Sonya apologized. She promised herself next time she'd keep her feelings to herself. It was just one of those things that she always thought. But this time she mistakenly verbalized it.

Sonya insinuating something could possibly happen to him really bothered Tone. He didn't understand why she would put that negative vibe into the air.

Tone snapped. "Don't be sorry, just don't do it."

Within a few moments things were seemingly back to normal, although the silence between them told a different story. After their verbal exchange, the vibe was noticeably different. Sonya noticed that the excitement that had been so apparent in Tone's eyes had been replaced by apprehension. His mood had suddenly changed. Inwardly, she was worried for Tone's safety, but she needed to keep up the brave act. However, she knew once Tone left her presence she'd worry about him all day long.

After exiting the apartment and getting in the car, Tone instructed his girlfriend on exactly where to drop him off. God forbid if anything happened to him at least Sonya would know where to come looking for him.

"Be careful," Sonya told him as the car came to a stop.

"I got this," Tone assured her as he kissed her goodbye. "See you later."

"What time you'll be home?" she asked.

"When I'm done," Tone replied without looking back.

She shook her head. Sonya watched her boyfriend as he walked away. Tone's over-confidence showed her that he needed protecting, if from no one else than himself.

"Yo, Shorty here?" Tone asked, staring at the skinny junkie who opened the door.

"Shorty!!!" the man hollered into the house. "Somebody here for you."

"Let him in," she called out.

Upon hearing her animated voice, the doorway opened up and Tone was allowed to enter. He was lead to the kitchen.

"You can have a seat. Shorty be right down," the man said before rushing off upstairs.

Tone took a look at the raggedy dinette set and the flimsy mismatch chairs that looked too weak to hold up under his body weight. Immediately he decided against sitting. With no one around he was free to take inventory of his shabby surroundings. He looked up and saw paint chips dangling from the ceiling, grease stained walls and roaches roaming freely almost everywhere he looked. Tone made a point not sit or lean against anything. He didn't want anything to crawl on him or take any roaches home with him.

This place was a crack house, a dope spot, shooting gallery or whatever else you wanted to call it. There was no way any human being not under the influence of drugs would willingly live here.

In plain sight on the kitchen table, he saw dozens of loose, multicolored crack vials scattered about. They were probably leftovers from a recent drug binge. Nearby an ashtray overflowed with cigarette butts and ashes spilling on the table. A few empty bottles of fifths of liquor, the inexpensive, strong kind that winos and junkies drink, seemed to litter the floor, cheap liquor with names like Night Train, Thunder Bird and Wild Irish Rose.

Tone had been in more than his share of drug houses back in New York, but this was amongst the worst. He could only imagine what the rest of the house looked like. In fact, he didn't even want to know. He was at the point where all he wanted to do was handle his business and leave.

"New fuckin' York," Shorty smiled, flashing a mouthful of missing or rotting teeth. "You ready to get this money this mornin', yo?"

"I was born ready," Tone stated.

"Show me what you got," Shorty told him.

Quickly, Tone stuck his hand inside his hoodie pocket and removed a clear sandwich bag. He handed the doubled sandwich bag over Shorty. It contained around a half an ounce of powder cocaine.

"That's it?" she wondered as she took possession of the drug.

"For now," he replied, seeing no need to explain himself further.

Shorty untied the knot from the outside bag then removed the bag that contained the cocaine. She held it up toward the light. Her eyes seemed to light up when she saw the silver shimmering particles of Fishscale cocaine. She opened the bag, dabbing a little bit on her finger to test its purity. It instantly numbed her tongue.

She proclaimed loudly, "New York, we gotta winner here!"

Tone was happy that Shorty thought so highly of his coke. If she felt that way about it, chances are customers on the streets would too.

Immediately, Shorty went to work. She quickly rinsed out the remnants of some left over Kool-Aid in a dirty jelly jar that lay in the sink. Then she went inside the refrigerator and grabbed a box of baking soda. Next, she dumped half of the product into the jar, along with a small amount of baking soda that she carefully measured with her eyes. Shorty poured some water inside the jar from the faucet, turned on the front stove pilot and sat the jar on the stove.

"We gone rock half of this up for the smokers and leave the other half just like it is for the shooters," Shorty advised.

"Shorty, you ever did this before?" Tone asked, knowing there was a risk involved whenever coke was transformed to crack.

Shorty sucked her teeth. "I do this shit in my sleep, New York."

The only reason Tone asked was because he was well aware that he could lose more than a few grams of cocaine in the process if Shorty didn't know what she was doing. Tone was in no position to lose anything.

"I cooked up kilos for some of the biggest dope boys in the city," she swore.

Tone had some reservations about that statement. But then again, he knew she had no reason to lie to him. Since she seemed to be telling the truth about everything else, he had no choice but to have faith in Shorty.

Tone's eyes were transfixed on the stove where the water inside the jar began to bubble. Shorty began to stir it repeatedly. Once the baking soda burned off and the cocaine began to gel, she removed the jar from the stove and filled it up with cold water. When the cocaine hardened, Shorty placed it on a paper towel. She had successfully transformed Tone's powder cocaine into what was known on the streets of Baltimore as *Ready Rock*.

"Waalaa," she announced. "This what I do."

"I see," Tone remarked playfully.

"Brought it all back," Shorty added, admiring the cookie shaped piece of cocaine inside the jar.

Tone nodded his head in agreement.

No sooner than the words were out of her mouth, Shorty did something strange, at least from Tone's point of view. She produced a small crack pipe from her back pocket and broke off a small sample of the drug, placing it inside the stem.

"Ain't no shame in my game, I do what I do," Shorty said as she lit the drug and inhaled deeply. "Don't you ever let me hear about you fuckin' wit' this shit, yo."

"Never that," he assured her.

With sympathetic eyes, Tone stared at Shorty, as if to say to each his own. This wasn't a surprise to him at all. He had suspected as much all along. But to know someone is getting high is one thing. To see it is something totally different.

Getting high was Shorty's weakness just like hustling crack was Tone's. Truthfully, Tone didn't care about her addiction, as long as it didn't interfere with them getting some money together. Shorty could do whatever, as far as he was concerned, she was grown.

For Shorty life wasn't always like this. She once was a law abiding, tax-paying citizen who suffered a severe broken leg on her job as a mail carrier. At the hospital she was prescribed morphine to help her cope with the pain from her injury. From the first time she tried the drug, Shorty got hooked. A monster was created. Her life began to spiral downhill. Drugs got a hold of her and never let go. Essentially, Shorty sacrificed a good life with her close-knit family for a dark, lonely life of addiction.

"That's some good shit there, yo," she swore while exhaling a thick cloud of crack smoke in the opposite direction. "Time to rock and roll yo."

Shorty put her makeshift crack pipe down and sprung into action. She went upstairs and retrieved a clear sandwich bag filled with black top vials. At the kitchen table the duo proceeded to bag up the entire batch they cooked up, placing the contents inside the vials. Whatever crumbs remained, Shorty convinced Tone to hand out as testers to a select group of drug addicts. Initially, it was those free testers that caused a buzz and sparked a cocaine feeding frenzy.

From his experience of hustling on the streets of New York, Tone knew people didn't sell drugs. Drugs sold themselves. All one had to do was be there to exchange the product for the currency. It was commerce, albeit an illegal one, supply and demand. The same business principles applied.

Tone sold out quickly, with Shorty working the streets. The news about the good coke traveled fast. He had to return home to get more drugs and repeat the process all over again. This time Tone brought even more cocaine than he had before. He had the idea that he was going to make more money than he did last time. And he did.

All day long Tone stayed inside the dope house guarding the stash, while Shorty sold the drugs, hand-to-hand on the street and in the alleys along Homewood Avenue. He had no idea if Shorty was tapping the vials or shorting him on money. Nor did he care. Everything went smoothly; he seemed to make money hand over fist. At the end of the day, just before all of the vials were sold, Tone paid Shorty in product and cash, at her insistence.

"I told you we was goin' to kill 'em, yo," Shorty bragged as they exited the house through the back door and walked through the alley toward the main street.

It was nighttime when Tone finally emerged from the stash house. The darkness that had descended over the city had suddenly made him realize the drastic shift in time. It was then that he came to the realization just how long he had been cooped up in the stash house. That didn't amaze him, it was the couple thousand dollars he had in his pockets that really impressed him.

Today was a good day, he thought. *Tomorrow gone be even better.*

With Shorty escorting him, they matched each other step for step as they walked a few blocks in search of a hack. Then suddenly Tone's search for a ride to take him home turned into looking for the first place they could find to get off the streets.

Tone heard it before he ever saw a thing.

"Yo, what the fuck is that?" Tone asked.

The loud chopping sound of a police helicopter's rotating blades flooded the area as people began to scatter. A spotlight soon encircled Tone and Shorty, dousing them in a bright light. Suddenly, Tone had his answer.

Oh my fuckin' God! he thought.

Never in his life had he experienced anything like this. This was something straight out of a movie. His heart sank to the pit of his stomach. As hard as he focused on staying cool, a nervous energy began surging through his body. Tone had no idea of what was going to happen next.

Ain't no way in hell I'm goin' out like this. I'm not gettin' arrested on my first day on the block, he vowed.

Shorty saw the look of concern on his face and quickly addressed it.

"Don't look up, New York," Shorty warned. "It's the police. Put ya head down and keep walkin' yo. Just follow me."

That was easier said than done. Tone found himself sneaking a peak upward through his peripheral vision. However, the spotlight was blinding and he couldn't get a good look at the helicopter. So he had to settle for feeling its threatening presence instead.

Tone's thoughts raced. Inwardly, he shook his head at his sudden reversal of fortune. One minute he was feeling like he was on top of the world, and the next he was feeling like he was going to jail. Tone abandoned his instinctive impulse of running. Instead he chose to take Shorty's advice. Something told him she knew what she was talking about.

The police helicopter continued to follow them as it hovered above, barely atop of the power lines and the rooftops of the row houses, sending trash and dust swirling around them. Yet side by side they continued to walk, remaining cool.

As quickly as it had started, it ended. The police helicopter suddenly raised its altitude, turned off its spotlight and disappeared into the East Baltimore City night skies. At the very last minute, Tone was able to lift his head and catch a glimpse of it.

Instantly Tone was relieved that the heat was off of them. Slowly he was able to pull himself together. The weird reaction he experienced to his first encounter with a Baltimore City police helicopter was understandable. It was then that Tone came to the realization that the drug game in Baltimore was a different kind of beast and nothing that he had experienced in his hood could have prepared him for it.

"New York you was scared to death, yo," Shorty joked.

"Man, that shit was crazy. These cops ain't playin' fair out here, huh?" Tone commented.

"Welcome to Baltimore," she exclaimed.

Tone's story may have begun in New York, but it was about to unfold in Baltimore.

CHAPTER 6

Tone was so immersed in the streets of Baltimore that he seemed to lose track of time. The days turned into weeks, and the weeks into months. This time period was more so a feeling out process to make sure that he and Shorty could work with each other. The vast amounts of money they began to make together assured him they could. Slowly but surely Tone grinded away and began to build a name for himself in the streets of East Baltimore. Piece by piece he started to assemble his own drug organization, the pitchers, lookouts and runners. All at his disposal. It started off with just him and Shorty. Whenever the mood struck him, Stew would get down too. Eventually, he bought his younger cousin Mann down from New York since he was running wild and getting into trouble in the city. Tone felt like since he was risking his freedom for nothing, he might as well make some money off his recklessness. But besides that,

Tone needed someone around him he could trust, unconditionally, and Mann was that person. He felt whom better to trust than family.

Once the proceeds from the drug sales began to come in, Tone was able to hire more help. This came in the form of local, young, hungry dudes from the neighborhood, native Baltimoreans. He knew this strategy would pay dividends moving forward. Tone did this deliberately to avoid the animosities and rivalries that an all New York drug crew might incur.

Long before Tone arrived in Baltimore, the rivalry between hustlers from New York and Baltimore had been perpetuated for years. Blood had been spilt and murders had been committed to strengthen each side's stranglehold on the drug trade. Tone hadn't done anything to fan those deadly flames. He merely inherited a lot of animosity because of where he was from, not because of anything he had done. Tone was a different kind of New Yorker, he heeded Shorty's words and chose to blend in. He was well aware of the anti-New York sentiment in certain sections of Baltimore. He made it a point to steer clear of those places, not because he was afraid, it was because feuding with someone over a drug block was pointless. Beef was a broke man's sport that Tone would rather not indulge in. He'd rather stay right in East Baltimore, where the streets had accepted him and the neighborhood had embraced him. Where he could flourish in relative anonymity.

In Baltimore, hustlers from New York were notorious for taking over neighborhoods and everything it had to offer and never giving anything back. Tone decided to make himself the exact opposite of everything that the streets were accustomed to when dealing with a New Yorker. He played fair and gave everyone their just due. If he ever did anything to someone, then they had it coming.

Man, fuck them New York boyz yo, Junkies often said to Tone. *No disrespect Tone, you the only New Yorker I fuck wit. You ain't like them other petty muthafuckas yo. You show love out here in these streets.*

Early on, Tone used strategic moves to defuse the anti-New Yorker sentiment. Whether it was by occasionally accepting short money from junkies or looking out for kids in the neighborhood by buying them new tennis shoes when their old one's wore out. He gave money to struggling single mothers who might be behind on a bill. These random acts of kindness deflected any distrust or misplaced reservations that anyone may have had about him. As a result, the community began to embrace him, overlooking the fact that he was a part of the drug problem that was ravaging the neighborhood.

Despite his best intentions, Tone's drug operation didn't get off the ground without a hitch. He struggled to keep a consistent flow of drugs. As quickly as he would get his drugs from New York, the quicker he would sell out. He couldn't maintain a big enough or constant supply of drugs. Because of this incontinency, he lost a few customers and a few workers too. Only the loyal ones remained as he worked out the kinks. In reality, Tone was running a nickel and dime drug operation, trying to find his footing in the drug trade in Baltimore. He was forming the cornerstones of what would some day be a drug empire.

No matter how good the quality of his cocaine was, Tone's unpredictability, accompanied with lack of sufficient weight, kept him cornering the drug market in the area. He was forced to rethink his game plan as a result, in an attempt to solve his problem. His thoughts turned to older, more established hustlers from his hood that he knew, maybe form some kind of partnership with them and really flood the streets of East Baltimore with coke. He quickly scratched that idea, fearing that they would take over his entire drug operation and leave him out in the cold once they saw all the money there was to be made.

Reluctantly, he sent his cousin Mann up to New York a time or two in an attempt to find a coke connection. But those trips yielded nothing.

Tone remained on the path of inconsistency until he made a bold move of returning to New York himself. It was in Manhattan, Washington Heights, that Tone finally met the solid cocaine supplier that he needed. After constantly copping weight on a weekly basis, his Dominican coke connection saw the value in Tone as a customer, and began giving him cocaine on consignment. Whatever amount of weight Tone bought, he matched. Once he found a reliable cocaine connection, things really took off for Tone in Baltimore.

With a consistent supply of cocaine, Tone was able to begin to make some real money. He worked around all the major drug operations in the area until his organization rivaled theirs. Then he surpassed them by using all kinds of gimmicks he had learned in New York to lure new clientele. He fed right into the greed of the junkies by offering two for ten-dollar specials, buy three get one free. He gave out full sized testers whenever he bought a new batch of coke out. Aside from giving out free, full sized testers, Tone was winning on two fronts, with quality and quantity.

With the right connection, Tone's drug block really began to pop. The streets of East Baltimore began to buzz with talk of *New York Tone* and his raw cocaine. Every day he was gaining more street notoriety, unlike anything he had ever experienced in New York. Quickly, Tone was becoming a star in the hood.

Leaving New York was looking like the best thing that ever happened to him. He went from a little fish in a big pond to big fish in a little pond. He was beginning to play the game on a level not even he had imagined.

"Black Tops! Ready Rock!" a worker's voice chanted.

"Got that Ready y'all," another worker shouted. "Don't beat yaself, treat yaself. If you wanna get high, then I'm ya guy, yo."

Dressed in black from head to toe, a black hoodie, black jeans and black Timberland boots, Tone sat quietly on the abandoned and boarded up row house steps doing his best to blend into the bleak, impoverished landscape while observing the daily activities. Each day Tone had taken up the same tactical position on the block. Try as he might to be incognito, his presence was unmistakable. He served as a deterrent for any stickup kid or would be robber. The gun in his waistband testified to that fact.

The junkies knew he was strapped, his workers knew he was strapped, and maybe even the occasional police patrol car that passed might have known too. It was no secret that Tone had a gun on him. East Baltimore was an extension of the world, guns were everywhere and violence could erupt anywhere.

Tone lead by example. Although he didn't have to be out there, he hit the block every day with his team to make sure things were run right. He never wanted to feel that he was too big or beyond getting his hands dirty by putting in some work. This was his thing, no one else had a more vested interest for seeing it go right besides him. His perception of the situation was in line with the reality. He stood to gain the most financially. With the demand for his coke steadily increasing along with his profits, Tone felt like he could be targeted for a robbery any day. For those reasons, Tone was willing to protect his drug operation with his life.

Tone glanced at the alley and smiled as he saw his workers serving a multitude of customers. He was proud of himself. He had taken a block that had been abandoned and built it back up into an open-air, 'round the clock drug market that junkies frequented in search of some of the best powder cocaine and ready rock that East Baltimore had to offer. Rain or shine, day or night, customers came and went.

Tone's eyes scoured the street for anything out of the ordinary before returning to the junkies on line. He searched each face, looking for anyone who seemed out of place. For the moment everything appeared to be in order, so Tone continued to sit on the stoop while keeping vigil on the block. One after another he watched the junkies get served their vials of coke until the line died down.

"I'll be right back, I gotta use the bathroom yo," Shorty said to him as she suddenly appeared from the alley before disappearing up the block.

Tone nodded his head slightly, barely acknowledging her. Though his suspicions lead him to believe her trip up the block wasn't to use the bathroom at all. Shorty was probably gone to get high. Tone didn't care though, Shorty had proven her loyalty and allegiance to him time and time again. If it wasn't for her, Tone wouldn't be in the position he was in. Besides that, he knew his drug operation would run itself until she returned. He employed a small team of workers to assure that it would.

Stone faced, Tone watched closely as a stranger approached. He eyed him suspiciously. The man hadn't even come in close proximity of him yet and he had already gotten a bad feeling about him.

"What's up, yo?" the man greeted him.

Tone replied slowly, "You!"

"You New York Tone?" he asked.

"Why?" Tone fired back. Whenever Tone felt uncomfortable with a question, he always put the onus back on the person asking the question by stating why.

Tone studied the man's physical features for a moment. The thing that jumped out at him was his dark jet-black skin and big potbelly. His dark beady eyes seemed to announce his griminess.

"Ain't nuttin', New York. I don't mean you no harm. I was just askin' that's all, yo," he explained. "You don't sound like you from Baltimore."

"Well what do somebody from Baltimore sound like?" Tone wondered.

"Not like you, yo," the man laughed in an attempt to ease the tension.

The man suddenly extended his hand in an attempt to formally introduce himself.

"They called me Ronnie Sykes, yo," he blurted out. "But everybody call me Sykes."

He stared at Sykes' dirty, black, swollen hand and declined to shake it. Instead Tone gave him a head nod. Seeing that Sykes coolly withdrew his hand. If he felt slighted or disrespected by Tone's actions, he did a good job of camouflaging it.

"Boy, you New York boyz go hard huh, yo," he laughed. "You remind of my boy Champ from New York. He usta be up on 20th Street and Greenmount Avenue. I think he from Brooklyn.... Queens or one of them places, yo... Don't start me to lyin' though... Anyway, you might know him?"

"Nah, I don't know 'em," Tone assured him. "New York's a big place."

He was beginning to sense Sykes was trying to run game on him. Making small talk in an attempt to hide the real reason for his sudden appearance.

"So I heard," Sykes proclaimed. "Yo, was the man wit' that China White."

"I hear you," Tone replied, sarcastically.

Sykes must have heard the sarcasm in his voice because he quickly changed the subject.

"Anyway," he began, "I just come home a few days ago. I'm tryin' to get back on my feet yo.... I was wonderin' if I could get in wit' you. I'll do whatever, New York. These niggas around here know me. They know I don't play.... I'm as thorough as they come."

As Sykes boasted about his exploits in the streets, Tone just stared blankly at him. Tone got the feeling that Sykes thought he was actually somebody. And maybe he was back in his day. However, right now, he was a nobody to him. Try as he might, Sykes couldn't convince him otherwise. Tone's mind was already made up.

"Yo fam, I got my team already," Tone told him. "I only deal wit' a select few. My circle small."

"Damn, New York. They said you the man around here yo. You getting' all the money and if I wanna get money to see you. They said you got the best coke in East Baltimore.... That you was a good dude.... Damn, New York, don't do me like that yo.... I messed up, I just came out the joint...." Sykes pleaded.

"They told you wrong. I ain't gettin' it. I'm gettin' a quarter over lunch money. I'm strugglin' just like everybody else," Tone announced, trying persuade him otherwise.

"I hear you, New York," Sykes said, regrettably. "If you ever need me yo, just holla."

"Aiight, cool. If a spot open up, I'll let you know," he lied.

"Say, New York," Sykes continued. "I know you said you ain't got no position for me right now, but I was wonderin' could I get a lil help?"

Tone stared at him for a moment. He knew exactly what Sykes was hinting at. Sykes wasn't really looking for a hand up. He was looking for a hand out. Tone was slowly becoming a victim of his own success. It seemed like word was getting around about how fair he played, how he looked out for certain junkies giving them a few vials of ready rock on credit. His acts of generosity made him a good dude to some, and a target for the low life's and leeches.

In Tone's book, that's exactly what Sykes was, a leech. He had seen his kind before, time and time again, undercover addicts looking to use him. Tone had helped a few local hustler's fresh out of jail, rehab or whatever, get on their feet by giving them packages of drugs to sell for themselves with the idea that when they got on their feet, they'd not only pay him back, but come buy weight from him. However, that never materialized. In the end, it turned out to be just talk on their part and wishful thinking on his. Their drug habits turned out to be bigger than their hustle. Making money was a ploy they used to cover their real intentions of getting high.

Tone had gotten burned too many times showing love to look out for another person other than himself.

"Help how?" Tone snapped.

"Lemme hold somethin'… just a couple vials yo… til a better day," Sykes reasoned. "I'll pay you back yo… You got my word on that…. I swear to God yo…."

Finally, Sykes had exposed his hand. Now Tone knew that his entire conversation was fraudulent from the start. What Sykes was really attempting to do was something called a friendly extortion. Asking for drugs in a friendly manner. Tone knew if he gave Sykes anything that it would open a door for him to keep coming back repeatedly. He would rather nip the situation in the bud now than have him feeling entitled to some free drugs anytime he felt like getting high.

"Ain't nuttin' free my nigga," Tone barked. "Can't support ya habit fam."

Sykes flipped out. "You New York boyz some disrespectful muthafuckas yo. I just ask you for a lil sumthin' yo and you gone do me like that? Me, Sykes? This ain't New York, this Baltimore yo. Pay homage.... You got me fuck up yo! You must not know who the fuck I am?"

Not liking what he just heard, Tone rose from the stoop. With his hand underneath his hoodie, he tightly gripped his gun, signaling to Sykes he was prepared to make this verbal altercation into a physical one.

Transforming from beggar to bully, Sykes was now attempting to throw his weight around and intimidate Tone. The problem was Tone wasn't easily intimidated. Despite the size differential favoring Sykes, he had the heart to stand up to him. He would meet aggression with aggression. He wasn't about to bow down to a bully and let him walk all over him. If it was a few vials today, it'll be something else tomorrow. Tone knew how he dealt with Sykes, or rather how the block saw how he dealt with him, would go a long way in determining how he was treated for the duration of his time there.

"Whore ass nigga, I'll run you from 'round here yo," he continued before taking a few steps toward Tone.

Quickly, Tone drew his gun. Placing his weapon close to the side of his leg. He menacingly pointed his finger in Sykes' direction. His actions caused Sykes to slowly backpedal with hands slightly raised.

Tone had drawn a line in the sand that he dared Sykes to cross.

"Yo, who the fuck you think you talking to? C'mon, play yaself my nigga and I'll leave you right where you stand," Tone threatened. "I don't give a fuck who you are!"

"You got it! You got it, New York," he repeated while backpedaling away.

"Yeah, I know I got it," Tone insisted. "Now get da fuck outta here. And don't let me catch you 'round here again, or you gone have a fuckin' problem."

By the time the last words exited Tone's mouth, it seemed like the entire block had stopped and taken notice of the altercation. Junkies and workers alike stopped what they were doing and openly stared. From the looks on their faces they seemed stunned to see Tone backing down Sykes. They continued to watch as humbled Sykes walked away.

Inwardly, Tone reveled in momentary victory. This was the first chance he got to flex his muscle. He thought the streets had been getting the wrong perception of him. Tone hoped the altercation with Sykes would go a long way in changing that. He knew he had to flip every once in a while to keep everyone in line.

Calmly, Tone put his gun away and sat right back down on the stoop. He acted as if nothing had happened. Soon everything went back to normal.

A few minutes later his cousin Mann exited the stash house and ran over to him.

"Yo, what's good Tone?" he uttered. "Heard you had some beef out here."

Mann had good intentions, but under no conditions was he supposed to leave the stash house unattended with money and drugs inside.

"Yo, my nigga, what are you doin' out here? Get the fuck back in there. It's over!" Tone chastised him.

"My fault! My fault!" he apologized. "Niggas said you was out here beefin' wit' some dope fiend nigga, so I jetted outside to see what's good."

Mann was Tone's responsibility, yet his younger cousin was very protective of him. Tone couldn't blame him for coming outside to check on him. Still, Tone bore the burden of not only providing for his cousin, but protecting his life with his own. If anything happened to Mann the blame would fall squarely on him. He vowed not to let nothing happen to his cousin, not on his watch.

"That's dead," he told him. "Go the fuck back up in the crib. We'll kick it later."

"Aiight," Mann replied as he turned and headed back to the stash house.

Meanwhile, Tone remained outside. It was business as usual for him. In the proceeding moment after the altercation, Sykes didn't cross his mind. Before long, Shorty returned to the block with the news of Tone's action having already reached her ears.

"What's this I hear you and Sykes got into it?" she suddenly asked.

"Fuck Sykes!" he stated. "That dope fiend nigga'. He was tryin' to get some free coke outta me. I told the fat nigga no. He ain't like it. He acted like he wanted to do something, so I backed out the joint on him."

Shorty replied, "Wham bam just like that huh? I heard you pulled a gun out and threatened to kill him. Tone, he not the type of nigga you threaten or pull a gun out on. He's the type of nigga you kill! Sykes ain't wrapped too tight, yo. He's comin' back, and he ain't comin' to talk!"

In Shorty's opinion, Tone didn't know who or what he was dealing with. She couldn't stress enough to Tone just how dangerous Sykes was. He might have been a dope fiend in appearance, but Sykes was a killer at heart. Shorty was trying to warn Tone exactly what he was up against. Clearly, Tone had missed the point.

Heated, Tone snapped. "I don't care about none of that shit! Ain't nobody afraid of that old ass dope fiend nigga. You think when they made his gun they only made one, huh?"

Tone thought just because Shorty disagreed with him that she didn't understand his position. That thought couldn't have been further from the truth.

Shorty explained. "I'm just warnin' you, yo, I ain't tryin' to say you can't hold ya own.... I'm just telling you so you'll watch your back."

Somehow Tone had mistaken Shorty's relaying of information as an act of her taking sides against him.

"Yo, fuck him. If he come back around, I'll handle it," he announced.

Oh he will, Shorty thought.

In this situation Shorty felt that New York arrogance was preventing Tone from heeding her message. She hoped that wasn't the case. However, whether he liked it or not, she felt like it was her job to at least warn him.

Tone continued, "You make this nigga out to be some kind of boogeyman. Yo, that nigga bleeds too!"

Tone felt like Shorty was blowing the situation way out of proportion. There was no way that Sykes was half as bad as she said he was. No way.

"Okay Tone, I'm done wit' that," she said. "I'm goin' back to handlin' my business, yo. Be careful..."

With that said, Shorty turned and walked away. Tone had too much pride at the moment to talk rationally to him. And on the streets of Baltimore pride would get you killed quicker than arrogance or disrespect.

Shorty made a mental note to keep an extra set of eyes on Tone. In her opinion, she was sure he would need it. Shorty knew as long as Tone hustled on this block, or in East Baltimore for that matter, seeing Sykes again was inevitable.

CHAPTER 7

Where the fuck is this nigga at? Sonya thought, wondering where her man was, or better yet, when he was coming home.

Sonya sat on the couch, completely frustrated. Her television flashed images from *The Arsenio Hall Show*. Her favorite R&B group, Jodeci, was on. Yet she barely paid them any attention. She just wasn't in the mood. Sonya had more pressing concerns. Her thoughts were focused on Tone's whereabouts, where he was or rather whom he might be with.

Try as she might to push those thoughts out of her mind, she couldn't. Sonya knew Tone was a good looking guy, coupled with the fact that he was making money in the streets and the fact that he was from New York, it was a recipe for disaster. She knew that chicks from the south, Baltimore in particular, had a natural attraction for dudes from New York. So Sonya made it a point to keep her eye on Tone. She knew temptation was everywhere and he wasn't an angel. Sonya had caught Tone cheating on her before in New York and she forgave him. On the surface she did anyway. But mentally, his prior infidelity was yet to be resolved within her. And probably never would.

For Sonya, there was sanctity in a committed relationship that one shouldn't violate. She was very traditional when it came to that. Her rules were simple, no cheating. And now that they were living together, *don't let the sun beat you home.* There was no excuse for staying out all night. Whatever Tone was doing in the streets in the nighttime he could do in the daytime as far as she was concerned. Violating those rules was the difference between Sonya's unconditional love and her removing you from her life, forever.

Although her boyfriend may have a newfound obsession with the streets, Sonya had remained deeply in love with him as ever. Whether she cared to admit it or not, Sonya had a soft spot in her heart for Tone. According to her rules, he should have been cut off after his first incident of cheating. Yet she couldn't bring herself to let him go. She really wanted this relationship to work. Sonya couldn't see herself with anyone else. He was her high school sweetheart, the man she lost her virginity to. Tone was the only dude she'd ever been with. In her mind this was a special relationship, something she would tell her grandkids about someday.

Sonya thought her love could change him. She was slowly coming to the realization that maybe it couldn't. The only thing that seemed to be changing Tone was money, and it was doing a good job of it, too.

On a daily basis, Tone wasn't measuring up to the expectations that Sonya had of him. There were days that she barely saw him. Every day without fail, Tone came home late. His street activities were at the center of their conflict. They had several heart to heart talks where Tone explained to her exactly what he was trying to do. Sonya seemed to understand that sacrifices had to be made for Tone to achieve his street dreams of making it in the drug game. However, she didn't know that she was going to be the sacrificial lamb. That their relationship was going to suffer because of his relentless pursuit of the almighty dollar.

In these instances, Tone was fond of saying, *Women remember the things that they shouldn't remember,* referring to his cheating. *And forget the things that they shouldn't forget,* referring to who was paying the bills. Love and relationships were the afterthought, money always came first with Tone.

Simply put, when it came to women Tone was a man with options. He was like a kid in a candy store, exploring a lot of them. He had a thing for women from Baltimore, and even more so they had a thing for him.

Suddenly, she grabbed the phone and punched in his pager number. Her fingers moved robotically over the keypad as they recalled Tone's number by heart. Angry, Sonya felt like she had done this for the umpteenth time and she swore she wasn't calling Tone any more. Who was she kidding? Even though he had ignored her phone calls, Sonya was going to keep calling Tone's pager until he returned her calls.

Was he locked up, shot or dead? Sonya mused. Those ill feelings were gnawing at her. Sonya's suspicious nature was quickly turning into fear.

After punching her home phone number into the pager, Sonya added the numerical code of 911. This was supposed to emphasize to Tone that this was an emergency. But Sonya had done this too many times before, in non-emergency situations, for Tone to fall for that again.

Once she was done, Sonya slammed the receiver down and continued to wait, impatiently, for a call that may or may not come.

On a good day, when Tone wasn't running the streets, which was rare, Sonya felt like a hustler's wife, pampered, spoiled, loved and appreciated. On a bad day, like today, she felt like a side chick, betrayed, lied to and disrespected.

That's when all the doubt and negativity seemed to seep in. A voice in the back of her mind told her to leave him, that she deserved to be treated better than this. Sonya had every reason in the world to leave and yet no reason at all.

For Sonya, life with Tone wasn't turning into all that she thought it would be. She thought the move to Baltimore would bring them closer together. But in all actuality, all it did was drive them apart. Ever since Tone arrived in Baltimore, the dynamic of their relationship changed. They weren't clicking. Or at least not like they use to. In her mind, Tone had lost sight of their relationship in the process of him becoming *the man in the streets*. Sonya was starting to feel like collateral damage. She couldn't remember a time that she was truly happy. Recently, she tried to stick it out and wait for things to get better, but they actually had gotten worst. Tone's selfishness was killing their relationship.

Sonya saw firsthand how the street life in Baltimore had steadily corrupted Tone more so than it had in New York. Over the past few months he had changed into someone she didn't know. Sonya had seen a side of Tone that she never knew existed. He was a one-track minded man who preferred running the streets to a quiet night at home.

Of course Sonya didn't mind all the benefits Tone's drug dealing lifestyle afforded them. His success in the streets had trickled down to her. They had moved from her small off-campus apartment into a rented home in Baltimore County. She loved the brand new white BMW 3 Series convertible she drove that drug money had paid for.

There was the MCM bags, Gucci designer shoes that her boyfriend showered on her. And what was not to like about the shopping sprees to Mondawmin Mall in Baltimore, Maryland, and Fifth Avenue in New York City. Tone had been more than generous to Sonya with his money. Although most times Sonya thought his generosity came with a price, the expensive gifts were to buy her silence. Those things were just material possessions, things she really didn't need.

Rrrrrriiinnngggg! The sudden sound of the telephone shattered the silence, interrupting Sonya's thoughts.

"Hello," she said with a nasty attitude, picking it up on the first ring.

"Yo, what's up?" Tone barked into the phone. "What's the emergency? Why you blowin' up my pager?"

The other end of the phone went silent as Sonya listened intently, trying to ear hustle and pick up on any background noise or voices that might indicate where Tone was at, or what he was doing.

"Yo, Sonya, what's up? You there?" he shouted.

"Yeah, I'm here," she spat. "Where you at?"

Tone began, "How many times I gotta tell you, I'm handlin' business."

"You so predictable, Tone. You keep givin' me the same lame excuse. What the fuck you brought ya cousin down here for if you still gotta do everything? Huh?" she complained.

"Yo, you buggin', Sonya," Tone told her. "I can't have this conversation that you wanna have right now over the phone. I ain't tryin' to get indicted explainin' myself to you. We'll talk when I get there, man."

Tone was beginning to realize that there was no pleasing Sonya. Either he could spend time with her by staying in the house and be broke, or he could hustle his ass off and spend crazy money on her. But he couldn't do both. His drug business needed his full attention. Though Sonya might beg to differ. She always preached moderation. Tone didn't seem to know the meaning of the word. To him drug dealing wasn't an occupation. It was a lifestyle.

He was fond of saying, *I'm doin' everything I can to get everything I can while I can.*

Sonya was right, Tone was predictable in a sense. She knew her inquisitive questions would lead to him giving her the cold shoulder. Tone wouldn't divulge any information over the phone, or anywhere else for that matter. Like most street dudes, he had a sneaky suspicion that the phones were being wiretapped by the police. This was his defense mechanism. Tone called himself protecting her, shielding her from the streets. She called it being secretive.

He once told her, *What you don't know, you can't tell.* It didn't matter to him what Sonya thought. He couldn't ease her fears of him cheating on her or leaving her. So he dealt with it the best way he could, by ignoring it.

"What time you plan on coming home?" Sonya asked reluctantly.

Tone replied, "Couple more minutes. I'm on my way home now."

"Don't have me waitin' fa you all night," she added. "You hear me?"

"Yeah man, I hear you!" he snapped. "Bye."

Sonya sighed. She really didn't have the patience to deal with his inconsiderateness right now, or any other time for that matter. Listlessly she sat on the couch as she continued to stew in her own anger. Time went by ever so slowly as she anxiously awaited Tone's arrival.

About an hour later, the squeaky sound of the door opening signaled his arrival home. Sonya was very much aware of Tone's presence. She listened intently as the soft sounds of his footsteps made their way toward her. Soon he was standing right before her, blocking the television with a smirk on his face. Rolling her eyes, she glared up at him evilly.

"Yo, what's up?" Tone said.

"You're what's up!" Sonya complained. "Tone, I'm beginning to feel like you don't got no kind of fuckin' respect for me. This is not what a man does when he lives wit' his woman. You waltz in here all hours of the night. Nigga, I barely see you. We hardly ever spend time together… All you do is eat, sleep, and run the streets. It's like you and me ain't a couple. And if that's the case, lemme know so I won't be sittin' here lookin' all stupid and shit."

"Are you alright?" he asked, hinting that there might be something else bothering her.

Honestly, Sonya wasn't doing well at all. She couldn't sleep. She couldn't focus in school. Stressing over Tone was beginning to affect her schoolwork.

"No, I'm not alright," she pointed out. "Are you alright wit' the way things are goin' wit' us? From how things appear, obviously you are."

He speculated. "What are you talking about?"

She just glared angrily at him, as if to say, *Really? Do I have to clarify that statement?*

"What are you talking about?" Tone repeated. "You can't be serious."

"To tell you the truth," she began, "I don't know how long I can keep puttin' up wit' this. Sooner or later you gonna have to make a decision, me or the streets."

The entire ride home, Tone thought of all the things he was going to say, all the valid points he would raise during their argument. Suddenly, he was having a tough time remembering it all.

"Stop givin' me ultimatums," he warned. "You knew what it was when you met me."

"Yeah that's true," Sonya replied. "But you ain't never spend this much time in the streets before."

"And I ain't never made this kind of money before either," he told her. "So I guess we even."

Tone turned and stormed out of the living room, heated at Sonya for having to explain himself. In hot pursuit, Sonya quickly got up out of her seat and followed him into the bedroom.

"It's funny how you always questionin' me about where I'm at or what I'm doin'. I don't even know if you fuckin' even goin' to school at all," he implied.

Tone could talk shit all he wanted to, but there was one thing he never had to question, and that was Sonya's loyalty to him. She was blind to a fault.

Sonya replied, "Tone, you gotta do better than that. I ain't about to let you turn this shit around on me. I don't know what you up to, but you up to something."

To Tone there was nothing more frustrating than being accused of something without any real proof.

"So now I'm up to something?" he echoed, while beginning to undress.

Tone felt like a hypocrite because he was cheating and lying to his girlfriend's face about it. For him there was no pussy like *new pussy*. But he knew Sonya was just mad that she hadn't caught him slipping up yet. To him, this relationship thing was beginning to be a contest of who tells the best lies.

"Like what?" he asked.

"To be honest, I think you gotta chick on the side. I really believe you fuckin' around on me," Sonya guessed.

"Sonya, you really need to get outside more often and stop stayin' cooped up in this crib, because home girl, you buggin' the fuck out!" he stated. "Why am I goin' out for hamburger, when I got steak right here at home, huh?"

"I don't know," she insisted. "You tell me."

"Ya too emotional," Tone swore. "Ya feelings is overriding ya common sense. And that's bad."

Sonya stared at Tone intensely, looking him directly in the eye, as if that would give her the answer that she sought. Tone told so many lies she didn't know what to believe any more. All she wanted was the truth so they could repair their relationship. *Why couldn't he understand that?*

Tone refused to make an effort to even understand Sonya's position because that required him to take some responsibility for his actions. Owning up to his mistakes was like admitting he was wrong. Tone was a man, so he could never admit that.

Making as minimal eye contact as possible, Tone continued to strip off his clothing until they were piled up in front of him in the middle of the floor. He stood before Sonya in only a white form fitting wife beater and a pair of Karl Kani boxers.

Sonya stood within inches of her boyfriend, looking awkwardly at him. "You finished? I'm bout to take a shower," he suddenly announced.

She replied, "No, I'm not finished. Before you jump in the shower, lemme smell ya dick."

"Huh?" Tone looked at her, confused.

"Huh my ass," she stated. "Drop ya draws and let me smell ya dick, since you ain't doin' nuttin' wit' nobody."

He didn't have a valid defense for that. Refusal to do what his girlfriend asked was like an admittance of guilt.

"You trust me?" Tone asked as he stalled for time, looking for a way out of the situation.

She stared at him blankly, not insulted by his question and most of all, not the least bit surprised.

"Nigga, cut the bullshit and do what I asked you to do. If you don't there's gonna be a problem," she advised.

In order to dispel her suspicions, Tone knew he had to do what she said or things might get physical. Sonya was known to go 'crazy' on him from time to time.

"Yo, I don't believe you, Sonya," he told her. "This what we come to..."

Sonya was betting Tone had just finished having sex, and she'd bet her life that his dick smelt like one of two things, pussy or fresh soap. She didn't care because either way, he had a problem.

"Well believe it! You ain't exactly been an angel, so don't act like I don't have my reasons either," she said, while dropping to her knees.

Immediately Sonya stuck her fingers in the slit of his underwear and removed his penis. She took his member into her hand, looking up disgustingly at Tone before taking a strong whiff. Her first smell was undecipherable. Her nostrils were unable detect the scent of a female on him. So Sonya smelled it again and again, only to find nothing out of the ordinary there.

From the look on her face, Tone could tell he passed the test with flying colors. If not, he knew he probably wouldn't have a dick; Sonya would have bit it off by now.

Tone had to admit that was a close one. He had a strategy for when he slept around and this time it was put to the test. First, he never took a shower at the motel or the chick's house. All he did was wash his private parts lightly enough to get the scent of the condom off his penis and pubic hairs. Secondly, he used the same soap to wash up that he always used at home. And last but not least, he put the heat on high in the car as he drove home so his body could sweat. Tone had it all figured out.

"You feel stupid?" he asked. "Told you I wasn't doin' nuttin'."

He continued, "Now gimme some head since you down there."

Literally, Sonya was in no position to tell him no. She complied with his request for some oral sex. She began sucking him off, as she if owed him something. For this couple the only thing better than sex, was make up sex.

After a night of fucking and sucking, it seemed like all was forgotten. Tone had sexually performed up to her expectations, so at least for tonight, Sonya's fears were eased.

The next few days things between them actually got better. Tone hung around the house a little more and was very attentive to his girlfriend. However, the good times didn't last long though, things quickly went back to normal with Tone ripping and running the streets.

One way or another, things had to change for these two. At least that's how Sonya felt.

CHAPTER 8

Unexpectedly for Tone, things seemed to go from bad in his personal life, to worst in the streets. The previous night Tone had placed his pager on silent mode, so he never felt the continuous pages from his cousin Mann. If he would have, it would've alerted him that something was seriously wrong on the block.

As Tone turned the corner, to his surprise the block was flooded with cop cars. A crowd of people, nosy neighbors and a significant number of bystanders, congregated near an alleyway, which was currently taped off by the police. This signaled that this was an active crime scene. Tone didn't know what was going on, but he was about to find out. Something was messing up his money and he wasn't happy about it. The police presence was bad for business.

What the fuck happened? he thought while advancing toward the commotion. His pulse quickened as he got close enough to get a glimpse of the body lying on the ground, blanketed by a white sheet.

Who the fuck is that? he wondered. Simultaneously, a young neighborhood girl turned around and spotted him. Her shoulders were slumped and her eyes blood shot red from crying.

"Tone…Shorty dead!" she blurted out.

"What?" he responded.

"Sorry for your loss." she said, walking away stunned. From the look on his face she realized she had said too much.

Tone was in complete denial. He couldn't believe Shorty was dead. By maneuvering his way through the crowd, he got a better view of the outline of the body. Still he didn't want to believe it was Shorty. Tone probably could take it better knowing Shorty got shot and survived. But seeing her lifeless body on the cold concrete was too much to bear.

He overheard two junkies talking. "Yo, they shot Shorty? Man, say it ain't so…" the man stated in disbelief.

"Yeah yo. Some rotten no-good muthafucka done killed Shorty!" Another cursed. "I hope they gotta special place in hell for that son of a bitch. She ain't deserve that…."

Just like that, bits and pieces of gossip began to reach Tone. It seemed like one by one people approached him to tell him what went down and whom they thought was responsible for it. However, no one actually saw anything, there were no witnesses. This may have been all assumptions, but Tone already knew who was behind this. There was only one logical answer…Sykes. But the only question was why? Why kill Shorty when it was him who he had a problem with.

It's all my fault, Tone thought. He felt a sense of guilt that he was alive and Shorty was dead. In his mind it was like Shorty had taken a bullet for him.

Shorty had warned him, but Tone thought it was an exaggeration. He thought Sykes wouldn't do anything, that he had more bark than bite. Now he realized just how wrong he was.

Tone couldn't think straight, there were too many people coming over to address him. The police began staring at him. His presence was beginning to draw too much unwanted attention. He had to get away from the area; already he was beginning to feel smothered by the hood expressing their condolences. The sentiments they displayed were coming from a place of love. Still, it was a somber scene. But through the outpouring of affection, Tone saw how beloved Shorty really was.

Tone felt like his world had just been turned upside down. Shorty was Tone's right hand. She had started off as a complete stranger but had evolved into his most trusted companion. With her help, Tone had built his drug business from the ground up. So surely he owed Shorty a debt of gratitude, at the very least.

Getting the person who did this lay at the forefront of his mind. Seeking revenge was the only thing that could possibly make Tone feel better about this situation. It was the only thing that would satisfy him. On the surface his rage was invisible, yet inwardly a violent storm brewed. At this point, it was wherever and whenever he ran into Sykes, it was on.

It didn't matter how long it would take, or what it may cost him in time or money, or what toll that the situation may extract from him, it had to be done. Nevertheless, if Tone had taken everything into account beforehand, the price of revenge may have been more than he was willing to pay.

"Yo, Cuzo," Mann whispered into his ear as he eased up on him. "I was hittin' you on the hip, you ain't get my pages?"

Tone didn't even turn his head, he sensed the familiar presence of his cousin Mann, now standing at his side.

"Nah," he said flatly.

Mann continued, "Anyway yo, let's be out! There's nuttin' we can do about this shit right now."

Tone shook his head, "I'm stayin'. I'ma wait til the Coroner come."

He felt that was the least he could do. He wasn't too good at saying goodbye and right now he didn't want to. But merely paying his respects was not enough. Tone was looking for some payback. Right now, Tone was in a dark place.

Mann sympathized with what his cousin was going through. He knew Tone always took death hard, especially when it came to the people he truly loved. Tone and Shorty had a bond that he never could really understand. But what was understood amongst them didn't have to be explained to him.

He often asked his cousin why was he still dealing with Shorty long after his need for her expertise had gone, after all her fuck ups.

"Shorty taught me everything I know about hustlin' in Baltimore," he once told him. *"I wouldn't be where I'm at without her."*

Shorty's murder really hurt Tone, to him she was one of them. She was a part of his inner circle, so he felt like he had been cheated of a good worker and robbed of a great friend.

After the Coroner van arrived and placed Shorty's remains in a black body bag, whisking it away to the city morgue to perform an autopsy, Tone collected himself and walked away as the crowd began to disperse. All he kept thinking was, he had some unfinished business to take care of, immediately.

Back at the apartment, Tone and his cousin Mann continued to discuss Shorty's murder. His cousin made it clear that he had no personal interest in revenge, his mind was on the money and he wasn't out here for anything else. It made no difference to him whether Sykes got away with it or not. As far as he was concerned, let someone in her family handle it, or let the police take care of it.

Tone didn't share those same sentiments. He wasn't going to let the beef end with Shorty's death, or wait for someone else to step up. He took it upon himself to be that someone else. So, this was far from over. Sykes had to deal with him now. And Tone would be shooting to kill.

"Yo, what happened today could have happened at any time to any one of us. That shit ain't on you. Don't beat yaself up over that kid," Mann advised. "Everything happens for a reason."

Tone leaned against the kitchen countertop with his eyes cast downward at the floor, his stressed facial features showed little interest in what his cousin was saying. Mann couldn't tell if he heard him or not. Suddenly, he looked up, needing a distraction from his thoughts.

"I know," he stated flatly. "I just feel bad. Shorty is dead because of me. It's as simple as that. She was just guilty by association."

Tone fell silent for a moment. He stared blankly at Mann, but there was nothing in his eyes, no fear, no pain, no sadness.

"Yo, word to mother, I'ma kill that bitch ass nigger!" he blurted out.

Mann interrupted, "Bosses don't kill people. They get people killed. Yo, you too valuable to even be thinkin' like that."

"Fuck that!" Tone shouted. "This shit is personal. He gotta know where this is comin' from and why."

"Tone, you ready to risk everything you built? We gettin' crazy money! Think about it. You said the nigga a dope fiend. If that's so, why even bother with him? He already killin' himself. Just let Karma handle it for you."

"Yeah, he is killin' himself. But a bullet will help him speed up the process," he snapped. "At some point in time, you gotta stand fa sumthin' or niggas will walk all over you. Can't just let this shit go."

Tone feared if he didn't handle this that his conscience would eat at him. He felt like Shorty would never forgive him. He talked the talk, now he had to walk the walk.

At that point, there was no talking Tone out of it. Mann knew it. His cousin loved him, and he knew that Tone knew that he loved him too. Mann had no choice in the matter. He had to ride with his cousin because if the shoe were on the other foot, Tone would be riding for him. No questions asked.

It was dark after Shorty's death. The streets just didn't feel the same to Tone any more. Every day he grew tenser. He was still making money, which was cool, but it just didn't feel right without Shorty. She had never been easy to work with, but her sudden absence affected Tone greatly. It was weird just to be out on Ashland Avenue and not see her serving a customer, collecting money or running around *all crazy*. It was her advice that he sought on anything from drug sales to woman problems, that he would miss the most.

The cold reality was Shorty was dead and Tone felt a debt of responsibility because of it. Mentally, he was having a hard time that she wasn't here.

Tone looked up and down the block, his eyes taking everything in. Like every day since it happened, he hoped and prayed Sykes would show his face. But he didn't. Tone was frustrated by his inability to locate Sykes, however, he knew he couldn't hide from him forever. Eventually he'd make a mistake, and Tone vowed it would be his last. All he had to do was wait patiently for the opportunity to present itself, then strike. Being a heroin addict, Sykes straddled that fine line between addiction and desperation. Tone knew something would give, he just didn't know when.

Out of sight didn't mean out of mind, thoughts of Sykes dominated Tone's attention. He hustled all day, then he and Mann rode around Baltimore City at nighttime to well known open air drug markets, in search of him.

"Here is somethin' you can't understand," rap group Cypress Hill sang through the car stereo. "How I could just kill a man."

"Yo, I'm gettin' tired of listenin' to this shit," Mann complained as he drove.

Tone ignored him. He sat stiffly in the passenger seat as his eyes scoured each drug block and each street the car passed. They went from East Baltimore, to West Baltimore,

Park Heights to Cherry Hill, on a search and destroy mission. He had his eyes peeled for Sykes or anyone who fit his physical description. He had a heightened sense of awareness about everything around him and everything in his vicinity. Tone didn't overlook a thing. He was anxious to get some payback for Shorty's sake, and for his as well. He knew the streets were watching, wondering how he would respond or if he would at all. Tone had the answer to that question tucked safely under his seat, in the form of a fully automatic tech-nine machine gun.

That night, or any other night that Tone went looking for Sykes, he didn't find him. So Tone decided to be more strategic in his approach to tracking Sykes down. He removed himself from the block in the hopes that his absence would lure Sykes into feeling comfortable enough to come back around. He struggled with the thought that his absence might be sending the wrong message, that people might think that Sykes ran him off the block, or that he was scared. But that wasn't the case at all.

"Let these niggas think what they wanna think," Mann replied after hearing his plan. "Fuck 'em!"

His cousin's endorsement of his idea meant a lot to Tone, especially at a time like this.

"I'm just gonna lay low," Tone told Mann. "As soon as anybody see 'em, hit my house phone and I'm out here…. On his ass!"

"To what do I owe this pleasure?" Sonya said, sarcastically. "You been home a whole lot lately. What's up Tone?"

She looked at him with a stern expression on her face, expecting Tone to tell her the real reason he had been in the house so much lately. Sonya knew something was up. They had been living together for close to a year now. She had studied his habits and routines. Being a homebody just wasn't him, so Sonya knew something was wrong. What it was she had no idea.

Instead of snapping at her, Tone chose to kill her with kindness.

"Yo, let's go to the movies," he said. "That new flick *New Jack City* just came out today."

"What?" she answered. "It's too early in the day boy."

"So what you sayin', you don't wanna go Sonya?" Tone accused her.

She stated, "That's not what I'm sayin'. I'm sayin' it's early. Why don't we wait till tonite?"

"There's no better time than the present," he tried convincing her. "You gotta be spontaneous… Let's make it a date. We can go to the movies at Security Mall, then we can go downtown and get somethin' to eat. You wit' it or what?"

"Okay," Sonya said excitedly. "Tone, what we gone see?"

"*New Jack City*, I already told you," he added. "Go get dressed. And don't take long."

Hurriedly, Sonya disappeared into her walk-in closet in search of a cute outfit to wear. Meanwhile, Tone dressed in black from head to toe, in a pair of black Levi's, black hoodie, black leather jacket and black Timberland Chukkas. He put his .380 caliber semi- automatic in his pocket, just in case. There was no way he was leaving his house without protection. Things were too nasty in the streets for him right now.

Sonya promptly reappeared, looking stunning in a pair of form fitting jeans and some high heels.

"Lookin' good girl," he stated, watching as her face lit up. "You ready?"

"Thank you," she acknowledged. "Yeah, I'm ready."

Tone threw her a set of car keys, which Sonya caught. "We takin' da MPV," he told her. "You drivin'."

Sonya sucked her teeth. "Why can't you drive?"

"Cause I'm not," he replied. "That's the least you can do. Damn, I'm takin' you to the movies, bout to feed you and fuck you. What else you want from a nigga?"

Tone and Sonya had a great time at the movies. They really enjoyed each other's company. Just being together for that long period of time bought back memories for Sonya on why she fell in love with him in the first place.

"To me the movie was dope. Nino Brown was that nigga until he took the stand and snitched," Tone commented.

"Because he snitched that ruined the movie for you?" Sonya wondered.

"Muthafuckin' right," he said. "See, I don't expect you to understand that, you not in the streets."

"I'll be glad when the day comes when you not in the streets either," she declared.

"I hear you," Tone responded. "That day will soon come."

Sonya had some apprehensions about that statement. If Tone really meant what he said, he could show her better than he could tell her. She had to admit, today was a good start. Now if he could be more consistent with spending quality time with her, then they might be able to get back to where they were, where he was as connected to her as she was to him.

Tone leaned over and kissed her on the cheek. "Don't worry, we gone be aiight. I promise you, my love. I'm doin' this shit for us."

It took her a moment to process what he said and to recover from his affectionate kiss. Sonya couldn't help but think what a romantic thing for Tone to say. Suddenly their relationship was beginning to feel hopeful again and not like they were doomed. "I love you, Tone," she said.

"I love you more," he replied. "But do me a favor, drive by Pennsylvania Avenue on our way downtown."

"Really?" Sonya snapped. "Tone, you really know how to kill a moment. Can't you handle that shit on ya time. You on my time right now."

"Just do me that favor," he asked. "I need to see somethin' real quick. It's only gone take a second."

Sonya drove down Security Blvd. to Edmonson Avenue, and then she took a left on Fulton Avenue and a right on North Avenue, which lead to the notorious Pennsylvania Avenue. Just as Tone suspected, there were plenty of people out and about. Like a hawk his eyes scanned each person's face, the addicts, the dealers, and the commuters on their way home from work, until he came across one that looked familiar. Suddenly, Tone sat up straight in the passenger seat as he began to stare more intensely. He thought his mind was playing tricks on him. He couldn't believe his luck. That face that looked eerily familiar to him belonged to none other than Sykes. It was a small world and suddenly it had just gotten smaller.

"Slo down," Tone suggested. His eyes were following Sykes' every movement.

Yeah, that's that fat nigger, he thought.

Tone took a shot in the dark by driving to Pennsylvania Avenue and Gold Street, a renowned drug block, and finding the unexpected Sykes, looking like he was going to cop.

"Pull over," Tone ordered Sonya.

"What the hell?" Sonya said, surprised. "What's so important?"

"Gotta go holler at somebody real quick," he replied.

"Whatever you say," she continued.

"Do me a favor. Whatever you do, don't cut off the car," Tone warned. "I'll be right back!"

The way he said that, the intensity in his voice, made Sonya pause momentarily and stare at him. As soon as Tone jumped out the car it made her question why they even came this way. Something wasn't right, she could tell. Her common sense told her as much. She knew there was more to the story.

With his hoodie pulled low over his head and his hands jammed inside his pockets, Tone walked quickly across the street. Suddenly people began moving out of his way, as if they could sense that he was up to no good. Tone continued to follow Sykes, who at this time was oblivious of his presence. Soon as he turned on to Gold Street, Tone picked up his pace. He steadily began to close the distance between them. Tone didn't want to shoot him in the back, especially not from far away. He wanted to get close enough to put a bullet in his head.

Unaware that he was being stalked, Sykes continued to walk toward his ride while clutching a few bags of dope. All that was on his mind was making it to the car and getting away from around here so he and his driver could go somewhere and get high.

Just as Tone removed the small caliber gun from his pocket and began to quicken his pace, Sykes must have felt his presence because he turned around just in time to see the weapon being raised and pointed in his direction. Tone saw the fear in his eyes. Sykes looked as if he'd seen a ghost. Immediately, he took off running.

Boom! Boom! The gun roared.

Two bullets quickly whizzed by his head. Sykes' surprisingly quick reaction had amazed Tone. He hadn't expected that.

The sound of the first shot immediately grabbed Sonya's attention. She doubted that it was gunfire until she heard it again. She turned to the direction that the noise had come from. Realizing it was the same direction that Tone had disappeared into, she began to wonder just what the hell was he up to.

Running behind Sykes, Tone quickly gained ground. He was so close that he could hear Sykes gasping for air. Stopping in his tracks, he aimed his gun. Tone's adrenaline was racing through his veins. His finger tightened on the trigger. His thoughts seemed to slow down as the surreal moment played itself out on that side street.

Tone desperately tried to steady his hand so he could get a clean shot at Sykes' head. He knew his first two shots had missed just by the ease of which his victim was still running.

"Yeah nigger, what's up now," Tone yelled, removing his hoodie.

In his mind Sykes was a dead man. Tone stood less than fifty feet away from him, thinking how easy it was to kill him before he got to the car. Now he would put this drama to an end once and for all.

Fearing for his life, Sykes summoned a burst of speed that even he didn't know he had. Thinking Tone was hot on his heels, Sykes began to run in a zig-zag pattern to his ride. As he ran, Sykes couldn't help but think that at any moment he was going to catch a bullet in his back or to the back of the head. In fact, he braced himself for it.

Just as Sykes reached the car door, Tone calmly took aim and pulled the trigger. Nothing happened. Tone stared at Sykes in disbelief as he scrambled to get inside the car. Once again he squeezed the trigger at the car window, because Sykes had already fled inside, and again nothing happened. It was then that Tone realized that there was a malfunction in the gun. It had jammed. As if his life depended on it, Tone quickly ejected the clip into his hand, removing the awkward angled, unspent shell. He then slammed the clip back into the gun. He cocked the gun back and prepared to fire, but it was too late. The getaway car was gone.

The sound of tires screeching signaled to Tone that his opportunity was getting away. So he did the only thing he could do. He chased the car, firing erratically at it while running.

Boom! Boom! Boom! The crackle and pop of gunfire sounded. Once the car was out of sight, Tone turned and ran back in the opposite direction. Sonya had already been looking in the direction where the loud gunshots had come from. Within a few seconds, Tone reappeared, running from that exact same corner.

"Drive!" he shouted as he entered the car.

"Was that you shooting?" she questioned.

When it came to certain things involving the streets, Tone had to spell it out for her. More than likely, this always took place at the wrong time. Now was one of those times. He didn't have time to offer an explanation. Sonya just needed to play her part, do as she was told, and drive.

"Yeah!" he barked. "Now let's get the fuck outta here."

"Oh my God!" she cried as she quickly drove away.

"Slow down!" Tone coached her. "You goin' too fast. You gone get me knocked."

Stunned, Sonya kept her eyes on the road and drove as best she could. Her nerves were shot. She was scared and angry at the same time. This was too much for her to handle. She felt like she didn't deserve to be an accessory to a crime. *What if that person was dead? What if someone had written down her tag number?* Then it would all come back to her since the car was insured under her name.

This was it for her, their quiet evening together was now officially over. She wanted to go home and calm her nerves.

When Tone finally turned around, convinced that there were no police cars behind them, he noticed that they weren't headed downtown in the direction of the restaurant.

"Where you goin'?" he wondered. "The restaurant ain't this way."

"I'm goin' home." She rolled her eyes. "I had enough of you for the night. Tone, I don't believe you did no dumb shit like that wit' me in the car. You put my life in danger...."

"What?" Tone snapped, searching her face for a sign that she was joking. Something that told him this wasn't real. He found none.

Tone knew he exercised poor judgment and this was bad timing. But he had to do what he had to do. He didn't know when he'd see Sykes again. Tone thought about explaining the whole situation to her. Quickly, he changed his mind. He felt no matter what he said, Sonya wouldn't understand. This was some *street shit* and a civilian would never understand it. There was no way he could ever justify the shooting. Tone figured Sonya would eventually get over it, she was a trooper.

It took every ounce of his willpower to bite his tongue and not get into an argument with Sonya. Out of frustration, Tone grinded his teeth together loudly. He had little else to say.

"Yeah, take me home!" he said aloud. *This is the last time I try be nice to yo ass,* he thought.

CHAPTER 9

"What?" Tone spat groggily into the telephone. "Say that again."

"This nigga Sykes came through and robbed a few workers and shot up the block," Mann repeated. "It's crazy hot out here right now. Mad police."

"What about the stash?" Tone asked. "Did he hit the stash house?"

"Nah, we good on that," Mann told him. "Shop closed."

"Where you at?" Tone wondered.

"I took a hack to my lil Shorty house out in Cedonia," Mann informed him.

Tone advised, "Stay right there, I'm on my way."

Damn, I can't believe this shit is happening...FUCK! Tone cursed, hanging up the phone.

Deep down inside he knew it was his own fault. Tone may have thought that he put the fear of God into Sykes, but that wasn't the case at all. He had gotten overconfident after the shooting and had forgot to call anyone and make his team aware of what had happened. Sykes made him pay for that oversight. The very next day he had swiftly retaliated against them, hitting Tone where it hurt, in his pockets. He felt fortunate because things could have been much worse.

Sykes was proving nothing was safe as long as he was around. He was playing a deadly game of hide and seek, in which whomever got caught would likely wind up dead. On the streets there was always someone out to get someone else, especially in East Baltimore, that was nothing new. It was just the way things were. Tone realized if it weren't Sykes, he'd probably have an issue with someone else.

Frustration simmered inside him. Sykes was becoming a big pain in his ass. To Tone he was more of a nuisance to the neighborhood, albeit a deadly one, than anything else. Tone jumped out the bed, threw on some clothes, and grabbed his gun. He hopped into his car and drove past the block before going to meet Mann.

Once again they strategized on ways to solve their problem, none of which sat too well with Tone. They discussed putting a hit out on Sykes, but he was sure that word would get back to him. They also thought about bringing down a shooter from New York to carry out the plot. Tone nixed that idea too, since there was no telling when or where Sykes would be seen again. With the shooting incident, Tone had proven to himself and Sykes that he had enough heart to get down and dirty whenever the situation called for it. More than ever the situation was calling for it now.

Besides Sykes, he had another problem. He had gotten some cocaine on consignment and he had to pay that bill as soon as possible. His connect didn't want to hear about his beef, all he wanted was his money. He managed to stash enough money to live off for a few months, and also to pay for whatever amount of cocaine he had got fronted. But he didn't want it to come to that. Quickly, Tone had to find a way to get it to him in a timely fashion. Or he had to face the fact that things might get worse before they got better.

In the days following the robbery, Sykes went on the offensive against Tone and his team. He launched assault after assault, doing everything in his power to disrupt his drug business. He began shooting at all of Tone's workers, anyone who had anything to do with Tone. If Sykes had it his way, he would run Tone and anyone who dealt with him from around Ashland Avenue and Madeira Street for good.

One by one, local dudes from the area quit working for Tone until his team dissolved into just him and his cousin Mann. He couldn't understand it, how was it possible that not one person from that area wanted to get money with him? He couldn't believe how much Sykes had the whole hood under pressure. He suspected that he had verbally threatened more than a few people's lives. And after what he had done to Shorty, no one was actually hanging around Tone to become his next victim.

In response to their cowardly actions, what Tone really wanted to do was call them out for being *pussies.* He had every reason and yet no reason at all to be pissed off at them. But something held him back from doing that. He couldn't think of what advantage that that would gain him. After all, this wasn't their beef, it was his. He just needed time to process things, to think this thing out. Tone thought time away from the block was the best thing right now. It was best to lay low until the drama died down. All this back and forth shit was taking a toll on him.

Tone glanced into his bathroom mirror, seeing the severity of his circumstances staring him in his face. He'd been staying in the house so much lately he didn't know what to do with himself. He replayed the events of the past two days yet again. He needed a solution and he needed it fast. Tone searched his brain for a long time, thinking about Sykes. He was beefing with a man twice his age. And way more dangerous. So he figured he had to be doubly as cautious. He knew Sykes' weakness was shooting dope. But it was one thing to know his weakness, and quite another to exploit it. Yet even another thing to find him. Sykes would weigh heavily on his mind for the next few days. That was until he got a phone call that would change everything.

"Yo," Mann spoke into the telephone. "I found out where that nigger Sykes is at."

Tone's ears pricked. "You know where the nigger rests his head?"

"Better than that," Mann responded.

"Say somethin' kid!" Tone demanded.

"City Jail," Mann told him.

"What?" Tone exclaimed. "How you know?"

"Bumped into a dope fiend at Lexington Market and he told me he seen the nigger. Sykes got picked up on a retail theft charge," Mann assured him.

"Word?" Tone added.

"Word!" Mann chimed in.

Tone sighed as he came to a sudden realization. "That information ain't gone do me no good. I can't get at him in jail."

"Listen," Mann began. "You can if you bail the nigger out."

Suddenly a light bulb went off in Tone's head. The wheels in his mind began to turn. Mann had said a mouthful. For all intents and purposes, he thought that the news of Sykes' arrest had put their beef on hold. Up until now it had been impossible to pinpoint Sykes' location, the dope houses he frequented, or where he rested his head. Now suddenly Sykes' advantage had just slipped away. For the first time since their altercation began, Tone had the upper hand. Now he could get some closure. Put an end to this dangerous game that he had been playing.

By bailing Sykes out, Tone would know exactly where he would be and at what time. He could take it from there. The moment had come. Tone put the plan in place, and he knew what had to be done. Later that evening, he had one of Mann's girlfriends pay the bond with a bail bondsman. Now all there was left to do was wait until the bail was posted and Sykes was released from City Jail on Eager Street. He would be right there watching and waiting.

It was a narrow window of opportunity, but Tone thought it was well worth the shot. He knew he had one thing in his favor, the element of surprise.

The conditions in Baltimore City Jail were deplorable; the place was unlivable, on a good day, unbearable on a bad day. Sykes thrived in these conditions, he was immune to them, having spent so much time in correctional facilities. He had lived in shooting galleries that weren't much better than this. Fortunately for him, this wasn't his first rodeo. He knew how to maneuver in jail.

The legal system was his personal revolving door. Sykes had spent more than half his life incarcerated in jails from Hagerstown to the Maryland Eastern Shore. He thrived in these conditions. He was well known throughout the system. He once bragged that he could do his time at Baltimore City Jail *standing on my head*, that he knew *how to bid*.

Sykes' heroin habit had gotten the best of him, resulting in him attempting to steal soap powder from a supermarket to feed his habit. Arrested, he was sent to City Jail in lieu of bail, not because of the severity of the crime, but because of his lengthy criminal history. Sykes was a repeat offender.

Slowly, his cell door mechanically began to open, shattering the peaceful night's silence that had engulfed the tier. The loud noise was enough to only make Sykes barely stir in his sleep. His cell door stood wide open for a few seconds without him so much as acknowledging it. Still in a deep sleep, Sykes hadn't realized yet that his cell door was even open.

"Sykes," a correctional officer called out. Sykes was like a famous basketball player, he was known on a first name basis.

No answer. "Sykes! Sykes!" He shouted again, this time louder. Sykes continued to lie on his back on his bunk, in a comatose state. He was enjoying the precious rest that jail afforded him. It was the same rest that evaded him whenever he was in the streets, and his drug habit kept him up for days and all hours of the night.

"Sykes! Yo!" An inmate from a neighboring cell called out. "Wake up! The C.O. callin' you."

He heard that.

Groggily, Sykes opened his eyes to discover his cell door wide open. *This is strange,* he thought. The minute he sat up on his bed, his large belly protruded over his waistline. Bare-chested and dressed only in a pair of dingy white boxers, he stumbled to his feet and walked over to the cell door. He leaned halfway out the cell as he looked down the tier.

"C.O., what the fuck is up, yo?" Sykes hollered down the tier.

"Pack ya shit," the Correctional Officer began. "You made bail. Let's go!"

"You whores better stop playin' wit' me, yo!" Sykes swore. "I just fuckin' got here the other day. I ain't even been to court yet. I ain't made no fuckin' bail, yo!… Now close my fuckin' cell door and stop playin' wit' me!"

Frustrated, Sykes re-entered his cell and laid back down on his bunk. He shook his head in disbelief.

"I made bail? Yeah right," he said to himself.

His luck didn't run like that. He didn't have a get-out-of-jail-free card in his back pocket. Sykes had done too much dirt to the people that loved him for them to ever come get him out of a jam. The only person who would come get him out of jail, his mother, had died over ten years ago. At any second, he fully expected his cell door to shut close and he could resume his slumber. Yet he watched and waited for something to happen that just didn't.

Click-Click, Click-Click.... His cell door methodically moved back and forth before moving back to an open position.

Angry, this time Sykes jumped out of bed barefoot and marched over to the cell door.

"C.O., stop playin' wit' me, yo!..." Sykes yelled.

The Correctional Officer snapped. "Sykes, you wanna go home or what? If so, let's get a move on now. I got other inmates to process out on bail. If you don't wanna go now, then you can try your luck on the next shift. The choice is yours. Make up your mind quick my man."

There was honesty in the man's voice, which led Sykes to fully believe him now. He saw past all the tough talk to the heart of the matter, the truth. Now something told him that the Correctional Officer wasn't playing at all. Sykes rushed back into his cell, quickly got dressed, grabbed a few meager belongings, some commissary items, and exited his cell.

Suddenly the tier was in an uproar. Prisoners began to call out to Sykes from nearby and down the tier as they bid him farewell.

"Sykes, stay out there this time, yo!...." someone yelled.

"Sykes, this Bey, holler at my people for me," another man shouted. "Tell 'em I'm short. All I need is a thousand dollars to get me out yo!"

"Alright, Bey!" Sykes lied, knowing damn well it would be the last thing on his mind once he hit the streets. "I got you, yo."

Happily, Sykes rushed down the tier, not believing his luck. In the back of his mind he thought it was a clerical error and it might be discovered once he got to admissions. He still was unsure. So on the way off the tier, he stopped at an old comrade of his that he had done some serious time with in the old jail in Hagerstown, Maryland.

"Chicken!" he shouted. "Here yo! I'm leavin' out. I just made bail. Take this commissary. If I come back, I want my shit. If I don't, it's yours, yo."

"Alright yo," Chicken replied, accepting the prison items. "Stay strong soldier. I'll see you when I get uptown."

"Sykes!" the Correctional Officer shouted. "We ain't got all day!"

"Alright, here I come," Sykes announced as he walked away from the cell door. "I'll holla at you niggas later yo. Y'all stay up!"

"You'll be back!" someone hollered out.

"Fuck you, you jealous whore!" he yelled back while strutting down the tier.

Sykes was still in denial by the time he got down to the admissions area of the jail. He was placed in a holding cell along with a few other inmates fortunate enough to make bail. Sykes exhibited a nervous energy that made him very talkative.

"Hey C.O., I wanna know, who bailed me out?" Sykes inquired nicely, with his face pressed to the steel bars.

"Listen Sykes, for the umpteen time," the Sergeant groaned, "you're not going to keep bothering me. I'm very busy. I have a job to do and that's to get you guys out of here and off the morning count. And, I don't have that information in front of me. End of story."

He continued to press. "Could you find out who it was? Please?"

The Sergeant snapped. "Jesus Christ! You wanna go home or what? If so, excuse me while I get back to work. You're about to go home now, that's all you need to know. If you really want to know, take it up with your bail bondsman tomorrow."

"Sorry Serg," Sykes spoke. "I just was wonderin', that's all."

The Sergeant was right, Sykes mused. He decided to give the man a break, relax and wait for his name to be called so he could go home. Suddenly his mind began to race about the things he wanted to do when he got home. The first thing he planned to do was get a shot of dope. That had been on his mind since he got arrested. So much so he had dreamt about it several times, even while he was dope sick.

Soon those thoughts would manifest themselves into reality as Sykes planned on visiting his old haunts in search of some good dope. A few days in jail weren't enough to kick his heroin habit. He had been shooting heroin on and off for twenty something years. The swelling in his hands and the nasty abscesses and scabs on his forearms were proof of that.

In an hour or so, Sykes was released after signing the necessary legal documents. He was given some court paperwork, telling him his next scheduled appearance in court. In the wee hours of the morning, he and a handful of other prisoners were released back into society, onto a dark block, on East Eager Street in East Baltimore.

"Lemme get a cigarette, yo," Sykes asked another recently released inmate who was smoking nearby.

The man handed over a cigarette and a lighter, which Sykes placed between his lips and lit. He handed him back his lighter and proceeded to go about his business.

"Thanks, yo," Sykes stated through a cloud of smoke.

"No problem," the man replied.

Quickly, Sykes began walking away from the jail as fast as he could, trying to put as much distance between him and the correctional institution as possible. He was nervous that his release had somehow all been a mistake, yet he was anxious to get to a dope spot. He knew an all night shop up on Greenmount Avenue, where he could get some credit or at the very least bum a blast. He had no inclination that he was being watched, followed, and stalked from the moment his feet hit the concrete pavement.

The further away he got from the jail, the more at ease he became. Sykes stopped looking over his shoulder for a police car a few blocks ago. At the moment his actions were primarily being dictated by his insatiable thirst to get high. The anticipation of his drug use put Sykes in a very vulnerable state. He wasn't moving as safely as he normally would.

Tone crept through the dark alley, gun drawn. In the near distance he heard a loud voice, which he identified as belonging to Sykes. He knew the sound of his loud mouth ass anywhere. Using an acute sense of hearing, Tone followed the sounds a few yards to a nearby row house. There a light from the kitchen window illuminated through the darkness. Tone cautiously approached. Carefully, he walked through a beat-up metal fence. Quietly, he approached the window. Tone walked gently on the ground, careful to avoid any sticks, glass or bottles, anything that would make noise. After accomplishing that feat, he settled into the shadows.

When Tone was close enough to sneak a peek inside, he carefully raised his head until his eyes were clear of the windowsill.

From his vantage point, he could barely see inside. A thick film of grease and dirt covered the windowpane of the scarcely furnished kitchen. Everything was blurry. He couldn't see much in terms of facial recognition. What he did see were two men standing next to each other, in stark physical contrast of one another. One was fat, with a big belly, which Tone knew to be Sykes. The other person was skinny and frail in appearance. This person's identity was unknown to him.

Tone continued to look in the window with great interest, waiting for the precise moment to strike. He had shadowed Sykes from the time he was released from jail to the house where he went to cop his dope, to this house, where he was about to shoot his dope. It was safe to say that

Tone didn't come this far to stop right here. If need be, he'd shoot or kill the other person too. As far as Tone was concerned, the man was in the way. He was in the wrong place at the wrong time.

"C'mon yo. Gimme a lil sumthin'," the man pleaded with Sykes. "I'm lettin' you shoot up in my house. This late at night man, I usually don't even open the door. I only did it cause it's you."

"Damn, I hate a whinin' ass nigga, yo," Sykes snapped. "That's all you do."

Now the man was having second thoughts about letting Sykes into his home. Sykes was trouble. He was known for not giving anyone a fair shake, especially when it came to sharing dope. With Sykes, the man felt he was damned if he did and damned if he didn't. Had he not opened the door for Sykes, tomorrow, the next day or whenever they saw each other again, Sykes would lay hands on him, humiliating the man wherever he saw him.

"Huh!" Sykes exclaimed, throwing a bag of dope on the kitchen table. "You and yo bitch better be happy wit' that, cause that's all the fuck you gettin' from me, yo."

Hurriedly the man snatched the bag of dope up off the table before Sykes could change his mind and take it back. He gripped the bag in the palm of his hand as if his life depended on it.

Sykes continued, "I need a set of works. You gotta extra set?"

"Yeah," the man replied. "Follow me upstairs."

Obediently Sykes followed the man as he exited the kitchen. Patiently, Tone waited in the darkness. Silently he debated in his mind when and where to make his move. He knew timing was everything. He decided to keep a close watch.. Tone felt now wasn't the time to strike. He'd let Sykes get high first before he decided to do anything. Then Sykes wouldn't know what hit him.

Soon Sykes returned to the kitchen. He sat down at the kitchen table and prepared himself to shoot heroin. He laid his hypodermic needle on the table next to a few bags of dope, a cigarette lighter, blood stained cottons balls, a soda bottle filled with water and a large silver spoon. Tone spied through the window as Sykes tied his belt around his arm in an effort to locate a good vein. Eventually, he found a vein that was suitable enough to use.

For the next few seconds, Tone watched and waited, praying no one would enter or exit the house until he was ready to spring into action. He reminded himself how easy Sykes would be to kill once he got high. His mind would be in a stupor and his reaction time would be slow at best. Tone clutched his pistol harder, just thinking that his target lay just beyond the cloudy glass. He lay in wait, watching for the precise time to attack.

Just as Tone raised his pistol and prepared to make a move for the backdoor, a large rat scampered across his foot. The rodent startled Tone, causing him to knock over a nearby trashcan. The noise from the alley attracted Sykes' attention. He got up and made his way over to the window to take a look. Quickly Tone pressed himself flat against the row house in an effort to conceal himself.

Sykes squinted his eyes in an effort to see through the dirty windowpane, but his vision was obstructed by the filth on the glass. He looked around in the darkness briefly before chalking the noise up to a stray alley cat.

Tone exhaled slowly when he saw Sykes' shadow suddenly disappear from the window. He knew he had blown a chance to shoot Sykes, but Tone would rather look Sykes in the eye, man to man, so he could know who did this to him and why. Once the shooting began, he wasn't worried about Sykes or anyone else seeing his face, because it would be the last face they would ever see.

Sykes busied himself, carefully dumping the brown contents of the pill into a spoon, along with a few drops of water. He grabbed the lighter and put the flame to the bottom of the spoon. Quickly, the brown powder and the water merged to form a dark, gooey substance. Sykes watched as the dope began to boil and bubble, dissolving the cutting agents. Satisfied it was ready, Sykes turned off the cigarette lighter, carefully placed the spoon on the table, and reached for a cotton ball and his needle. He stuck his cotton ball onto the spoon and then inserted his needle into the cotton ball, using it as a filter, as he slowly drew up the entire contents of the spoon into his syringe.

Gently, Sykes placed the hypodermic needle between his teeth as he slapped his arm, looking for the perfect vein to invade. When he found one suitable enough for his purpose, he took hold of the needle, stabbed his flesh, and slowly released the poison into his bloodstream.

Tone studied Sykes' every movement until he was sure he was completely under the spell of the dope. He saw Sykes' eyelids begin to droop until they closed as his chin slumped into his chest. Periodically, his head jerked as he began going into a deep nod.

Silently, Tone walked toward the back door. With a sudden burst of fury, he raised his leg and with all the strength he could muster, he exploded in the direction of the flimsy door. Fragments of wood spewed into the air as Tone burst into the kitchen. He stood before Sykes, gun drawn, prepared to settle the score once and for all.

"What's up now, muthafucka?" Tone said through clenched teeth.

Sykes' eyes displayed a look of surprise. He didn't plan on running into Tone, definitely not now. Sykes did the only thing he could do at the moment. He begged for his life.

"New York, it ain't gotta go down like this," Sykes stated, with droopy eyes and a slurred voice.

Suddenly, Sykes knew who bailed him out and why. He had been caught slipping.

Tone gave Sykes an evil grimace as he approached. He noticed Sykes' eyes open wide. There was a flash of fear in them, although his pleas were less than convincing. The fact of the matter was, Sykes was too dangerous to be left alive.

Tone announced, "It's too late to cop a plea!... This is for Shorty." Tone winced as he let off a barrage of shots from a nine-millimeter. The first shot caught Sykes directly in the middle of his chest. The impact of the bullet sent him sprawling onto the kitchen floor. Sykes staggered to his knees while one bloody hand clutched his chest. Tone pumped slug after slug into Sykes' body until the impact of the shots forced him to lay on his back. Then he walked over to his body and dumped at least three more shots into his head and face. When the shooting was done and there were no signs of life left in Sykes' body, Tone fled, leaving just the scent of gunpowder and blood in his wake. He disappeared into the chilly Baltimore night, assured that his nemesis was dead.

CHAPTER 10

Netta violently pushed the thin hospital blanket away from her body. Her subconscious was being rocked by another bad dream. Once again she was in a fight for her life. The blanket represented her attacker's grasp, which she, by any means necessary, had to free herself from. She struggled long and hard until his grip was broken. But this altercation was far from over. Netta continued flailing her arms in self-defense, but little good did that do. As he rushed her, Netta used her nails to claw at his face until she drew blood.

"You fuckin' bitch!" Black spat. "I'ma kill you this time, yo!"

Netta knew she had to get away. But unfortunately, nothing that she did could break this death grip.

Her attacker had broken into her home while she was asleep, not to commit rape or burglarize her home. His sole intent was to kill her. Whatever physical resistance she was putting up just wasn't enough to stop him. It was Black, he had come back to kill her. He had come back to finish the job.

In a last ditch effort, Netta tried to scream as loud as she possibly could. She opened her mouth wide, but nothing came out, not a sound or a syllable. This scared the hell out of her. She began to panic as Black's large hands clamped down around her throat, slowly crushing her windpipe. A sinister smile spread across his lips as he proceeded to strangle Netta. Her eyes began to bulge out of her head as she desperately clawed at his hands in an effort to break his grip.

Black could have killed her in a multitude of ways, but he wanted to look Netta in the eye. With all the strength that he could muster, he continued applying all the pressure he could, until he succeeded in cutting off all the oxygen to her brain. Everything went black. At that point Netta's body went limp. Her lifeless form crumpled to the floor with Black's hands still applying the deadly chokehold.

This wasn't the first time she had dreamt that her former boyfriend Black tried to kill her. However, this was the first time he had succeeded. Netta usually managed to escape or wake up out of her dream before he completed his task. This time she didn't, and that was the scary part.

Netta could put up a brave front as if she didn't fear Black, but her subconscious suggested otherwise.

Slowly, Netta began to awaken from her medically induced coma. The constant beeps from the life support machines in a strange way were soothing. Those noises let her know that she was still alive. In her hospital bed, she lay motionless, unwilling to move, maybe even believing that she couldn't. For the moment she hadn't yet opened her eyes, instead she relied on her keen sense of hearing, and it told her that she was in the hospital. She didn't know how long she had been there or even her medical condition, still she was there.

Ever so gently, she pried her eyes open; they took a few more moments to adjust to the sunlight after being plunged so long in darkness. The bright lighting of the room caused her some immediate discomfort. She squinted her eyes to minimize the amount of light that she took in. Netta was saddened to find herself alone, in a hospital room, with none of her so-called friends. Mimi and the other members of the Pussy Pound were nowhere to be found. If she had died, would anyone have known? Would anyone have cared?

Just as she was gathering her bearings, Netta was hit with an intense migraine headache. She began to feel the aches and pains exploding all over her body as she attempted to move. She reached for the nurse call button that dangled on the side of her bed and immediately requested a nurse's assistance.

A buzzer at the nurse's station alerted the medical staff members to Netta's request for help.

"I got this one. You look a little busy," Nurse McNeil said as she watched her co- worker fill out some medical paperwork.

The African American middle-aged nurse rose from her seat and headed to the room in question. Within seconds Nurse McNeil was standing in front of Netta.

"Oh my goodness. You finally woke up, chile," the nurse marveled. "Praise the Lord … I've been waiting on this day. I've been praying for you, Shanetta."

Netta was confused. She hadn't the slightest idea how long she had be laid up in the hospital or why this nurse was so excited to see her awake.

"I need something for the pain.… My head, my body, hurts like hell. Excuse my language," Netta admitted.

"Hush your mouth, it's understandable. Especially for a patient in your condition," Nurse McNeil told her. "There were days where we were wondering if you were going to make it at all. But God is good."

At the moment Netta didn't need a sermon. She wanted some pain medication and she wanted it right now.

"You think you can get somethin' for the pain now?" she reiterated.

"Give me one second, Sweetie, I'll be right back," the nurse replied.

"Nurse?" Netta called out. "One more thing, where am I?" Netta was suddenly unaware of her exact surroundings.

"You're in Maryland General Hospital. You've been here in a medically induced coma for almost a week. When I come back, I'll tell you everything else you need to know," the nurse said as she rushed out the room.

Netta watched as the big-boned, big-breasted nurse strolled out of her hospital room. In an instant, she closed her eyes, seeking temporary relief from the pain, while processing her current predicament. She slowly began to remember her ambulance ride to the hospital.

"Here you go, darling," Nurse McNeil said as she entered the room with a small white cup with two pills inside. "This should make you feel better."

The nurse proceeded over to Netta's bed, slowly propping her up until she was in an upright position. She reached for the small pink pitcher filled with water that had been placed on a nearby counter and poured Netta a cup of water.

"Open your mouth," she said.

After gently dumping the contents of the cup in her mouth, Nurse McNeil poured a slow, steady stream of water down her throat. The bitterness of the pills caused Netta to grimace.

"What was that?" Netta suddenly thought to ask. The nurse replied, "100 milligrams of Tramadol."

Netta snapped. "I don't know what that is, but from here on out bring me some Tylenol. I didn't come in this hospital with a habit and I'll be damned if I leave with one."

The nurse shook her head. "Okay, calm down, Sweetie. I'm just following doctor's orders. But I'll make a note of your concerns on your medical chart. I'll see what other medical options we have to relieve all that pain you're in."

All Netta could think of was the street stigma that was attached to these opioid pills with funny names. How heroin addicts easily exchanged a dependence on dope for another legal high. Netta despised all junkies, even though her mother Renee had been one. She hated the fact that her mother couldn't ever overcome her demons; that her addiction never gave Netta a fair shot at a normal childhood.

So in no way, shape, or form did she ever want to become anything like her mother.

The nurse continued, "There are medicinal uses for Tramadol. You're thinking about the ways people misuse it. It's a pain reliever. And if a patient is in constant pain, then the body doesn't heal properly. If the body doesn't heal properly, then you can't recover quickly. And if you don't recover quickly, then you can't go home when you want to. You wanna go home, don't you?"

"Sure," Netta assured her. "But it's just that I'd feel more comfortable takin' Tylenol. Drug addiction runs in my family. It's like a defective gene."

"Okay, I understand. I can't argue with that, Miss Jackson," she said, placing the water pitcher back on the counter before moving to the foot of the bed to examine her medical chart.

Nurse McNeil began checking all the medical machinery that had been used to monitor Netta's condition. It all seemed to read normally. She began detaching some of the attachments from Netta's body, then she adjusted the bed, putting Netta in a more comfortable position to talk. She was feeling trapped in her hospital bed.

"Sorry, Nurse McNeil, I didn't mean to get stank wit' you earlier," she apologized. "You've been nothing but kind to me. I know you just doing your job."

Fortunately, the nurse was a true professional who had heard a lot worse. Netta's words or tone of voice hadn't offended her at all. She knew not to take most things that a patient said personally.

"Sweetie, I understand how you feel," the nurse explained. "I only dispense the medication that the doctor prescribes."

She continued, "Medication or no medication, all things considered, you're lucky to even be alive. From my understanding, when they brought you in here, you were in very bad shape young lady. You were rushed in here suffering from trauma and multiple contusions. You went into shock on the operating table from the loss of so much blood internally...The doctors say they almost lost you.... For the past week you've been in a medically induced coma."

Wow, Netta thought when the nurse explained to her about the period of uncertainty as to whether if she would survive.

Slowly, bits and pieces of her memory came back as Netta forced herself to think. She forced herself to recall exactly what happened that fateful night. Unsettling images of the assault began to replay in her mind. She recalled vividly the rage in Black's face, and the savagery of the beating. Then she remembered the dream she just had. Now she understood the reason behind it. Suddenly it all made sense.

"Sweetheart, you are one tough cookie. God has blessed you. I've seen people pass away from much less. When it ain't your time to go, it ain't your time to go. No man can change that." The nurse added, "Shanetta Jackson, you are truly blessed. The Lord has His hands all over you. He has something better in store for you once you heal up and get back on your feet."

Netta was glad that the nurse was singing her praises, because she wasn't so sure about that, or anything else at this point. She had a lot of soul searching to do.

Exactly who the hell am I? she wondered.

That was a good question. Was she Shanetta Jackson from Murphy Homes? Or Netta from the Pussy Pound? She had been so many things to so many people in her life that she had lost sight of her true identity.

She had no idea what the real answer was. After all that she had just been through, physically and emotionally, it was no wonder she couldn't think clearly. Her thoughts were all over the place, in a state of confusion.

Netta wasn't sure what the future looked like, but she wasn't going back to what she had been.

"Thank you. I appreciate everything you've told me," Netta admitted humbly.

"It's the truth, Sweetie. I don't say this of my own accord. The Lord told me to tell you. You are going to be alright," the nurse claimed. "Amen."

Once the nurse got off her pulpit, she succeeded in putting the proper perspective on Netta's current situation while at the same time giving her hope for a full recovery. Now Netta knew beyond a shadow of a doubt that she would survive this, just like she had every other blow that life had dealt her. Netta's internal scars would heal quickly. But it would take a lot of time for her mental scars to mend.

The nurse confessed, "You know, while you was in that coma, the police been coming by every day to check on you. They wanted to see if you were feeling well enough to talk. Or if things had taken a turn for the worst. Of course you were incapacitated, so I used that to run them away."

The mere mention of the police had Netta's full attention. There were a thousand things going on in her mind. Her future. Her past. What she was going to do next. Now this. She was the victim. They had to know that. The police probably wanted to protect her. Maybe even save her, but she didn't need them to do that. Netta felt she could hold her own.

However true or untrue that notion was, one thing she wasn't going to do was snitch. Netta wasn't pointing any fingers or making any statements in regards to Black. What happened to her was going to stay in the streets.

The nurse continued, "I don't know if I'll be able to keep the police from talking to you now. But beside the police, there were a few young ladies here. They said that they were friends of yours. Didn't catch all their names, there were so many. And this handsome looking young man with a New York accent came to check on you too. I think he said his name was Antonio?.... Tony?..."

"You mean Tone?" Netta replied.

"Yes, that sounds about right," she concluded. "That's his name. Now if you would excuse me Sweetie, I got some other rounds to make and some paperwork to do. The doctor will be in to see you soon. But in the meantime, I'll call down to the kitchen and have them send you up some lunch."

"Okay. Thanks," Netta replied. "Nurse, I hate to bother you, but could you help me out of bed. I need to get a look at myself."

The nurse adjusted the high bed railing, moving it into a lower position so that Netta could place her legs on the side of the bed and prepare to take her first steps since coming out of her coma. She was feeling a little self-conscious dressed in her paper-thin hospital gown, parts of her nude body were exposed by the slit in the back.

Netta needed assistance just lifting her upper body off the bed. Nurse McNeil gave her a helping hand, pulling her to an upright position with her legs dangling off the bed. That little bit of movement took a lot of energy and effort on Netta's part. Her back began to stiffen and her muscles started to ache from not using them for the past week.

"You okay Sweetie?" the nurse asked.

"Yes, other than a few aches and pains here and there, I'm fine," she admitted.

"Just take your time trying to walk. Your mind might be telling you one thing, but your body may have other ideas," the nurse said. "We don't want you to fall."

The nurse reached out both her hands, offering Netta some support. Netta took hold of her hands and slowly stepped off the bed. Instantly she felt unsteady on her feet as he legs began to tremble under her body weight. Her legs were shaky at first. The socks she had on were no help either. The floor was more slippery than it should have been. This reaction cast doubt in her mind, it made her hesitant to take her first step.

"Come on, you can do it Shanetta," the nurse assured her. "I know you can."

Those words removed any doubts that Netta had. Suddenly, she took a step forward. It was followed by another and another. She moved gingerly toward the bathroom, with about as much speed as an elderly person. Each step she took awakened muscles and joints that had stiffened during her coma. Quickly, the uneasiness in which she first stood disappeared and was replaced by confidence.

Netta smiled at the nurse. It was a silent thank you for her assistance.

"I got it from here," Netta told the nurse.

She let go of one hand, then the other, proving she could walk under her own power. Still, the nurse kept a cautious eye on her, while standing nearby. By the time they arrived at the bathroom, Netta was slightly fatigued.

"I'm good," Netta pronounced as she placed her hands on the sink.

"You sure now baby?" Nurse McNeil asked.

"Yeah, I'm fine," Netta replied while using one hand to close the door.

"There's an emergency button in there if you should need anything," the nurse informed her.

Instantly, Netta was drawn to the mirror. She slowly surveyed the damage Black had done to her face. There was a large knot almost in the center of her forehead. She had a black eye and a busted swollen lower lip to accompany the other minor bumps, cuts and bruises on her face. Her hair was in total disarray. Netta had to admit to herself, she looked horrible.

Netta couldn't stand the sight of herself anymore. In her current condition she felt like the mystique that had once surrounded her was forever tarnished because of the vicious beating that Black had administered to her. It made her ashamed to show her face in the streets.

If she could at that moment, Netta would have covered the mirror, just to block out the battered reflection of herself that she was seeing. She turned away, unable to look at her reflection any longer. She angrily began the journey back to her bed, to commiserate in her misery.

A million thoughts ran through Netta's mind. She was angrier at what had been done to her more than being fearful of almost losing her life. It was at that point that Netta realized that her anger wasn't going to bring her the peace of mind she needed to heal. So she decided to just let it go.

As if it were just that easy. She couldn't control her hateful thoughts. Just like she couldn't control those bad dreams from reoccurring.

Sonya looked out her bedroom window, watching Tone as he jumped into his car, headed to the block to ply his trade. Whenever he exited the house, her mind went astray. She couldn't think straight. She woke up every day with so much anxiety and emotional distress. She worried herself wondering what he was doing. Or better yet, whom he was with. She wasn't buying his weak excuses any more. She saw the large amounts of money Tone stashed in the house. She was aware of his team of workers. So she knew he didn't have to be on the block every day like he claimed. That was just an excuse to get out the house as far as she was concerned, and do his thing with other women.

No one had ever made her feel like this, sexually or emotionally. In the past she never had a problem controlling her feelings for a man. She usually was able to keep them under control. But there was something about Tone that made her go overboard. There was something that brought out the craziness in her. Lately, their conversations felt more like interrogations. She placed the blame for that solely on Tone. If she was a certain kind of way, it was clearly because he made her that way. Point blank period.

"There wasn't a truth that had been concealed that time won't reveal," her mother was fond of saying. Sonya believed it too.

She felt now was the time to know the truth about Tone's extracurricular activities, for them to manifest itself to her. With a suggestion from her best friend Bri, they were going around Tone's drug block to see exactly what was good with him.

Sonya had done all the crying. She had experienced all the negative feelings and been through all the turbulent emotions that Tone's cheating had caused. Now it was time to act.

Beep! Beep! The sound of the car horn snapped Sonya out of her thoughts.

"Comin' down now," Sonya yelled out the window.

"Hurry up heifer," Bri shouted back.

The moment Sonya climbed into her front seat, Bri was grinning ear to ear. This was the moment they both had been waiting for.

"You ready?" Bri laughed.

"Ready as I'll ever be," Sonya replied.

"Then here we go," Bri teased.

Bri wasn't nosey, she didn't ask Sonya to tell her their business. She had only agreed to Sonya's plan because she was a concerned friend.

Netta forced herself to eat as much of the bland food as she could possibly stomach. She hoped the food would give her some nourishment and help promote healing within her body, even though the baked chicken looked half cooked and tasted rubbery. Her mash potatoes tasted like mush and the vegetables didn't even look edible. At the very least she hoped the food would settle her stomach.

Within a half hour a member of the kitchen staff entered her room to collect the tray. The lady seemed to sense Netta's disdain for her barely eaten lunch.

"Wasn't in the mood to eat, huh?" the lady asked sarcastically.

"You wouldn't be either if your meal tasted like hot garbage," Netta remarked.

"Yeah, it takes a little getting used to it," the lady said before giving Netta a sympathetic look and carting the picked over meal away.

Netta sat through a long boring day at the hospital, with visits from multiple doctors and specialists. The prognosis was the same yet she was still fearful and frustrated. Frustrated with being in the hospital alone, and fearful that Black may just come to the hospital and finish the job. She hoped the issue was dead between them. She had robbed him and he had extracted his revenge. As far as she was concerned, they were even. She hoped he would eventually forget about her and go on about his business.

She hoped.

However, Black played by a different set of rules than everyone else. There was no telling what was going through his mind. Getting some revenge might have felt good to him, but getting more may have felt even better.

Netta understood his mindset, so she prepared herself for the worst. She trained her mind to expect the unexpected. Planning to defend herself was one thing, but the reality could be a whole lot different.

Just as Netta tried to soothe her mind with some positive thoughts, two well built, Caucasian, plain-clothes police officers entered her room. The two silver police badges that swung from their necks announced who they were before they had a chance to speak.

One police officer began. "Sorry to disturb you, Miss Jackson. We'll try to be as brief as possible. I'm Police Officer Jason Campbell and this is my partner, Police Officer John Hastings. We're with the Baltimore Police Department's Anti-Crime Division. It's come to our attention that you were badly beaten in a downtown hotel by an unknown assailant. Well, we were able to lift some fingerprints from that hotel room and we brought along a few photos of some suspects. If you would be so kind as to take a look at them and..."

"I can't help you. I didn't see the person who did this," Netta said, cutting the cop off.

"Would you at least take a look before you jump to that conclusion. There could be a face in there that might jar your memory," Officer Campbell suggested.

"I already told you. I didn't see a thing," she spoke defiantly.

The cops weren't buying Netta's story one bit. They didn't believe anything she said. They knew that Netta could indeed identify her attacker. They knew she knew him personally. They knew more about the situation than they were letting on. Quickly they changed their tactics, becoming more confrontational.

"Listen, Miss Jackson, you're not fooling anyone over here. You expect us to believe that? That you were just strolling down the street and then suddenly you were kidnapped, blindfolded, driven to a hotel where you registered for the hotel room under your name. And you don't know the person responsible for doing this to you? You must be nuts," Officer Campbell explained.

"Maybe I am. But the fact of the matter is this, you can believe what you want to believe. I ain't got nuttin' to say. Case closed," Netta said.

To her last dying breath, Netta was sticking to the code of the streets. She was playing the game the way she was taught that it should be played. See no evil, speak no evil, and hear no evil. If she was a civilian and Black had committed this atrocity to her, then that would have been different. Netta wouldn't be held responsible to uphold the code of the streets. But as it stood now, that was not the case.

She thought, that's what was wrong with the game now. There were too many so- called hustlers, drug dealers, thugs and killers that were turning into snitches. They were too weak to deal with their own street situation so they turned to the law to take out their opposition. They get charged in a criminal case, so they turned confidential informant to save their own skin or to get less time. They committed the crime, but all of a sudden they don't want to do the time.

Snitching to Netta was a choice. A choice she wouldn't make. That stigma would never be attached to her name, not if she could help it.

Netta had never cooperated with the police before and she wouldn't do so now.

"So that's your story and you sticking to it, huh?" Officer Hastings inquired, as if he were giving her one last chance to come clean.

"That's what I'm sayin'," she declared adamantly.

"Well, hypothetically speaking, let's say this guy, who you say you don't know, comes after you again. And you do know that that's a real possibility, right? Especially since you refuse to ID the perp. He is still out there and free as a bird. We know you and Dashaun Williams, aka Black, were in that room having sex when things, for whatever reason, turned ugly. You made him pretty angry at you. He did a number on you as a result of that. He damn near killed you. Only by luck, fate, chance or whatever you wanna call it, are you still breathing. This guy is the real deal, a killer without a conscious. He has no problem killing people. He's done it before. So just know, if he ever lay eyes on you again, your luck just may run out. Ms. Jackson, be smart, we're begging you to point this guy out. And I promise you we'll take care of the rest. We'll see that this guy is put back away for a very long time."

Netta stood silent. Instead of speaking she let her defiant stare do all the talking. She was seemingly unfazed by his big bad boogieman story.

"I wish I could help you officer, but I can't," she said coolly. "As I said before, I don't know who did it. I don't know what he looks like. And for the record, I don't know no Dashaun Williams, Black, or whatever his name is."

"Oh you know!" Officer Hastings interjected. "You know more than what you're willing to say. We know that at one time you guys were romantically involved. Right before he did that stretch in the pen."

Tempers were beginning to flair quickly, so his partner intervened.

"Listen, honey, take my card just in case you have a change of heart or you begin to remember faces again. It could be tomorrow, next week or next month.... Just gimme a call," he said, laying his business card on her night table.

"Mr., please take that card off my dresser. I ain't goin' to be needin' that," she assured him. "I don't play those games."

"You sure?" the police officer asked unbelievably.

"Trust me. I'm as sure as I'll ever be," she explained.

Suddenly there was a knock on the door. The policemen took that as their cue to exit the room. They were frustrated that they hadn't gotten anywhere with the victim.

"I hope this decision that you've made doesn't come back to haunt you, young lady. Your life could be in grave danger," Police Officer Campbell said as he removed his business card from the table.

Another knock on the door only served to hasten the police officers' exit.

"Sorry for disturbing you," Officer Campbell commented, replacing his business card back in his wallet. "Enjoy the rest of your day. Get well soon."

At the door, Tone contemplated for a few seconds, thinking maybe it wasn't a good idea to visit Netta now. Maybe he should come back later. He didn't like the police. He didn't want to make himself a target of any investigation that they might already have underway. He didn't want to jump from the frying pan into the fire.

Tone had been at the door for a few minutes, he practically overheard their entire conversation. He was proud how Netta had stood up to the police and didn't snitch. Personally, he knew more than a few dudes who would have told if placed in the same situation, if their life was on the line and they felt like they weren't going to make it. He couldn't heap enough praise on her for holding her tongue.

"Yes, come in," Netta answered, anxious to end this conversation.

As the cops marched out the room, pissed off after dealing with a hostile witness, they literally ran into Tone as he entered the room.

"Pardon me," Tone said as he sidestepped the duo.

The police officers nodded their heads, curiously eyeing Tone as he walked past.

"I'm not even suppose to be up here. They was sayin' you still couldn't have no visitors, but I snuck up here anyway. Good to see you pulled through. I don't mean to scare you, but shit wasn't lookin' too good for a minute," Tone said, handing her a bouquet of flowers. "I ain't tryin' to be all up in ya bizness, but what was that all about?"

"The cops came to pay me a visit. They wanted to talk about my lil incident," Netta explained.

Looking at the beautiful flowers, Netta had suddenly become self-conscious. She became aware how off her game she was. How messy her physical appearance must be with most of her weave snatched out of her head. With her broken nails and her face all battered and bruised.

Tone noticed the sudden change in her facial expression. Somehow he sensed how insecure Netta must feel. He told her a few words of encouragement.

"Yo, you good Ma. Don't even sweat it. I know you seen way better days," he proclaimed.

His vote of confidence went a long way with Netta as she relaxed around him, feeling good enough to drop her guard. The comment made her smile. Tone could have been anywhere in Baltimore at the moment, doing god knows what, but he thought enough about her to come be at her bedside.

"Excuse my hair, face and nails. I know I must look a mess, but under the circumstances it is what it is," she admitted.

"Shit happens," he added. "It's just not ya fault."

There was an awkward pause between them as Netta took time to deeply inhale the perfume scented roses. She was showing her appreciation for everything since God had given her a new lease on life.

She continued, "Could you do me a favor?"

"Yeah, what is it?" Tone wondered.

"Could you go downstairs and buy me a scarf for my head. At least until I can do somethin' wit' my hair," she asked.

"I got you," Tone told her. "Yo, I'll be right back."

Quickly, Tone returned with a decent headscarf from the gift shop. He handed it over to Netta and she immediately pulled her hair back and put the scarf on her head. Finally, she felt halfway decent.

"Anything else I could get you?" he asked before taking a seat in a lounge chair next to the bed.

"No, I'm good," she said.

"Some food or something to drink?" he declared.

"Not right now, maybe later," she confessed. "I know you probably wonderin' what happened to me that night you found me."

"Nah," Tone lied. "You don't owe me no explanations."

Secretly, Tone was dying to know what happened. However, he didn't want to ask. He thought it might be a sensitive subject and he didn't want to run the risk of rubbing her wrong.

"I feel like I do," she told him. "Shit, if it wasn't for you I might not be alive today."

Netta was distrusting of people by nature, but she found herself trusting Tone despite all her apprehensions she had about strangers.

Tone wasn't a complete stranger, she reasoned. *He saved my life.* Netta didn't know where to begin, but she decided to put all her cards on the table. Tone was too deeply involved as it was to leave anything out.

"Hope you got time, it's a long story." Netta began giving him a firsthand account of how she first met Black.

"So the dude that put me in this fucked up situation, I know him. He's my ex..."

Recounting the story, Netta began to zone out as she relived one of the most prosperous times of her life, when she really had it going on and money wasn't a thing. When she was the undisputed queen of the streets of Baltimore and Black's girl. She spoke of the lavish gifts, like the Mercedes Benz coupe Black bought her for Christmas that she crashed. They had the his and hers matching chinchilla fur coats. Netta could envision it all now, her eyes lighting up every time Black surprised her with an expensive gift. He used to worship the ground she walked on. But that all changed when Black went to jail, and Netta committed the treacherous act.

Netta didn't care if the information she gave up painted her in a negative light, or if she portrayed herself as a gold digger or not. She was going to keep it real with Tone, even if it killed her.

As he listened intently, Tone had this underlying feeling that there was more to the story. What she was telling him really wasn't adding up. There was a disconnection there. He kept waiting for her to get to the good part. It was hard for him to take this loving image that Netta painted of Black from the animal who had beat her so brutally. Tone knew that something caused him to flip. Normal dudes just don't flip out for no apparent reason. He knew Netta had to have done something to him. She just hadn't gotten around to telling him about that yet. Something had to have been done to arouse anger like that in a man, to drive him to such great lengths to make him want to kill you.

She continued, telling him about their engagement. How Black really loved her and how she never loved him. How she was playing him. Black had been another notch on her belt, the final step in her quest for the good life.

Her careful words and vivid depictions evoked memories of exactly what it was like to be a hustler's wife. She also told him how Black's murder charge derailed their life together, eventually sending him to prison, and set the stage for her to steal his money.

"… I know what I did was wrong. I shouldn't have took that man's money. So when he got out of jail, he came looking for me. When he found me, he told me to get into his car with him. How could I refuse? Maybe if I had, who's to say that he wouldn't have killed me right there on the spot," Netta sobbed.

Netta was on a guilt trip. She had to accept the blame. She knew what she had done. She had brought Black's wrath on herself. Next time, she promised she would be strong enough to give as good as she got. All she could do now was take it as a lesson learned.

Netta wasn't the type to sit next to someone she barely knew and pour her heart out. Her doing so was indicative of how much she was feeling Tone. She wasn't begging for sympathy or asking to be saved. She didn't want to drag him into this mess. Especially when there was still a remote possibility of Black launching another attack against her.

Every so often Netta looked in Tone's direction for any sort of indication he wasn't following the story, or he wasn't feeling what she was saying. There was none. Tone sat in the chair absorbing every word she said, expressionless. He could hear the pain in her voice as she drowned in her own sorrows. Regrettably, she had been too stupid to think about the consequences.

Suddenly it all made sense. So that's why Black went on a rampage against her. Over the years, he had built up a great deal of animosity toward her. Black must have become obsessed with her. He sat in prison, plotting, planning and scheming on ways to get revenge. Finally, when his day came, when he was a free man, he retaliated.

Although Tone understood why he did what he did, he still couldn't justify Black's actions. That kind of struck him as odd. He couldn't justify him violating a female the way he had. But dudes moved differently, this he knew. A broken heart or a sign of disloyalty could turn the nicest guy cold hearted.

Tone refused to acknowledge that he had heard of Black a time or two. His name still rang bells in the streets of East Baltimore. Depending on who he talked to about the guy, he was a tyrant, a good dude, or a plain bad guy. On the streets, versions of him differed just like opinions on him varied.

It was obvious that Black was a man who commanded respect and instilled fear. It was probably never about the money with him, it was the principle. Netta had bitten the hand that fed her and she paid dearly for it.

"Tone, I ain't gone sit here and try to portray myself as a saint, yo. Nah, I'm far from that. I was just tryin' to get mine, just like you down here tryin' to get yours. We just go about it differently."

Netta and the street hustlers of the world needed no introduction, that's why her and Tone clicked from the moment he met her on that West Baltimore block. The two were kindred spirits, more or less. Their faces may not have been familiar to one another, but they were cut from the same cloth, and that cloth was called the struggle.

At this point the story became easier to digest. The more she told him the more he needed to know.

Netta was just getting started. She told him everything, from her upbringing in Murphy Homes, to her dope fiend mother dying of AIDS, to her joining the infamous Pussy Pound. She spared no details. At the moment her life was an open book, and she let Tone thumb through the pages.

In those vulnerable moments there was an instant and deep connection between the two. Without thinking, Tone reached over and grabbed her hand, something he probably would never have done if she were some other chick. He felt a spark in that physical contact, like the first time he lusted after her on Monroe and Fayette Street. Those same feelings were suddenly rekindled.

Tone began to sympathize with Netta. He didn't look at the larceny in her heart or the malice in her past actions. He simply understood. He placed himself in her shoes and asked himself what would he have done.

Slowly, in the crucial moments of conversation, she had won him over. He was beginning to understand who she was and what made her tick. Because of the emotional attachment he was beginning to feel, Tone was able to separate her act of thievery from the young lady he was just beginning to know.

Tone thought Netta's life story was amongst the realest he had ever heard. He loved that survival trait that was embedded deep within her. Her circumstances had forced her to the streets and her hunger for a better life had formed her into a hustler. To him, her mentality was both fascinating and diabolical at the same time. Through the course of their conversation, he could see Netta's worth. She brought more to the table than just pussy. In his book she was a hustler, not a hoe. Someone he wouldn't mind having on his team. He could picture Netta by his side as his girl.

From Netta's perspective, it felt good to get that off her chest. She felt like a burden had been lifted. She needed to vent to someone and Tone was gracious enough to lend an ear and he was so easy to talk to. For her it was like having a conversation with an old friend.

Once she clarified her position on Black, and the more Tone heard Netta speak, the more he began to dig her. It was in those moments that Tone saw her in a new light. He accepted her shortcomings and told Netta she was capable of more.

"You know you ain't gotta live like this no more. Not if you don't want to. I'm here. What happened between you and Black is history. And ya history doesn't have to be your destiny," he confided in her.

Silently, Netta agreed with Tone. The winds of change were beginning to blow. She knew she had to make a change in her life before it was too late. God hadn't given her a second chance for her to revert back to that same lifestyle, to do the same things that put her in this predicament.

Something had to give and it was beginning to. "Yo, lemme ask you a question," Tone interrupted.

"Yeah, go right ahead," she replied.

"You think Black was gonna let you live that night?" Tone wondered. "I mean, homeboy was goin' hard."

"That's a good question," Netta answered. "I never really thought about that, even though I came close to dyin'."

Although Tone never said it out loud, because he didn't want to scare Netta, he knew that there would probably be more drama involving Black. This dude would be a problem somewhere along the line. However, at this point, he wasn't his problem.

Tone peppered Netta with questions here and there. He didn't want to seem too intrusive, so most of the time he let her dictate the course of the conversation. He realized Netta had been hurt and humiliated enough. She didn't need him to keep interrogating her. But if there was a chance of them having a meaningful relationship, he needed to know everything.

Netta whole-heartedly answered every question honestly. Her explanations were so clear and concise it made it easy for them to be accepted and understood.

"Black's different. It's not a game wit' him, yo," Netta emphasized. "And here I was playin' wit' a nigga that ain't playin'."

All this talk about Black was depressing. Netta had mentioned Black's name so much that Tone had grown to resent him. His facial expression began to sour every time he heard it. He tried changing the subject whenever he came up. Yet all avenues of their conversation led right back to Black.

Tone thought Black might need time to forgive and forget. While Netta might need time to grow, heal and evolve. But whatever the case may be, Tone was feeling real confident. Fresh off of his execution of Sykes, he felt unburdened by Black's fearsome reputation. Black was just another dragon to be slayed, if need be.

"Yo, I'm sick of hearin' about homeboy, let's kill that noise," he interrupted her. "You hungry, you want somethin' to eat?"

Netta laughed. There was something about his arrogance that she liked. Before she could put a finger on it he was taking her order.

"I'm in the mood for some crab cakes, I could really go for that," she announced.

"You got it," Tone said. "I'll be right back."

Tone left the hospital and went and got Netta some crab cakes from Lexington Market. When he returned, they wolfed the meal down without saying too much more. Netta was real hungry and it showed. The food not only satisfied her hunger, but it made her very sleepy. After a long tense afternoon, she was tired.

"Yo, I'ma see you tomorrow," Tone promised, kissing her on the forehead. "Get some rest."

"Why you leavin'?" she protested, as lines of worry creased her forehead. "I'm up."

Immediately, Tone sat back down in an effort to calm Netta down. Before long the heaviness of her eyelids were too difficult to fight off the tiredness. Suddenly, she fell into a deep sleep. Seeing this, Tone quietly eased out of her room, leaving Netta sound asleep. Silently, he promised to be back tomorrow.

As Tone exited the hospital, he never noticed a late model Ford Tempo lying in wait. He went about his day not knowing he was being followed.

"There he go right there," Bri said as soon as she spotted his car.

"Follow him," Sonya replied.

"I don't know who this nigga been in there seein' all damn day, but obviously they pretty important to him," Bri commented. "You think it's a nurse or a patient? Or what?"

"I don't know, but we're gonna soon find out. Believe that," Sonya said.

Right now everything was such a mystery, but Sonya knew the pieces of the puzzle were coming together, and soon it would all make sense.

CHAPTER 11

Sitting on his bed reading the Baltimore Sun newspaper in the early morning silence, Black's mind slipped back to last week's violent confrontation with Netta. He laughed to himself while recalling how badly he had beaten her. Although he had beat Netta like a dog, Black still fumed that she didn't begged for her life.

Fuckin' bitch! he thought. *Hope ya ass is dead, yo.*

In the days that followed the attack, Black's search for Netta had turned up nothing. No one had heard anything about her. Nor had she been seen. Personally, Black thought she was dead. He took to reading the obituary section in the paper in search of her name. If Netta was indeed dead, nothing would make him happier. Netta had gotten too cute for herself while he was away. She was the talk of the town while he was in prison, her and the Pussy Pound. She was a major source of embarrassment to him. That's why he had paid her back in the manner that he had. Black felt like she deserved it. Besides, he had his reputation to protect.

Nobody steals from Black and lives. Nobody! he thought.

Once upon a time ago, Black fucked with Netta heavy. Now he didn't fuck with her at all. If she was still alive, then Netta was a target marked for termination. There would be no love lost and no love given.

Black finished reading the newspaper, as clueless about Netta as when he began. Was she alive or was she dead? He didn't have the slightest idea. However, it gave him something to think about.

"You ready yo?" Stink said as he stuck his head inside Black's downtown condo bedroom.

"Gimme a second," he told his younger brother.

Stink stood in the doorway as he watched his brother's chiseled physique partially disappear into the closet and retrieve the jacket to his sweat suit.

"You hear anything about that bitch, yo?" Black asked as he put on his jacket.

"No, I don't know where that whore at," he answered. "That bitch Netta just disappeared off the face of the earth. I told you yo, you should have been let me handle that hooker while you was locked up. I woulda put that bitch on a t-shirt."

Stink and Black may have been blood brothers, but they literally couldn't have been more different. Black put in a lot of work on the streets, he was self-made; while Stink had rode the coattails of his brother's success in the streets. The streets only truly acknowledged him because of who his brother was. Stink was all bark, while Black was all bite.

"Stink, I already told you that that shit was personal," he stated. "You know how many niggas wanted to do her in for me for free. I told them just what I told you, I'ma handle it, yo. I didn't want that shit comin' from nobody else but me."

"I know, but…" Stink protested.

"But nuttin' yo. That wasn't ya beef, it was mine. And I handled it the way I wanted to handle it. Don't question me. End of discussion," he spat.

Stink had pissed his brother off questioning him about Netta. Now Black had an attitude, he had no idea which version of himself he'd present to the streets today, the moneymaking hustler or the stone, cold killer who had the streets of Baltimore on edge. Whatever he decided, the streets were powerless to stop it. Black was home and he was back to reclaim his spot, the easy way or the hard way, however the streets wanted it.

Black continued, "Grab the keys, I want you to drive."

"I got 'em already, yo," Stink announced.

Stink was glad his brother was taking him with him to meet his dope connection. He didn't care if he had to drive to California to meet him, just as long as he was in the presence of his brother. As it stood they were just driving a few hours away to Maryland's eastern shore. Stink felt good about playing a major role in his brother's drug operation. Previously, before Black went to prison, he felt his brother was too young to participate in his illegal activities. His mother would kill him if she found out that Black had corrupted his little brother. But while he was away, Stink had dove head first into the street life. Now it was only right that Black took him under his wing and showed him the ropes.

"When we get back from down the Eastern Shore, we gone put that shit up and go see about them niggas you been hollerin' about. Them corner boys who want some work," Black said.

"Okay yo," Stink replied. "I got everything all set up already. They waitin' on you."

By late afternoon, Black and Stink had arrived back into Baltimore. After putting a kilo of pure heroin up for safekeeping, they jumped back into the car and headed to 21st and Barclay, in East Baltimore. This was a gritty, drug-infested neighborhood with more than it's fair share of open-air drug markets. This was exactly what Black had been looking for.

When Black's black Mercedes Benz pulled into the block with Stink at the wheel, it drew stares. As usual, there was a makeshift dice game going on. But upon seeing Stink driving the car, the game suddenly came to a halt. One young hustler made his way over to the vehicle.

"Stink, what's up yo?" he said, sticking his face halfway into the window.

"What up Rudy," Stink greeted as they shook hands.

In the passenger seat, Black was his usual strong, silent self, communicating non-verbally, speaking only when he was spoken to.

The kid continued, "And you must be Black. I heard so much about you growin' up. It's good to finally meet you."

Rudy leaned into the car and extended his hand. Black took his hand while looking him square in the eyes, and gave him a firm handshake. Black was big on giving handshakes and first impressions. He wanted to set the tone early that he wasn't a joke.

"Hope y'all niggas don't hustle the same way y'all shoot dice," Black said, releasing his grip.

He started to say something else, but he closed his mouth. He wanted to lecture the kid on the do's and don'ts of running a heroin operation; what his years in the game had taught him. He wanted to tell him how the drug game was changing, the strides that law enforcement was making and how they needed to take preventive measures to assure that they had a long run. However, right now wasn't the time for all of that. These were his brother's peoples and anything he had to say, he would tell Stink and let him relay the message to them. Everything would be done through Stink. He didn't know these dudes well enough to trust them.

"Nah yo, we just fuckin' around right now. We ain't got no work," the kid explained.

Stink interrupted, "Well, this ya lucky day yo."

Immediately the kid's face lit up, he was excited about the prospect of working for Black.

"I'ma come holler at you tomorrow. Early yo," Stink promised. "Have all ya niggas out here. We bout to open this strip up, bright and early tomorrow morning."

Black didn't say another word, it wasn't his place. Instead, he did like his brother had done. He offered his goodbyes as they drove off. Black knew that they had a long night of cutting and bagging up dope. It was a necessary evil that they had to perform if they wanted to open up shop tomorrow.

"Stink, you gonna be runnin' shit out here," Black told his brother. "You gotta be smart though. You gotta pay attention to everything and always be aware of your surroundings."

"Don't worry, yo," Stink said. "I got this. You gone seen how thorough I am, Black. Watch!"

Black didn't say another word, he chose to stay quiet as he mulled over the long night ahead of them.

CHAPTER 12

The next day, Netta's morning began with a parade of doctors and nurses visits. She was subjected to a physical examination and lots of medical terminology. Under the circumstances, Netta often felt like they were talking about her rather than talking to her. During these conversations about her physical welfare, Netta's mind tended to drift to life outside her hospital room. She had spent most of the night mulling over the idea, so she didn't have a hard time picturing herself leaving the hospital. Not that she'd tell her doctors that. Still, it was a thought, one that was cause for alarm in her battered condition.

Black's unpredictable nature would ultimately factor heavily into her decision. Her fears were beginning to get the best of her.

By the time Tone arrived at the hospital later that morning, Netta was lost in her thoughts, seriously weighing her medical options. His presence was a welcomed distraction.

"Yo, what's up?" Tone announced as he entered the room.

Almost instantly he took notice of her somber mood. Netta's facial expression was easy to read. Her face was full of frustration. Her emotional state wouldn't change anytime soon, since she had been contemplating the same thoughts all morning over and over again. However, Tone did his best to cheer her up.

He continued, "Why you look so sad?"

"I wanna go home," she replied.

"What the doctors say?" he asked.

"I don't give a damn what the doctors say!" Netta insisted. "I'm ready to go."

"Damn, it's like that?" he said.

"Yup. I'm gettin' tired of this shit," she announced.

"Aiight, I guess you gotta do what you gotta do," Tone commented. "Just keep me posted."

"Oh, you'll be the first to know, Tone. Trust me on that," Netta answered.

Tone smiled, flashing a set of pearly white teeth. "Anyway, I gotta surprise for you this morning. Hopefully this will cheer you up. Yo, Aja, come in," he yelled out.

"Who you inviting into my room yo?" Netta asked as she suddenly became self- conscious about her appearance.

"Chill, don't worry about it. I got you," he said.

"Chill my ass!" Netta snapped. "What type of games is you playin' yo? I don't want nobody to see me like this."

An innocent looking teenage female, short, dark skinned with braces, enters the room with a black knapsack on her back.

"Who you?" Netta snapped.

"I'm Aja," she replied meekly.

"Yeah, this is Aja. Aja that's Netta. I bought her here to braid ya hair. Thank me later," he told her.

Tone knew better than to bring an older chick to Netta's hospital room, out of fear they just might recognize her.

"I don't know what I'm gonna do wit' you boy." She smiled, thinking this was so sweet and thoughtful. "But thank you. I didn't know how much longer I could have kept wearing this damn scarf on my head."

Tone was glad Netta was receptive to his idea, that she didn't take offense to him bringing someone to her hospital room to braid her hair. He knew if Netta was anything like most black women, then she was funny about her hair. Anyone couldn't just do a black woman's hair. But under the circumstances, she had to roll with the punches because her hair was a mess and any style that the girl provided would be an upgrade from the way her hair looked now.

Netta climbed out her bed, and sat down in a nearby chair while her hairstylist positioned herself in back of her. She placed her knapsack on the table and began removing all the things she needed, a comb, a brush, a mirror, some hair gel and a few packs of -32inch virgin Remy weave. Gently, she parted Netta's hair straight down the middle. Aja had to be very careful doing this since Netta still had bumps and bruises from the beating. This caused her to be tender headed. From time to time, Netta winced and grimaced, even though Aja was being as gentle as possible and moving at a slower pace.

The painful twinge that throbbed in Netta's head turned into a full-blown pain. She ignored it. She had to.

Netta decided to grin and bear it. She wanted her hair done in the worst way.

"Yo, I'll be back," Tone suddenly announced, he felt awkward standing there watching the process. "Anybody need anything while I'm gone? Soda? Juice? Bag of chips? Somethin' to eat?"

Aja remained quiet. She shook her head as she continued doing Netta's hair.

"You could bring me a bag of chips," Netta suggested. "That'll hold me over til later. Aja you want somethin' baby?"

"No, thank you," she replied. "I ate before I got here."

"Aiight, I'll be right back," Tone said, exiting the room.

While the two females busied themselves with the hair braiding, Tone had more things on his agenda than just going to get refreshments. He also went and got the television and the phone turned on in the room. He paid for it a week in advance, even though he was unsure of how long Netta was going to stay. However long she planned to be there, Tone wanted her to at least be comfortable.

Sonya sat patiently in the car as she watched Bri approaching. She hoped her friend had some information on the person Tone was going to visit.

"Busted!" Bri announced, jumping into the driver's seat. "Got his azz!"

"Who is he up there seein'?" Sonya asked.

"Some bitch named Shanetta Jackson," Bri replied. "You know her? Does that name ring a bell? Huh?"

"No," Sonya said somberly.

Sonya was barely able to look her friend in the eye, not because she was embarrassed, but because she was so mad.

"How you find out?" she wondered.

Bri answered, "I went right up to the security guard at the visitation desk a few seconds after Tone and that young girl got on the elevator. I told him my boyfriend just went upstairs, but I didn't know what room he went to. The security guard gave me the name and room number."

She sighed. "Let's go before I go up there and do somethin' I regret. Like gettin' arrested."

Bri did as she was told without saying another word. This was Sonya's situation, so if she wanted to deal with it in this manner, then she had every right to. Bri didn't want to influence her one way or another. She wouldn't make any awkward attempts at small talk. Tone's cheating was the elephant in the room. Bri had done her job, now she was just there for support.

In Sonya's mind it was a good time to be alone. She just wanted to go home and bury her head underneath the covers and cry her eyes out.

The young girl worked quickly and Netta's braids were done by lunchtime. Netta picked up the mirror and examined herself. Finally, she looked presentable. Putting braids in her hair was always a good idea, but depending on who did them and how they were styled, the end result could be a different story. Fortunately Netta liked her braids. She thought the young girl did a real good job.

"Thank you, Aja. You really took care of me," Netta complimented her.

"You welcome," the young girl replied.

Now Netta felt dignified. This was a step in the right direction to getting back to normal. That's all she craved, a little normalcy after her world had been turned upside down.

Suddenly, the nurse walked into the room just as Netta was admiring herself. It was time for Netta to take her pain medication.

"Well, well, good morning ladies," she spoke as she handed Netta a small cup filled with two pills. "Looks like you have been busy this morning, Shanetta," Nurse McNeil said. "I like the braids, they really fit you."

"Thanks, Nurse McNeil," Netta remarked while dumping the contents of the cup into her mouth.

"Here you go," the nurse said, handing her a cup of water.

Netta washed the medication down and then handed her back the cup.

"Do you mind if I take this lunch tray away," the nurse asked.

"Be my guest," she replied as she waved her hand at the bland food. "I wasn't plannin' on eatin' that."

"I see," Nurse McNeil stated, grabbing the tray and exiting the room.

Simultaneously, as the nurse exited the room, Tone entered. They greeted each other while headed in the opposite direction.

"That's more like it," Tone said, admiring her braids.

"You tellin' me," Netta replied sarcastically. "I feel like a new woman."

"Well lemme take Aja home and I'll be right back," Tone mentioned.

By the time she had packed up her things to leave, Netta thanked Aja a million times as she walked out the door. Acting as her escort, Tone drove her back to East Baltimore.

Once again Netta was alone with her thoughts. However, her isolation didn't last long, Rasheeda, Fila and Petey entered the room.

"Netta!" They all seemed to say in unison.

Individually they all went over to her, hugging and kissing Netta and wishing her well. Her eyes were wide as she soaked in all the love from the Pussy Pound. Netta couldn't but wonder where the missing member, Mimi, was.

"What's up with Mimi?" Netta asked.

Rasheeda responded, "She's a mess. We don't fuck wit' her. Her ass strung out on dope."

"What?" Netta speculated. "I don't believe you!"

Netta was stunned by the news. This wasn't your average he say she say or your typical ghetto gossip. This was a bad bone to put on someone if it weren't true. So there must be some validity in what they were saying. Everyone couldn't be conspiring to throw dirt on Mimi's name.

"You don't gotta believe me," Rasheeda answered. "Wait til you get up outta here. I guarantee you'll hear about her. The streets can tell you better than me." The information that she had received didn't sit well with her.

Netta was deeply disappointed in Mimi, her best friend, her ace, her everything, now turned drug addict. How or why Mimi got hooked on dope was beyond her. They all knew how she felt about drug usage. Netta had voiced her opinion on several different occasions.

"I swear, I ain't never going out like that. I'd rather die first than live like that. And if any of you bitches get hooked on dope, y'all cut the fuck off," Netta once said.

"Man, Mimi doin' her," Fila added. "She out there."

For once in her life Netta didn't have too much to say about Mimi. She merely shook her head in disbelief, but behind that smile lay a totally different emotion, disgust. Her thoughts began to race. She remembered the countless times that she tried to school each member of the Pussy Pound. Sometimes she did it through hypothetical discussions. Sometimes allowing them to eavesdrop on her phone conversations that she had with a particular hustler, just so they could see for themselves just how she played them.

"Like Rasheeda said, the streets can tell you better than we can," Fila told her. "You'll see."

Netta was disgusted. Her emotions were hard to hide while her thoughts began to race.

"I swear, I ain't ever goin' out like that. I'd rather die first than be a dope fiend," she said.

Netta spoke with conviction, always giving her clique the best advice that she could. She had no compassion or sympathy for a dope fiend or any kind of drug addict for that matter. Her childhood had been marred by her mother's drug abuse.

In light of her current situation and Mimi's drug habit, Netta was beginning to rethink this whole Pussy Pound situation. Maybe she never should have been a part of it in the first place, quickly becoming it's leader. Was it possible that she had corrupted them? Thus she had to take the blame for whatever happened thereafter. Netta's prolonged stay in the hospital had caused her to experience a feeling very foreign to her…regret.

Quickly, Netta shook off that thought. She reminded herself that the Pussy Pound was never naïve or innocent to begin with. However, maybe she should have let someone else take the reins. She had been instrumental in making their lives so comfortable, their hustle so easy, while hers had been anything but.

Once upon a time ago, Netta felt like she was giving them too much game. She had to check Mimi hard when she had gotten beside herself.

"I taught you everything you know, not everything I know," Netta once told her.

In her bitterness she reminded herself that she should have known better, especially about Mimi. Their friendship had blinded Netta to her faults and weaknesses. She couldn't make Mimi be her friend, especially now in her time of need. Netta knew things not given freely like love, then loyalty was never worth having, especially from a so-called friend.

Netta hated to admit it, but maybe they were wrong for each other from the start, her, Mimi and the entire Pussy Pound. Maybe they weren't built for the game like she was. It took a certain type of bitch to succeed at this shit, one who was heartless and ruthless. Netta had embodied those two traits while the other members of the Pussy Pound only pretended that they had it.

Netta was coming to the slow realization that these chicks weren't built for this type of hustle. They were all fair-weather friends who loved her for who they thought she was.

Right then and there, Netta decided to fall back and let the Pussy Pound do them.

"We can't wait til you get the fuck up outta this hospital, it's gonna be on…" Petey said, eagerly anticipating Netta's release from the hospital.

Netta thought, *I'm not fuckin' around no more. You bitches can do whatever y'all like. I'm done!*

Black had given her a real reason to change her lifestyle. It's funny how a brush with death can change one's perspective on life.

Netta sat in the bed and faked a smile. She knew her immediate future didn't involve any member of the Pussy Pound. She didn't long to be in their presence as she once had. She didn't crave being the center of attention, the center of their universe. She was going about her business without them and hoped that they would do likewise.

Now, the Pussy Pound was old news to her. She was putting them and every other bad experience she had in the streets behind her. That life she was living was pointless. Those material things that she attained were now worthless.

An hour after they had gone, Tone returned to the hospital. He sat next to her on the edge of the bed. Netta wondered if now would be a good time to bring up what she had been thinking. She needed some clarity on a subject. Netta was developing feelings for Tone. Now that she knew the truth, who was she to downplay her emotions; she'd be lying to herself if she didn't acknowledge them.

Tone had come into her life and made an immediate impact on her. She felt a deep sense of gratitude toward him for everything he had done, including saving her life. Still, she was unsure on where they stood. Was this thing that they were doing going to lead to a relationship? They were beginning to spend a great deal of time together. Before things went any further, Netta needed to know.

"Tone, I been wonderin'…" she began, "….I fucks wit' you. You definitely my type. But I need to know what we doin'. We gone be together? Or is you just comin' up here everyday cause you feel sorry for me?"

"Nah Netta, it ain't like that," Tone explained. "You already know I fuck wit' you. But if you need me to make dis shit official, then the answer is yeah, we together."

If Netta was who Tone wanted to be with, then she wanted to be with him. She knew if her feelings weren't genuinely reciprocated, then she wouldn't force the issue. She just needed to feel like she really mattered to him.

Netta answered, "I don't know what ya situation is, but I can only imagine that you got somebody or somebodies. You can't tell me otherwise. So what I'm tellin' you is, take care of whatever it is you gotta take care of. I ain't tryin' to be a part of no love triangle. I want a monogamous relationship. We not goin' to entertain other people. If we gone do this, we gone do this right, or not at all."

Although they hadn't known each other long, Tone knew this was where he wanted to be. He had come to that conclusion after the first conversation they had. Tone felt like he never connected with any other female, including his girlfriend Sonya, like he had with Netta. It had grown so strong, so fast. Everything was so real with them.

With that in mind, Tone knew what he had to do, leave Sonya. Which was probably easier said than done.

“I got you,” Tone said confidently. “It’s a done deal. I’ma live up to my part of the bargain, home girl.”

This was the most intimate conversation the two of them had, relationship wise. It felt good for Tone to be real with Netta. He promised himself that he would make a concerted effort to always keep it real with her. She deserved it and so did their relationship.

“Yeah, you do that,” Netta replied without giving him a chance to make more promises. “If this is what you want, you better act like it.”

CHAPTER 13

As a result of the conversation Tone had with Netta earlier, he was in a quiet mood. He drove home wondering just how he was going to break it off with his current girlfriend, Sonya, without getting into a big argument or a physical confrontation. Realistically, Tone knew that probably wasn't going to happen. Whatever the outcome was, he knew it needed to be done. It was time to place all of his cards on the table, if he wanted this relationship with Netta to work.

Tone continued to make his way home while various scenarios played out in his head. He could try to anticipate Sonya's reaction all he wanted to, however, he wouldn't know exactly what she was going to do until he broke the news to her.

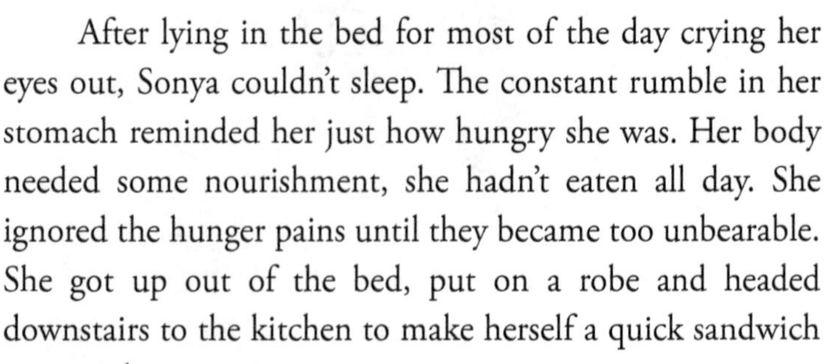

After lying in the bed for most of the day crying her eyes out, Sonya couldn't sleep. The constant rumble in her stomach reminded her just how hungry she was. Her body needed some nourishment, she hadn't eaten all day. She ignored the hunger pains until they became too unbearable. She got up out of the bed, put on a robe and headed downstairs to the kitchen to make herself a quick sandwich or something.

Sonya flicked the lights on in the kitchen before going over and opening the refrigerator. The well stocked fridge held too many options, none of which she really wanted to explore at the time. She didn't want anything she had to reheat or throw in the microwave, like leftovers. She loved ramen instant soups, but she didn't have the energy to make that. At this point all she wanted was to quell the noises in her stomach.

Suddenly, Sonya turned her attention to the fruit bowl, where colorful and delicious looking oranges, apples and bananas sat. She tore off a banana from the bunch, hoping it would do the trick. She took two bites of the banana before tossing the remainder of the fruit in the trash. Grabbing a glass of water to wash it down, she forced herself to swallow.

Instantly, her stomach seemed to settle down. Now if she could only get something to solve the rumblings in her heart.

As she leaned against the sink finishing up her glass of water, the day's events began to flash through her mind. Her worst fears had been confirmed. She felt she was justified in following Tone when she discovered that he was going to see a female at the hospital. Sonya didn't have to catch him in the act of cheating. Her intuition told her everything she needed to know. Now all that was on her mind was, where do they go from here?

Sonya turned to leave the kitchen after placing the glass in the sink. When she heard the sound of Tone's car pulling up, she decided to stay right where she was at so that she could confront him as soon as he opened the door.

"We need to talk," Sonya blurted out as soon as he walked through the door. "Right now!"

Cautiously, Tone entered the kitchen feeling a little uneasy, wondering what Sonya wanted to talk about.

Something in his mind told him, *Go head and admit it. Tell her you cheating. Tell her you love her, but you not in love with her.*

"Yo, you got somethin' you wanna tell me?" she asked.

Tone looked at his girlfriend without saying a word, a puzzled expression donned his face as if he didn't have the slightest idea of what she was talking about. Even if he did, he wasn't going to volunteer any information. Tone was smart enough not to tell on himself.

"So, where you been all day?" Sonya continued. "Gettin' money? Sellin' drugs? Or maybe baggin' up some coke? Am I missin' somethin'? Cause these some of your favorite excuses…"

Sonya paced the kitchen floor like she was a prosecutor making her closing arguments to the jury.

She continued, "….Or maybe fuckin' wit' some bitches, huh? Yeah, that sounds about right. What you have to say about that one, Tone?"

Sonya's comment was met with silence as Tone refused to be baited into going down that path. Rather than defending himself, he wanted Sonya to reveal her hand.

Just what was she getting at, he wondered. "I was outside, handlin' my business, makin' moves. You know, regular shit." he responded. "Why?"

"No, I don't know, tell me. Or maybe I should tell you," she explained. "How's that lil bitch at the hospital you been seein'? What's that all about? Huh?"

How she find out about Netta? Tone thought.

"Nigga, you thought you was slick? But yo ass is busted," she commented. "I knew you was doin' somethin',

I just didn't know with who. You fuckin' Shanetta Jackson? You takin' this bitch flowers and shit...."

"Busted doin' what? She's just a friend." Tone denied all the allegations his girlfriend was making.

"Ya friend my ass," Sonya vowed. "You must think I'm super stupid. But my thing is this, you runnin' 'round here actin' like I'm da muthafuckin' problem. When the whole time it's you. You seem to have a problem keepin' ya dick in your pants."

"You buggin' right now," he suggested.

"Yeah, nigga, I heard that before, too many times. All I ever asked you was not to lie to me and don't bring me back no fuckin' STD," she said.

It wasn't exactly bitterness in her voice when she spoke to Tone, it was more like frustration. Sonya felt she deserved better than this. However, Tone knew that falling for Netta was not in the plan. It was something that just happened.

Sonya felt so stupid, she was young, dumb, and in love. Caught up in her college studies and her sorority functions. Overall she was emotionally spent trying to make a husband out of a hustler. Trying to change a person who didn't necessarily want to change. Someone who wasn't loyal to her. Someone who loved the excitement of new pussy.

Tone stood there expressionless as Sonya went through her theatrics. Her performance was really starting to get under his skin.

"If you not fuckin' this bitch, who is she to you? Why are you takin' her roses up at the hospital?" she asked. "Tone, I'm tellin' you, you better have a good excuse, like this bitch is ya long lost relative that you just found out was terminally ill.... If you don't have a damn good explanation, it's over!" she snapped.

Tone didn't see the point in explaining his position any more. He saw a way to get out of this relationship without causing unnecessary harm to a woman he loved but was no longer in love with, so he took it.

"Yo, this shit ain't workin' out for neither one of us. Maybe it's better if we go our separate ways. I don't wanna stress you out no more than I already have," Tone stated.

Sonya's blood began to boil. She couldn't believe her ears. She loved Tone dearly, but lately they were just drifting apart, in every aspect she could think of, mentally, emotionally and even sexually. The fact that he could just break up with her so easily and that he could say it so matter-of-factly angered her. She unleashed a verbal tirade on him, spewing venom everywhere.

This can't be happening, Sonya thought. She was stressed out in every sense of the word. She had put her heart and soul into this man and all she got in return was rejection.

"So you really think that this girl could love you like I do? You willin' to throw this away for her? Nigga, she gone be gone soon as ya money get funny. If you wasn't doin' good you think she'd even want you? If you do, you better think again. That bitch ain't nuttin' but a gold digger. I helped you get on, she ain't gone do nuttin' but help you spend that money and disappear when it's gone. You don't even know her."

Sonya paused for a moment to let her words sink in as she glared evilly at Tone.

She continued. "Fuck you and that bitch, nigga. I hope you fuckin' die. You and that bitch can go to hell!" She cursed. "Bitch ass nigga.... If it wasn't for me ya ass would be up in New York broke. Nigga, I'm the one that brought ya dirty ass down here.... Now that you on ya feet you actin' real funny. You know, I liked you better when you was broke. Niggas get a couple dollars and get brand new. Nigga you ain't shit, fuck you and ya money. Let's see if that bum bitch, Nita, Netta, whatever the fuck her name is, will help you get back on when you fall off... "

A tearful Sonya looked Tone dead in his eyes and shook her head. She wanted to ask, *How could they make things right? How could they work this out?* However, her pride wouldn't let her utter those words.

Tone just stood there and let her vent. He knew he should have parted ways with her by now. The longer he stayed the more emotionally charged the situation could get. *The less I say the quicker this whole situation will be over with,* he thought.

Just take the high road, my nigga. Don't feed into her nonsense.

Sonya continued on for a while until finally Tone interrupted her.

"You done?" he said coolly. "Cause I'm goin' upstairs and grab some things. I'm out."

As Tone passed her to exit the kitchen, he studied Sonya closely. In her face he saw signs of old hurts, pain that he had already caused her, that she had been carrying around with her for a long time. He didn't know what to do but leave. Things were turning uglier by the second.

"Do it fuckin' look like I'm fuckin' done?" Sonya snapped. "You fuckin' loser! I'm still talkin'… You gone regret this shit one day, watch…."

Sonya blurted out whatever came to her mind, everything she was feeling and all her anger seemed to surface at once. Everything that she had been secretly thinking, she voiced.

Her anger had made Tone keep his distance. In her emotional state he thought anything could happen. A physical altercation could erupt between them at any moment.

Tone went upstairs to the bedroom, gathered up a few items of clothes, his money and whatever amount of drugs he had stashed in the house. Sonya followed him everywhere he went, cursing, screaming and even threatening to call the cops.

"You know karma is a muthafucka, Tone. The same way you did me, I hope this bitch do you … Even twenty times worst!" she announced.

Sonya stood in the doorway, still cursing at him as he drove off. Tone didn't leave anything of value behind. He knew once he was gone, whatever he left behind, Sonya would destroy. He knew she was probably inside the house pouring bleach on his clothes right now. He knew she was vindictive like that.

It was a nasty break up with Sonya. As he drove, Tone replayed in his mind all the spiteful things that she had said. There was so much malice in her words that Tone felt like he could never recover from. He still couldn't believe that she wished death on him. At the moment she wasn't fighting fair. Anything she could say that was disrespectful, she said. Anything she could say to get a rise out of him, she said that too. Tone knew Sonya was in an extremely volatile state, but that didn't excuse her from saying those crazy things. If the shoe was on the other foot, he would have never gone that far. Sure, he deserved to be cursed out and maybe disrespected, but death? There was no coming back from that. Now Tone was in his feelings too. Yet he remained respectful, never calling Sonya out of her name. He could never forgive her for this. Not that she cared.

For Sonya, things didn't work out like she thought. So she was bitter. She had envisioned marrying Tone, but now it looked like that day wouldn't come. In her mind she refused to accept the fact that it was over. No matter how bright her future was, Sonya had a hard time imagining it without Tone in the picture.

Walking away from this relationship unscathed was virtually impossible now. Sonya had taken things too far, to a dark place were they didn't need to go. He had hoped that they could at least be civil.

The couple used to say, *"If anything was to ever happen to their relationship, albeit a fallout or break up, that they would always be cool."* Needless to say, that was just talk, that wasn't the case now. Sonya would never honor such an agreement.

Tone just hoped his choice to leave didn't cost him someday. He thought he left a good thing for an even more promising one.

CHAPTER 14

"... Please take your ass out to that damn hospital to see about Netta," Ms. Tina yelled into the phone. *"Don't you do that girl like that...."*

As Mimi drove through the streets of East Baltimore, she thought the world was ganging up on her, she was hearing about herself on both ends, all because she hadn't gone to see Netta in the hospital. The Pussy Pound wasn't talking to her and her mother had verbally chastised her on several different occasions. Well, today would not be the day that she paid Netta a visit either. She had better things to do, like get high. She had no excuse for her failure to appear at her friend's bedside, but she made up every excuse in the book not to.

In her mind her and Netta weren't friends. They were merely friendly. There was a difference, a big difference. Netta didn't give a fuck about anyone but herself. She had proven that time and time again by what she said and how she treated her so-called friends. So why should she care about Netta's ignorant ass. To Mimi, they had been more like rivals than friends. Vying for the same hustlers, the same money, the same street fame had indirectly put them in direct competition with each other. Oftentimes Mimi got the short end of the stick. Which made her envious and jealous of Netta. Netta was always one tough act to follow, she had more personality, more swagger, and was more intelligence. Too bad Mimi never saw it that way. All she knew was she despised being relegated to her shadows.

Her jealousy stopped just short of seeing her friend dead. She was glad Black had whipped her ass for stealing his money, that someone finally knocked Netta off her high horse.

Mimi wasn't in her right mind, her thoughts and opinions were too clouded by her drug use to understand that her issues with Netta were one-sided. Netta didn't express those same sentiments toward her.

Fuck Netta, she thought, as she drove to a new dope shop she had heard about earlier in the day, somewhere her credit might be good but her body might be better.

Mimi turned on 21st Street and Barclay. She slowly drove down the block. She was anxious to find the right dope boy to talk to. Someone who was authorized to play let's make a deal with her. Someone who would willingly exchange some dope for some sex.

Every day Mimi's habit was getting worst. Her drug consumption had grown to a bundle a day. Ms. Tina, her mother, had tried to hide it the best she could, checking her daughter into drug rehabilitation centers, which Mimi promptly walked away from after a day or two. Now there was no hiding it, Mimi was a full-blown junkie. She exposed herself to the world for friends and family to see. Reports filtered in to her parents and friends alike, about how they had seen her here and there, on notorious drug blocks across the city and how bad she looked.

This shamed both her mother and father. Dollar would prefer his daughter have a life threatening illness than her to be stricken down by the same poison he sold. He thought he had taught her better than that.

"....You need to leave that shit alone so you can stick around and see your future grandbabies," he once told her. *"Don't you wanna do that?"*

There was nothing malicious about her father's words. They came from a good place, deep in his heart. Dealing dope was the life that he had chosen to make a better way for his family. Dollar had profited handsomely off of other people's afflictions. He was one of the biggest heroin distributors in Baltimore City. It was ironic how the same drug that had gotten him rich, had ensnared his three children.

Still, it seemed like his involvement in drugs was coming back to haunt him in the form of his children. First his twin boys Tommy and Timmy. One was violently murdered and the other was sentenced to life in the Baltimore penitentiary for killing the man who murdered his brother. Now his baby girl, his only daughter, was strung out on heroin. Dollar had lost three lives all while maintaining his stranglehold of the heroin trade in Baltimore.

Dollar had yet to figure out that heroin claimed the lives of the rich and the poor, the guilty and the innocent, the educated and the ignorant. His children weren't exempt from that.

As Mimi pulled closer to the action, she felt a wave of nausea. She knew the exact cause of her unsettled stomach. Whatever she was feeling was due to her lack of heroin, she was dope sick. She couldn't stay in the bed all day, unable to move, fighting her physical cravings for the drug. Kicking her habit was a scary proposition, one she wasn't ready to make.

It was the dawn of another day, yet it didn't change her reality. She was an addict. Mimi wished she could wake up from this nightmare of addiction, but she couldn't. Going cold turkey for her wasn't an option. There was no way she was going to put herself through that kind of sickness again. She was going to get herself some dope, some way, somehow.

The only thing she knew for sure was she needed her daily blast of heroin and she needed it fast. But with no money to purchase her drug of choice, her only option was to exchange a sexual favor for the drug.

Despite her dope habit, Mimi knew she was still attractive to drug dealers. She kept her appearance up, somewhat, enough to the point that dope boys still made unwanted sexual advances toward her. She was light skin complexioned, long black hair, average height, shapely, a soft beautiful face with straight white teeth. To everyone that just met her, she was a dime. But those that knew her, she had seen better days.

"C'mere, yo," she said, rolling down her car window calling over a kid she knew. "Let me holla at you."

Hope this lil muthafucka horny, she thought.

"What's up yo?" the kid answered.

"You remember me?" she asked, smiling seductively as she replayed a sexual act she performed on him.

"How could I forget you, yo," he shot back, mentally recalling the same incident. "As hard as you go."

Mimi's sexual exploits were practically legendary amongst the younger boys around there. If they knew she was out here they would literally be lining up to get a crack at her. If Mimi were your average dick sucker, he would have given her the cold shoulder and let someone else fall victim to her charms. However, as it stood, she was above average. So he openly flirted with her and entertained her.

"So what's up? You tryin' to go or what," she demanded to know.

"Hell yeah, yo," he said excitedly.

"You got some place for us to go? Or we gone do it in the car," Mimi inquired.

The kid commented, "I gotta place we can go. Park ya car, yo."

"Same deal as last time right?" she reminded him.

"Yeah, I got you, yo. You know I don't even play those type of games," he replied. "Don't I always take care of you?"

"Yeah, you do," she admitted. "You one of the realest ones out here."

"Ain't nuttin' changed," he bragged.

A few minutes of work for Mimi quickly turned into a few days of being held captive by her own drug habit, in a drug house, bartering her body for drugs. The neighborhood boys ran in and out the house for days. For some of them, it would be their first sexual experience. She was blinded to the faces of the males she serviced. Some were young, some were old, some were handsome and some were ugly. Some paid her with dope, and some gamed her and got a sexual favor for free. The one thing that was consistent was the high potency of heroin in her system.

When Mimi binged on drugs for days, like she was doing now, she retreated to some dark, remote space within herself and was totally uninterested in everything around her, her son, her mother or her friends. All she wanted, all that she needed, was inside a bag or a pill of heroin.

In this state she turned into a savage, doing whatever to whomever to feed that unquenchable thirst.

"We got this whore upstairs. Her head is the truth, yo," Stink confessed to Black.

"Fuck is you tellin' me that for, yo? I could care less about these raggedy ass bitches around here," Black cursed.

"Stop bein' so serious yo, just come take a look at the broad. You ain't gotta fuck her. Just come look," Stink pleaded.

"What's so special about this broad? You seen one hoe you seen them all," Black maintained.

"You'll see," his little brother promised him. "Now c'mon, yo!"

Black relented, following his younger brother upstairs to a dark, decrepit area of the row house. Stink opened the door of a nearby bedroom, stepping to the side so Black could get a full view.

"Bitch, arch ya back," one boy commanded Mimi, who was in the middle of a threesome. The other boy laid back enjoying the fellatio that he was receiving. They all appeared to be oblivious to both Stink and Black's presence.

"You know who that is yo?" Stink whispered.

"I don't know that whore," Black answered.

"Look closer," Stink suggested. "That's Netta's buddy Mimi, yo."

Damn, sure if it ain't, Black thought after taking a second look.

Seeing the sideshow that Mimi was engaged in wasn't sexually arousing. Still, Black didn't know why, but it made him feel good. Mimi was the missing link, she was his clue to Netta's whereabouts. He had looked in the newspapers and on the news and there was no mention about what he did to her. But now it should be easy to find out exactly where she was.

Black could not stop staring at Mimi. It was the first time he had seen her in five years. He looked at her and wondered what happened to the bad bitch he knew before he went to jail. The drop dead gorgeous chick that half the hustlers in Baltimore wanted. Now she was this pathetic drug addict. *What happened* he thought. Somehow it had all gone wrong.

Damn, how the mighty have fallen, he mused.

"Alright yo, y'all lil hoppers done had enough," Black said, seizing control of the situation. "Y'all put ya clothes on and get on up outta here."

The show suddenly came to a halt as all the participating parties got dressed or pulled up their clothes and prepared to leave. The boys exited the room first. It took Mimi a little longer to get herself together. When she tried to leave, Black blocked the door with his body, preventing her from exiting.

"Mimi, where you think you goin'," he asked. "It's me, Black. It's been a long time yo."

"Black?" Mimi repeated, as she stared at his face intensely. Although Mimi was under the influence of heroin, she was under no delusions about who this man was. Black was a very dangerous and powerful man on the streets of Baltimore.

Mimi woke up in at a hotel, the Holiday Inn on Route 40, not knowing how she had gotten there. She had been dead to the world, fast asleep for at least a few hours. In that span she had lost all track of time. Partially clothed, she stared at Black, blinking her eyes, but not saying anything.

Black sat at the desk reading the newspaper, a habit he had picked up in prison, until he noticed movement coming from the bed.

"Mimi, it's about time you woke up," he said, folding up the paper. "You sleep too hard, anything could happened to you in ya sleep."

"Where am I?" she wondered.

"Route 40," Black replied. "Don't worry shorty, you in good hands yo. I brought you here to sober up and recover. Them lil niggas was runnin' a train on you. You don't remember? I saved ya ass. Who knows what would've happened to you up in that house."

Mimi was too embarrassed to speak. She was ashamed that Black had seen her at her lowest point.

"Don't worry Mimi, that's our little secret. I won't tell a soul," he confided in her. "My lips are sealed."

Black knew he had to tear Mimi down before her built her back up. He had to make her feel comfortable around him. He wanted her to drop her guard so he had to be very careful how he questioned her. So quickly he formulated a plan to get her high first, then interrogate her extensively.

"Huh, get yaself off E," he said, tossing Mimi a few gel caps filled with dope.

Mimi caught the plastic bag in mid air, tore it open and began dumping the contents on the back of her hand, snorting it up. Nearby, Black watched in disgust as she vacuumed the drug into both nostrils, pill after pill.

"Slow down Mimi, that dope ain't goin' nowhere," Black laughed.

Only when Mimi had had enough, when all the pills of dope were gone, did she finally pick up her head and look at Black. He stared at her with pity. By the way she inhaled the dope, she had passed the threshold of a recreational user a long time ago. His eyes stayed on her, watching Mimi's every move.

It took a few minutes for the effects of the drug to kick in. When it did, Black could see Mimi was high. She began nodding off, her chin coming to rest in her chest. Now it was time for him to move in for the kill.

"What's up wit' Netta, yo? Where's she at?" he began. Mimi remained silent in her drug-fueled stupor.

"Bitch, you hear me talkin' to you, yo?" Black yelled loud enough to grab her attention.

"Nnnnneeettttaaa…" she said, slurring her speech and moving robotically. "…. Nnnneeetttaaa, in the hospital."

"How you know, yo," he wondered.

"My, my mother told me. She went to go see her," Mimi informed him.

There was no way of determining if Mimi was telling the truth to get back at Netta, or lying to protect her friend. However, it made sense. Which explained why he hadn't been able to find Netta's name in the paper. She wasn't dead.

"I hear you two fell out. Y'all not fuckin' wit' each other any more?" Black inquired.

"Fuck that bitch! She ain't right…" she began.

Black had Mimi right where he wanted her, talking. All he did was bait her into a conversation and Mimi started spilling the beans. She began telling him everything he needed to know, like which hospital she was in and what floor. She even rambled on about whom Netta was dealing with now, too.

Mimi had given him so much information. The thought that Netta had moved on from him and was with another man, a New Yorker at that, made him hot. She knew how much Black hated New Yorkers.

A lump of emotion suddenly formed in Black's throat. The idea of Netta cutting him loose to build a life with another man enraged him. He had some news for Netta. If she thought he was going to let her live happily ever after, then she'd better think again.

Black had tried to kill Netta once. And with Mimi's help, he would attempt it again. For some unjustifiable reason, Black wouldn't let this thing go.

CHAPTER 15

It all started with a phone call. That's all it took to ignite Netta's paranoia. The prank caller on the other end of the phone never said a word. They would remain silent for a few seconds before abruptly hanging up. This went on for a few days. Someone was playing on the phone, but Netta had no idea as to whom. These strange events put her on edge, as if the walls were closing in around her. She thought she was a sitting duck and Black was coming to kill her any day now.

Suddenly, the phone rang in her room. Netta stared at the phone undecidedly before picking it up. Even before her train of thought could reach a logical conclusion, she aggressively grabbed the telephone receiver.

"Hello!" She barked into the phone. Netta was tired of being played with.

"Hello, can I speak to Netta?" A female spoke softly into the phone.

"Speaking. Who is this?" Netta said defiantly. "And why is you playin' on my phone?"

"That wasn't me. I don't get down like that," the female answered. "This is Sonya, Tone's girlfriend. You don't know me but I know of you."

"Listen, I ain't got no time for this shit," Netta said with a nasty attitude. "Whatever happened between you two ain't got nothin' to do wit' me. You don't know me and I don't know you."

"Yes it does. It has everything to do with me and you," Sonya said, trying to appeal to Netta's sense of decency.

There is nothing more resourceful than a scorned woman. In a few days Sonya had found out everything there was to know about Netta; her full name, where she was from and her affiliation with the Pussy Pound. She had done a thorough background check and found all there was to know about her. For now she wouldn't expose her hand.

"Listen, whatever your name is, this ain't cool callin' no other chick about some nigga who don't wanna be wit' you. Get a grip…" Netta commented.

Sonya listened intently to Netta, resisting the urge to pump her for information, the what's, the where's and the how's.

She continued. "…For however long y'all were together, I wasn't in the picture. I don't know what was happenin' wit' y'all, if things were workin' out or not. That's not my business. But what I do know is this, girlfriend, if you were on your job, I couldn't exist. If you was keepin' ya man happy, then there is no me. So before you point the finger at me, you need to take a long hard look at yourself. You shouldn't be callin' me or callin' yaself trying to check me. You shouldn't have a problem with me, not personally. You don't know me to like me or dislike me. I have no beef with you."

Each word that Netta spoke seemed to pierce Sonya's heart and lodged inside her brain. She was giving her food for thought. Netta was trying to be more real than harsh with this stranger. It was time for the woman on the other end of the line to face the fact that her relationship was over. Sonya and Tone were a thing of the past.

But she sensed Sonya wasn't going out without a fight of some sort.

Netta continued, "The way you make it sound like is, I took ya man. Well, I didn't take anything. He chose me. So my advice to you is, see him about that. Seems like one of y'all got some explainin' to do."

Sonya mulled over everything Netta was saying. But instead of taking some sort of responsibility for her role in their breakup, she laid the blame solely on Netta. She believed that Netta posed the only threat to her relationship. So being angry with her was easy. She thought her and Tone had had a wonderful relationship. However, it had changed drastically in the year that Tone had arrived in Baltimore.

"Listen, bitch. You not nuttin' but a hoe!" Sonya exclaimed. "I know all about you and the fuckin' Pussy Pound. Y'all bitches ain't nuttin' but some gold diggin' hoes…"

Entertaining the call was a mistake, Netta knew that. However, it had been an impulsive, emotional response. All the back and forth was giving her a migraine headache, which she hadn't experienced in a few days. Now she regretted trying to reason with Sonya.

"Oh, was that suppose hurt my feelings," Netta replied. "Well, it don't! Listen little girl. Stop runnin' around like you got something. You might know my name, but you don't know my story. The shit I been through would break a weak bitch like you."

"Who you callin' a bitch? Bitch!" Sonya argued. "I will come up to that hospital right now and fuck you up."

"Come on. Bring ya bad ass up here," Netta suggested. "Ain't nuttin' between me and you but air and yo fear. Listen, you better do yaself a favor and ask about me. I might have a pussy, but I ain't never been no pussy. See, the problem is bitches like you ain't never ran into a bitch like me. Cause if you had you wouldn't be runnin' ya mouth so crazy."

Netta's tone of voice oozed with confidence. There was something fierce about her that even over the phone, Sonya could tell. There was something about her that commanded respect. She had just let Sonya know she was prepared to take their verbal altercation wherever it had to go.

"Whenever you feel like gettin' beat up, bring ya ass up here. You know my name, have the security guard give you my room number. I'm not wit' all this arguin' shit. I'd rather talk wit' my hands. Now, enjoy ya day little girl. Stay the fuck off this phone. Bye!"

Netta slammed down the receiver of the phone before Sonya could get another word in. She almost felt sorry for Sonya. Almost. To Netta it was a sad situation. But it was life, someone had to win and someone had to lose.

Needless to say, after their phone call Netta lost all respect for Sonya. All she knew was she would never react like this, under no circumstance. The day a man didn't want her would be the same day she didn't want that man. She didn't care who it was. There was no way she was staying in a situation where she wasn't wanted.

Rrrrriiiiinnnnnnggggg! Once again the phone rang. Netta snatched it off the hook with such fury that it threatened to break the phone.

"Netta, you dead! They gone find ya ass in Druid Hill Park with a bullet in your head," the male caller said before quickly hanging up.

All she heard was heavy breathing. Suddenly, a familiar chill ran down her spine. Someone had just threatened her life. The call had successfully shaken Netta up. She took this seriously. She was under no impression that the caller was bluffing.

These were strange days for Netta. Her mind was filled with confusion while being confined to a hospital bed as her body healed. She never got the face-to-face confrontation with Sonya that she sought. But she was all right with that. And she never breathed a word about the phone calls to Tone either.

Netta paced in her hospital room. She was already fully dressed in some blue jeans, black heels and a red silk blouse as she waited for the necessary paperwork to sign herself out the hospital. Over the course of the last few weeks, she had grown very paranoid about being in the hospital. It was ironic, the thing that saved her life she thought might be responsible for her death. No one could tell her anything about her personal safety. She wouldn't hear of it. She became very delusional about Black retaliating against her again. He wasn't some figment of her imagination; he was a threat and the threat to her life was real.

Netta was deep in thought when her physician entered her room. He was a bald, older white man, dressed in a white overcoat, a pair of beige khakis and black soft bottom wing tipped shoes. He held a clipboard as he calmly strolled over to her. He had stopped making his rounds so that he could address Netta personally.

"How you doing today, Miss Jackson?" he began.

"I'm good," she said flatly.

"It's come to my attention that you'd like to sign yourself out of the hospital," he said.. "Is that true?"

"Yes," she responded. "Is that my paperwork in your hand?"

"Yes. Now hold on a minute," he warned. "Before we get to that, I would like to have a brief conversation with you, if you don't mind."

There was no talking Netta out of leaving. She wasn't waiting for a clean bill of health. Whatever the doctor had to say, no matter how serious it may be, she truly didn't care. Her medical problems were her own to deal with.

He continued, "As you know, you're leaving the hospital against our wishes. The injuries you sustained in the attack were quite serious. Head trauma and internal bleeding are nothing to play with. I strongly suggest that you reconsider leaving, at least for a few days, until another CAT scan of your brain can be performed. I would feel a heck of a lot better discharging you knowing that you've healed properly. I understand the monotony of being in the hospital is getting the best of you, but it's for your own good."

"Thank you for your concern, Doc. I appreciate everything that you and the medical staff have done for me. But all things being equal, I'm still signing myself out, today," she explained.

"If you insist, Miss Jackson," he replied, finally giving up. Regrettably, there were no friends or family in the room that the doctor could enlist to convince her to stay. "So what I have here is a form called an AMA discharge. It's an acronym for Against Medical Advice. It's a release form freeing the hospital and its staff from any medical complications that should arise as a result of you leaving. It basically frees us from any malpractice suit that you may bring against us. You will not be able to sue for future monetary compensation. By you signing this form, you waive all your rights. Is that clear?"

"Yes," Netta acknowledged. "Where do I sign?"

"Please sign next to the x's at the bottom of each form," the physician informed her, while handing over the clipboard and a pen.

Hurriedly Netta scribbled her name on the documents and handed the clipboard back to the doctor.

"Well, Miss Jackson, it's been a pleasure helping you on your road to recovery," the physician said politely. "I wish you a speedy recovery and nothing but success in your future endeavors."

"Thanks Doc," she announced, while shaking his hand. "I appreciate all the things y'all have done for me. And y'all will forever be in my prayers."

"Your first few days home try to take it easy. No strenuous physical activity. Try to avoid stress. And get plenty of rest and relaxation," the physician suggested. "If I were you, I really would reconsider. However, I understand it's not my call to make."

Netta told him, "You're absolutely right. It's not your call, it's mine."

"I wish things could have been different," the physician announced as he turned to exit the room.

"Me too, Doc. Me too," she replied.

When Netta arrived at the main entrance of the hospital, she waited in the lobby for a precious few minutes, just lingering and thinking. Her thoughts turned to Tone, and the burden that he bore for her. He had paid professional movers to pack up her things and place them in storage. He had also rented a one-bedroom apartment in Randallstown for them to live in. Her living situation now was different from the one she left behind when she entered the hospital.

Quickly Netta grew tired of waiting inside the lobby. She navigated her way through the revolving doors, passing patients in wheelchairs being released to their families care. She stopped in her tracks, looking around trying to spot Tone's Mazda MPV mini van she thought he was picking her up in. She became visibly upset when she didn't spot it. Just then a shiny, white BMW M3 with dark tinted windows and a wide body kit came to a halt right in front of her. Slowly, the passenger window rolled down.

"Get in." Tone smiled, trying to make a good impression on Netta.

Netta grinned as she got into the car. She was thoroughly impressed by Tone's ride.

"When you get this?" she asked.

"A few weeks ago," he explained. "I haven't really driven it yet. You the only person that's been in it besides my cousin Mann. I only bring this joint out on special occasions. I ain't never even drove this joint in the hood yet."

"Oh, so I'm special, huh?" Netta remarked.

"You got that right!" Tone added. "If you wasn't I wouldn't be here."

For a while the two occupants of the car remained silent as they allowed Tone's last words to sink in. Skillfully, Tone maneuvered the five speed, European sedan through the downtown streets of Baltimore.

Netta admired the beautiful warm weather and all the people that were outside enjoying their lunch. It was the little things like this that reminded her to always be appreciative, since she could have had it all taken away from her that night in the hotel.

"Where we goin'?" Netta suddenly said as the car ventured onto the highway.

"Just chill Ma!" Tone explained. "I gotta big surprise for you."

Netta smiled again, as she wondered what lay in store for her next.

Meanwhile, Tone continued driving on Interstate 295 South, quickly putting Baltimore City in his rearview mirror. Soon signs for Baltimore Washington International airport began to pop up. Tone followed the signs until he came to a stop at the airport's long-term parking lot.

"What's goin' on, Tone? Why are we parked in the airport parking lot? You picking somebody up?" she wondered.

"Yeah, you," he told her. "C'mon, we gotta flight to catch."

"What?" Netta protested. "How am I gonna go on a trip if I ain't got no clothes? Please, explain that part to me."

"Easy, I got you," he replied as they exited the car. "I ain't got no luggage either, so we even. I figured that we can go shoppin' in Miami for some clothes since we don't board our cruise ship until tomorrow."

When Netta had told him her plans of checking out the hospital a few days in advance, Tone had taken the liberty of booking them a getaway from Baltimore. He thought a cruise would be therapeutic for her, all things considered. The trip wasn't just something he wanted to do for her. It was something that he needed to do for them, relationship wise.

"Ahhhhh!!!" Netta screamed, running over and jumping into his arms. "A cruise? Really? I never been on one of those before."

Tone smiled as he held Netta close in his arms. He enjoyed every moment of this affectionate embrace. He was happy that Netta was happy. She was happy that Tone was mindful enough to put the time and effort into booking a well needed vacation, a break from the streets of Baltimore.

"Where we goin'?" she shouted.

"The Bahamas and a few other islands in the Caribbean," he told her. "I really don't know. I paid a travel agent to set this whole thing up to be honest."

The prospect of going on a trip out the country gave her something to look forward to besides the loneliness she had experienced while in the hospital. This was all such a pleasant surprise. Netta's thoughts shifted back to Tone and how their relationship was beginning to blossom so unexpectedly.

The three-hour, non-stop flight from Baltimore to Miami felt shorter than it actually was. Tone and Netta disembarked the flight and went straight to the exclusive Bal Harbour shopping district to shop at some of the trendiest designer boutiques they could find. They made purchases at Neiman Marcus and Saks Fifth Avenue before hitting up Versace, Gucci and the Prada stores.

Tone had to miss out on some of the fun since he was too big to wear most of the European designers' wardrobe. Most of the stores didn't carry his size. Still, that didn't stop him from copping a designer belt and a pair of designer flip-flop sandals. He even bought a pair of Cartier sunglasses for the beach. Tone purchased most of his wardrobe from the mall. He bought a lot of Nike and Adidas athletic apparel, while Netta splurged on the high-end garments.

On their brief layover in Miami, Tone showed Netta money wasn't a thing. He might not have been a kingpin like her former boyfriend Black, but the money he was making on the streets of Baltimore wasn't anything to frown upon either. Tone was making a statement as far as what he was doing in the streets.

If he was hoping that it would impress Netta, it very well did. She loved being pampered and spoiled by her man. She loved the fact that he never once said no. That she was able to get anything she wanted. The Louis Vuitton luggage sealed the deal for her. She knew Tone had spent a pretty penny on this trip already.

Tone had a taste for some Spanish food, so after shopping, they checked into a hotel, showered, changed clothes then headed back out for an early evening dinner. They wound up at some Cuban restaurant in South Beach.

"Thank you, Tone." Netta gushed over her food. "This has been one of the best days of my life."

"Damn, we ain't even go on the cruise yet," he said. "I thought they always said the best is yet to come."

Whether Netta knew it or not, Tone was laying the foundation with her. That was what he was doing, making an emotional connection. Their relationship wouldn't be built on what he could do for her financially or how she could please him sexually. Every time Netta looked at him, she blushed. Every time while he was out in the streets doing his thing, he had thought about her. All the quality time they spent together took their relationship up another notch.

Suddenly Netta reached over and gave Tone a kiss on the lips. He could only concentrate on so many things at once, being in the middle of a conversation, eating dinner and now getting kissed was too much for him. He stopped eating to focus solely on the beautiful woman in front of him.

"You know, we could consider this trip a honeymoon," he told her between kisses. "That way we can consummate the marriage."

"Oh really … honeymoon, huh?" she mused. "That's a thought. And that other thing you said is very doable."

"Listen, Netta, you mine and you'll always be mine," he told her convincingly, letting her know that the thought wasn't open for debate.

Netta believed that Tone was the man for her, one hundred percent.

"I hear you," she answered.

Tone smiled at the thought of finally having sex with Netta. He was getting so much sex from other women that he could afford to be patient. He knew eventually it would happen because she was an attractive woman and he was an attractive man. They would be in close quarters for the next five days, so sex of some sort was virtually a given. He just wanted their union to be spontaneous. He didn't want to put her in a position where she felt like she owed him.

It was midday the next afternoon and the couple checked out of their hotel and took a taxicab to the port to board the gigantic luxury liner cruise ship. Seamlessly, Tone and Netta blended in with the countless other couples, families and vacationers that were setting sail for warm, exotic and romantic destinations.

"Close ya eyes," Tone said as they arrived at their suite's door.

"Why? I wanna see," she playfully commented. With one hand covering Netta's eyes and the other unlocking the door, they slowly entered the room.

"Walla," he pronounced, as if he were doing a magic trick.

Netta opened her eyes at the precise moment to see that they were staying in a luxurious hotel on water. The suite was plush with too many amenities to even name. Netta walked around the suite in amazement. The more she saw, the more she liked the suite. She walked out on the balcony and imagined the breathtaking seaside view they would have once the cruise ship departed.

She wanted nothing more than the comfort, rest and relaxation that this suite provided. She envisioned having sex with Tone in every inch of this room. This was a place Netta could definitely get used to. And she hadn't even seen what other activities lay in store for them on the ship.

"Tone, I must admit, you really rolled out the red carpet for me," Netta praised him.

"It's only right, Netta," he replied. "You deserve nuttin' but the best. Especially after all you've been through."

The fact that he put his own personal enjoyment behind hers wasn't lost on Netta.

"Keep it up Tone, and I'ma fall head over heals in love with you and you not gonna be able to get rid of me, yo," Netta assured him, turning to give him a hug and kiss.

"Well, I'ma hold you to that," he promised. Their first day at sea was pretty much non eventful. They ate and then wandered around the ship, trying to get a full account of all the entertainment and activities they would get involved with in the upcoming days. At Netta's suggestion, they went back to their suite and sat out on the balcony, watching the sunset. Netta kept her gaze riveted on the horizon as the sun slowly set. The view was awe-inspiring. They had witnessed one of the wonders of nature. The thought wasn't lost on either of them.

Soon after they headed back to the deck, sitting poolside. They dangled their feet in the pool and watched the ripple effects they created. Tone downed a few alcoholic mixed drinks while Netta drank seltzer water. Her physician's advice stayed in her head, warning her to shun alcohol. They talked a lot about everything and at times they talked about nothing at all. The care and concern that they expressed for each other was impressive. However, the most important thing they did was spend time together.

Tone and Netta walked back to their suite, hand in hand, high off life. They entered the suite like two giggling kids. Netta liked the fact that he hadn't asked or pressured her into having sex, despite the fact that they had shared the same bed for the first time the night before. The fact that he had been a gentleman, that he respected her boundaries when he could have easily been a savage, made her want him even more.

"Let's take a shower," Netta suddenly suggested, leading Tone to the bedroom area. She immediately disrobed and wrapped her braids in a scarf before placing a shower cap on her head. The time was now; there was no place for shoulda, coulda or woulda. Netta was going to let it all hang out tonight and give herself to him. All the effort and the control she had expended to keep from appearing easy to Tone was gone now.

By the time she did all of that, Tone had already hopped in the shower and began bathing himself. He stood underneath the water, the remnants of soapsuds remaining still high around his neck and ears. Netta admired Tone's lean and muscular body through the steamed up glass partition of the shower.

She entered the shower and slid up right behind him. Before things got heated, Netta picked up a washcloth and some body wash and began washing up. Once she lathered up, she and Tone swapped positions in the tiny shower. Netta lathered and rinsed numerous times, until she felt fresh.

There they were, body to body in the shower as the water splashed down around them. Tone ran his tongue across her earlobe, down the nape of her neck all the way to the small of her back. Netta moaned softly in appreciation.

When Netta spun around he kissed her passionately before reaching his arms around her and grabbing two hands full of her ass. Aggressively, Tone began feeling her up. Meanwhile, Netta reached down and took hold of his penis. Gently, she stroked it until his manhood came to life. Feeling his rock hard penis in her hand, Netta dropped to her knees and began giving him head. Slowly, her head bobbed back and forth as she amazingly took the whole of Tone into her mouth. From time to time she'd stop to spit on his penis, as if the water from the shower wasn't lubricating it enough. Tone leaned back on the wall, eyes closed as he received his sexual pleasure.

However, there was only so much they could do in the shower. Netta got off her knees, reached behind her, and turned off the water. Their bodies were still wet as they made their way to the queen size bed. None of that seemed to matter when they landed on the bed, and Tone's mouth found her nipples and began hungrily devouring them. Soon he worked his way down to her navel, and then to her private area as he returned the oral favor that Netta had given him earlier.

Netta moaned loudly as she spread she legs wide so Tone could have full access to her vagina. His mouth continued to work its magic. He alternated between feverishly licking and gently rubbing her clit. The end result was it drove Netta wild. She buried his face in her private area and then clamped her legs tightly around his head. Tone continued to stimulate Netta's clitoris with his tongue until she was on the verge of climaxing.

"Aaaaaahhhhhh!!!" she screamed as her entire body stiffened while letting loose her creaminess all over his face.

"You okay?" Tone joked, coming up for air.

"Oh, that was so good. You did ya thing, yo," Netta said in a low husky voice. "God Damn."

Tone smiled, knowing he wasn't done yet. He had more in store. Quickly, he mounted Netta in the missionary position. He looked in her eyes while kissing her deeply, using his free hand to guide his manhood inside her. Methodically, Tone began to stroke Netta, going side to side, hitting her walls. He wasn't in a rush. He wanted Netta to remember this. He wanted her to remember whom she got the good dick from.

Netta watched his penis disappear into her vagina over and over again. But what really turned her on was how Tone kept whispering how bad he wanted her. A few moans escaped Netta's lips while she was being pleased by his slow, deliberate strokes. At the end of each stroke, Netta would clench her pussy around the shaft of his dick. The foreign sensation took him by surprise, as he looked her passionately in the eyes and smiled.

Tone was making a conscious effort to please Netta. He knew he was hitting the right spot when he saw her begin to vigorously rub her clit with her fingers.

"Fuck me harder!" Netta cried out softly.

It was instinct that made Tone drive his manhood harder and deeper inside her. They both made ugly fuck faces as they had worked each other into a sexual frenzy. A thin layer of sweat glistened on their bodies as the room got hotter and hotter. It was a very intense situation that seemed to go on and on.

Netta began to shake violently as she climaxed, simultaneously Tone began to cum too. A strong surge of sperm raced from his scrotum to the head of his dick, exploding inside of her. He remained in that position until every drop of semen drained from his body. Netta gladly accepted it all.

In many ways Netta realized that she was making love to the man of her dreams. In this picturesque setting, she couldn't imagine it being any better. Now that she knew what it felt like to have sex with Tone, it was a feeling that she wanted to repeat over and over again.

That night, Tone and Netta made love time and time again, all over the suite, from the bed to the couch to the balcony, they both experienced multiple orgasms. They had given each other a sexual experience that they wouldn't soon forget. When they were done, they crashed in each other's arms on the bed, as the warm sea breeze cooled their hot, sweaty bodies.

The couple made the most of their makeshift vacation, taking land excursions of the Caribbean islands, exploring different villages, cultures and towns. Netta admired the laid back feel of it all as she wondered what it was like to live there. They went sightseeing by Jeep, venturing into dense tropical jungles to see wildlife they had only seen on television. The experience opened up a whole new world, for not only Netta, but for Tone too. They dined on different dishes, awakening new taste buds. They smelled new scents and felt the warm Caribbean sun against their skin.

On the trip everything felt better. The air was cleaner, the sun was warmer and the fruit was sweeter. Even when the rain clouds formed it seemed it was only a sun shower that only lasted for a few minutes. Never long enough to spoil their fun or dampen their mood. Netta's anxieties died down, as it appeared that the world had gotten bigger and her problems had gotten smaller.

One day during their five day cruise, as they walked the white sand beaches and waded in the crystal clear, emerald green waters, Netta looked at Tone and realized she loved him. She fell in love with him because he was unlike any of the other hustlers she had met in the streets. Tone could think for himself. He actually had an exit plan, a monetary goal in mind, to get out the drug game and open his own business. He was smarter than she thought and more complex than he initially seemed.

Sexually, Tone really put it on her and vice versa. Netta thought that if she could have created the perfect lover, then it would have been him. He fit so perfectly inside her it felt like a hand in a glove when they made love. It was impossible for her not to fall in love with him, especially after the sex.

It was as if they were destined to be with each other.

Being in love with Tone slowly changed her outlook on life; she had to eliminate that gold digger mindset. At times she even refused some of the most expensive gifts Tone offered to buy her. Netta wanted him to understand she wanted him for him, not for the material items that he could give her.

"Promise me you won't…" Her voice trailed off.

"Won't what?" he asked, confused.

Netta continued, "…. You won't ever leave me."

"I won't. I promise," Tone said intensely.

Netta felt a connection with Tone unlike anything she had ever felt with a man in her life. She reached over and tongue kissed him deeply. After she was done, she affectionately stroked his chin while looking deeply into his eyes. She saw strength in them, enough for both of them.

"You ain't gotta worry about Black no more. I'll take care of that if I have to," Tone announced suddenly, as if he could read her mind. "Netta, I'll kill or die for you. But either way, I hope this nigga don't make me prove it."

Tone's words seemed so final. He wanted Netta to know he was prepared to take this situation wherever it had to go. His words resonated with her. Tone wasn't bragging or trying to sound tough. He was just letting her know where he stood in case she ever wondered.

Netta didn't want to lose him, especially to a situation not of his making. She had his back just as much as he had hers.

"I love you, Tone," Netta found herself saying.

"Love you too, Ma," Tone replied. Whether he said it or not, the feeling was mutual.

Initially, Netta wanted Tone because Black frightened her. She wanted him because he made her feel safe. Now, she wanted him for a whole different reason, she had fallen in love with him.

The last few days of the vacation were the happiest of Netta's life. Although she had been through so much drama with Black and her medical condition wasn't the best, none of that seemed to matter. It was as if she and Tone made their very own footprints in the sands of time, on a tropical island where nothing could touch them. They had bonded and fallen in love on a spur-of-the-moment vacation.

The couple's relationship was growing closer by the day. They had spent a great deal of time talking about the past, the present, and the future. Particularly the future.

"… I wanna have a baby some day soon," Netta confessed. "But I don't wanna raise my kid in Baltimore."

"We ain't got to," Tone assured her. "Just let me get a couple more dollars and we out…"

Netta would recall that conversation, over and over again, as she pondered the realization of actually leaving Baltimore. The city wasn't the end all be all. Though it had been to her for quite sometime now. From this point on, Netta planned on looking at life in the grand scheme of things and which direction her life was headed.

CHAPTER 16

Soon as the couple arrived back in Baltimore from the cruise, Tone's first order of business was to get Netta settled into their new one-bedroom apartment that they would be sharing in Owing Mills, a small suburb just outside of Baltimore City. Tone carried the luggage inside the first floor apartment and promptly sat them down in the hallway. He then began showing Netta around.

"This is the bathroom," he commented. "It's kinda small, but it'll do since we won't be livin' here long."

It was hard to read Netta's body language. She was so quiet that Tone thought something was wrong. For some crazy reason he was expecting her to shoot down the whole idea of moving in.

"Something wrong?" he asked, while Netta looked nonchalant. "You don't like the apartment?"

"No, of course not," Netta responded, looking around the small apartment. "I'm grateful that you thought so much of me to find an apartment for us."

Netta was deeply moved. Today marked a turning point in her life. Tone getting this apartment for her meant the world to Netta.

Good, he thought. Tone needed to know that his efforts weren't in vain. The apartment was a last minute thing so he had to settle for what was available.

Looking around the apartment, Netta could tell that everything in it was brand new. Everything from the pots, towels, linen, television, the bedroom set to the brown leather three-piece couch. Netta could literally smell the newness in the apartment. She took a seat on the couch and laid back, imaging her and Tone spending a lot of time together there.

There was no doubt in her mind she was happy to escape her old home. The mere fact that no one knew where she lived was a plus. After everything that she had been through, Netta felt like she needed a safe haven and this was it.

"Gimme a second. I got somethin' for you," Tone suddenly announced before disappearing into the bedroom.

When Tone reappeared standing at the entrance of the living room empty-handed, Netta was puzzled.

"Well, where's it at?" she wondered.

"Hold ya horses," Tone said while extending his hand to help her off the couch.

Netta grabbed hold of his hand and he pulled her to her feet. Then Tone reached in his back pocket and produced a small black stainless steel gun.

"Here, this for you," he announced. "I want you to feel safe when I'm not here."

Netta took the gun in her hand and carefully looked it over. There was a feeling of calmness that the firearm evoked in her. She liked the idea of having the gun around. Suddenly she didn't feel so defenseless.

"You know how to use it?" Tone asked, interrupting her thoughts.

"Yeah, this ain't the first time I had a gun in my possession. Trust me, I know how they work," she assured him.

"Aiight, home girl, I was just checkin'," he replied. "There's eight shots in there. Not enough to go to war, but enough to get a nigga up off you."

Netta continued to admire the gun, tinkering with the trigger safety. Every muscle in her body tensed up as she imagined all the damage she could do. She thought from this point on, she wouldn't have to worry about a thing.

"This was a nice surprise," Netta admitted.

"I thought you'd like it," Tone replied. "Now put that away, you scarin' me wit' that gun."

Netta cut her eyes playfully in his direction. "Stop playin' yo. I would never hurt you."

"I know, I'm just jokin'," he told her. "I'ma leave you here to straighten up the place. I gotta go handle some business. I'll be back as soon as I can."

"Okay. Tone, be safe out there," Netta told him. "Love you."

"I will," he assured her as he exited the house.

For the next few hours Netta busied herself around the house cleaning, unpacking and settling in, trying not to think, trying to keep her mind off what was really bothering her. In this case, it was Black. She had a bad feeling that things between them were going to come to a head very soon. She didn't know how or when. Still, it's what she believed.

While Tone was in the streets taking care of business, Netta's thoughts were on him the whole time. Her most pressing thought was when would he be back? She didn't like being home alone. She felt more comfortable with him there. Every little sound that the home or the surrounding apartment made put Netta on edge.

Netta was afraid to be alone in the house, gun or no gun. The hours that Tone spent hustling drugs in the streets felt like a punishment of some kind. Although she never expressed the fact that she was afraid of being alone in the apartment, Netta was very afraid. Afraid that Black would return and finish the job. Whether that thought was just plain paranoia or not, it took hold of her psyche just the same. Her thoughts were that of a person who was terrified of being killed or physically hurt again.

She couldn't just go on with her life in Baltimore like she hadn't been damaged by what Black had done to her. As if her life hadn't been altered by the vicious beating he had administered. Netta knew better, only time and distance would cure what ills.

As night fell, Tone put his plan to kill Black in motion. He never told Netta of his intentions, this involved only he and his cousin Mann, acting as the get-away driver. Baltimore City was small, if one didn't know where a particular drug dealer sold drugs, it wasn't hard to find out. As soon as word of Black's new shop reached Tone's ears, he reacted swiftly.

Tone promised himself the next time he got into an altercation with anyone in Baltimore, he would be the aggressor.

Tone believed if Netta was to have a prayer of surviving Black, of living her life without fear, without constantly looking over her shoulder, he needed to end things now. He had made up his mind on the cruise that when he got back to Baltimore, he was going to launch a surprise attack on Black. This was a risky strategy for Tone. He was counting on the element of surprise to help him emerge victorious.

If he hurts her, he hurts me. And I can't let that happen, Tone thought. *What kind of man would I be if I couldn't protect my girl?*

Tone had kept his intentions secret from everyone. Whatever information he shared was on a need to know basis. Netta wasn't involved so she didn't need to know. Tone was doing this on her behalf, so with that in mind, he would rather beg her for forgiveness than ask her for permission. He would endure all the rain just so Netta could bask in the sunshine. If that meant risking his life or his liberty to protect her, then so be it. One of Tone's greatest pleasures in life was protecting the people that he loved. As long as he was around, Tone swore no harm would come to Netta.

Tone slid into the passenger seat of the car with a no nonsense look on his face. The look said he was one hundred percent serious about what he was going to do. For him there was no more worrying about getting caught up in a beef that wasn't his. Or doing something he had no business doing. He was all in, the Uzi submachine gun sitting in his lap said as much to his murderous agenda.

"Take me to where this nigga be at," he instructed his cousin Mann.

Mann nodded and proceeded to drive. Meanwhile, Tone shifted his attention to the task at hand. There was nothing left to talk about. Because of Netta, their paths were destined to cross.

Cautiously, Mann drove to 21st and Barclay Avenue. Slowly they crept up the block, on a search and destroy mission. This block was a crucial location to Black's sprawling dope empire that he hoped to build. They had heard that he was out there on a daily basis, running the show. Mann had taken a few test runs through the area so he knew exactly what he looked like. He was just waiting for Black to show his face to point him out to Tone. Then he would handle the rest.

Once upon a time ago, one wouldn't catch Black dead on the block. He had an army of workers to insulate him from the police and from the streets. But that was then, and this was now. With his release from prison, he was starting his dope operation from the ground up. He was looking to regain that lofty status again, as the gatekeeper of the heroin trade in East Baltimore. However, he knew that he had to take a hands-on approach. Black had to be out on the block with his team.

With Black's level of success came a certain amount of confidence, a certain amount of arrogance, a way of thinking that made him feel untouchable. He didn't count on anyone trying to derail his plans.

Black stood amongst his young workers, watching as they made dope sale after dope sale, unaware of the danger that was lurking.

"That's that nigga right there," Mann told him, pointing Black out.

Immediately, Tone hopped out the car and sprung into action. He raised the compact submachine gun to his chest, barely having to brace himself. An eerie silence seemed to engulf the block seconds before the attack. Black's sixth sense seemed to alert him of the assassination attempt. He turned just as Tone pointed the weapon at him. Black was able to duck a millisecond before Tone began to fire.

The heart pounding sounds of automatic gunfire shattered the tranquility of the block. Sounds of broken glass, running feet and screams soon filled the air. Tone was thoughtless in his firing of the Uzi. He unleashed a high volume of bullets that no target could sustain to an extended period of time. He fired at Black and anyone else he thought was a threat. He wasn't really thinking, a gun of that magnitude didn't require him to. All he needed to do was point and squeeze the trigger.

Tone was sure he hit a few people. He could tell by the screams and the sudden collapses to the ground. Yet he wasn't for sure if he had hit Black, his primary target.

After a few tense moments of hiding behind a car and listening for Tone's footsteps, Black was able to slip away amongst the ongoing confusion.

For the entirety of the shootout, all Tone kept thinking about in the back of his mind was the police. He kept a silent count in his head of how long things had been going on. Right now it was telling him it was time to go. So Tone hopped back into the car, automatic gunfire erupted from the interior as they sped off.

Humiliated, Black ran through the alley a few blocks away. He knew he was lucky to have escaped with his life. He also knew he might not be so lucky next time. He didn't know who that guy was that was shooting at him, but one thing he knew for sure, he was going to find out.

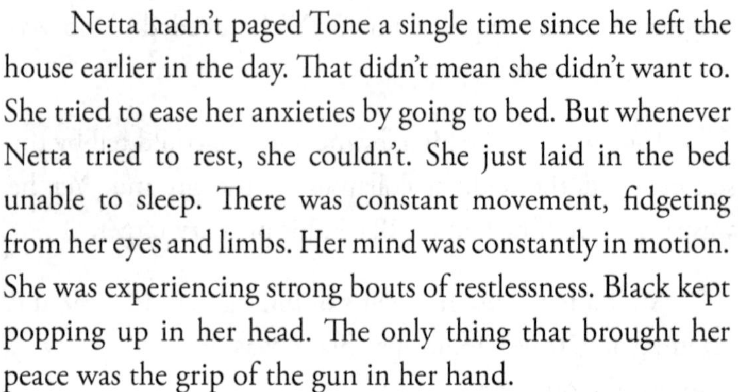

Netta hadn't paged Tone a single time since he left the house earlier in the day. That didn't mean she didn't want to. She tried to ease her anxieties by going to bed. But whenever Netta tried to rest, she couldn't. She just laid in the bed unable to sleep. There was constant movement, fidgeting from her eyes and limbs. Her mind was constantly in motion. She was experiencing strong bouts of restlessness. Black kept popping up in her head. The only thing that brought her peace was the grip of the gun in her hand.

She was having second thoughts about her new living arrangements. Netta felt she had rushed into this living arrangement knowing it was what he wanted, but not knowing if this was what she really wanted.

A sudden opening of the apartment door broke up those negative thoughts. When Tone finally arrived home, Netta had never been so glad to see someone in her life.

"What's wrong with you?" Tone asked as Netta embraced him.

"Nothin', I just missed you." She smiled in an attempt to divert him from the truth.

Tone knew something was up even though he didn't bother to press her about it. He had deeper concerns at the moment.

"I took care of that nigga," he suddenly stated.

After shooting at Black, the only regret on Tone's part was he didn't let Netta know his plans before hand. However, he knew Black's modus operandi, violence was his calling card. Black was a killer many times over. So Tone had made up his mind to strike first. He wasn't waiting on Black to make the first move.

"Who?" Netta wondered, not having the slightest idea of whom he was talking about.

"Black!" Tone answered. "I think I got him."

You think, Netta wondered. *Either you did or you didn't.*

Tone continued, "Shit was crazy out there. I was just shootin'…"

"Black ain't the type of nigga you shoot. He's the type of nigga you kill," Netta told him.

Those words hung in the air for what seemed like an eternity, with each person left to determine the true meaning.

Instantly, Netta's mind was flooded with fears and what ifs. Her warning seemed to allude to something. Like there was trouble brewing on the horizon. This would be a tit for tat situation. Right now, Tone was up, but Black owed him one. She knew that if he ever caught up with them, Black would be out for blood.

Suddenly, things were getting too real, too serious, and too dangerous for them both. Now there were consequences to pay.

"Now we really gotta get up out of Baltimore, yo..." Netta stated.

After speaking she fell silent. Now she was left to ponder what Black's next move would be.

CHAPTER 17

Netta lay in the bed, half asleep. She was emotionally drained and exhausted from having been up all night. She had talked to Tone briefly during the night, just to make sure that they were on the same page with their exit strategy. Yet the reality of what he had done weighed heavily on her. There was no coming back from the mistake Tone had made. The incident only served to accelerate their departure.

In her sleep a sense of complete isolation had overtaken her. Netta had forgotten that she wasn't sleeping alone. When Tone wrapped his arms around her trying to cuddle, panic suddenly gripped her. She elbowed him hard in his midsection, while retrieving the firearm from under her pillow. She raised the weapon high into a firing position at the same time whirling around to face her would-be attacker.

Tone rushed into action, making a grab for the gun and began wrestling it away from her.

"Yo! Yo! Netta it's me!" Tone shouted out as they tussled.

Netta struggled with Tone briefly before she came to her senses and recognized whom he was and where she was.

"Sorry," she apologized. "I was havin' a bad dream."

She winced faintly in the darkness as a throbbing sensation signaled that she was experiencing another chronic headache.

"Gimme the gun," Tone ordered. "Ma, you about to kill me up in here. Lemme put that shit away."

Tone rose from the bed in nothing but his boxer drawers and flipped on the light. He took the gun and placed it in a shoebox in the closet, for safekeeping.

"I got a little paranoid when you touched me," she explained. The possibility of Black returning was never far from her thoughts, while getting as much money as possible was the main thing on his mind.

"I see," he replied, feeling that she didn't have to worry about repercussions from Black, at least not with him there.

Tone's plan of gathering up as much money as possible before they left Baltimore, before Black made a move against them, was now in jeopardy. Netta's paranoia was complicating matters.

"Tone, we gotta get up outta here. I'm not goin' to feel safe until we do," she admitted.

Tone had to push all thoughts of Black aside and try to place himself in her shoes. How would he feel if a certified killer wanted him dead. He realized who was he to tell Netta about her safety? Who was he to tell her how to feel? If anything happened to her, he would have to live with that guilty feeling, especially after she had expressed her apprehensions.

"I hear you," Tone stated, sitting on the edge of the bed.

"We need to leave Baltimore a.s.a.p." Netta suggested. "Get all your money off the streets or either leave the work wit' your cousin Mann and let him Western Union you the money."

Tone wasn't too sure about that. After all, he had built this thing up from scratch on his own. He wasn't too sure about handing over the keys to his empire to anyone.

"I'll be ready in a few days," Tone admitted. "I just need to take care of some things."

Netta didn't like what she was hearing. The risk factor of staying too long in Baltimore was unacceptable. She wished that he would realize that they were wasting precious time and they needed to make their escape a top priority. She felt his response was inappropriate, considering the circumstances. She blamed her ill feelings on the high stress of the situation. Still, she tried to understand his position.

Tone couldn't just leave, pick up and drop everything. He was running a drug business and other people depended on him for their livelihood. It was silly to think that he could.

"You gotta few days to wrap this shit up," she explained. "Cause I'm leavin' with you or without you. But I'd rather it be with you."

Tone would keep Netta's sense of urgency in mind, like he didn't have enough to worry about right now.

"Okay, say no more, I'm on it," Tone promised, unsure exactly how he was going to make it happen.

"Good," Netta replied as she snuggled up underneath him.

At least now he wouldn't have a valid excuse for not being ready. Tone said he would be ready and Netta planned on making him keep his word. Or else.

Though she had Tone's word that they were moving, she recognized his heart really wasn't in it. Still, everyday until they moved, Netta complained about it to Tone. She was beginning to fear that he wasn't taking this situation seriously. While on the other hand, Tone was more than somewhat annoyed by her constant reminders.

The days leading up to their exodus took on an uneasy rhythm for Netta. She busied herself running errands, going to her storage and packing clothes. She was making all the necessary arraignments with a moving company to have her household items moved to Atlanta, once they found a suitable place to live.

"We gotta get outta here," she would say.

Since the attack Netta had lived in fear of what could happen. Her mind was being controlled by what might happen again.

Her belief of getting out of Baltimore alive began to wane over the next few days. Netta felt if she ran fast enough and went far enough, that she would escape Black's wrath. He would never catch up to her.

Netta hoped everything worked out for Tone on his end, because her only other option would be to leave him behind.

Tone arrived at Mann's crib out in Carroll County. His reason for seeing him was he needed to pick up all the proceeds that had been made while he was away and to get an account of how much product they had left. The elephant in the room was Tone had yet to tell his cousin of his imminent departure. He knew he had to choose those words carefully.

"…this is a little of over forty-five thousand," Mann said, handing over a duffel back filled with cash. "As far as the work go, we still good, but we gone need to re-up in a few days."

"Well, that's what I wanted to talk to you about," Tone announced.

There was intensity in his words that really made Mann pay attention.

Tone continued, "Yo, after this shit done, I'm out!"

Mann looked at him, puzzled, as if he couldn't comprehend what he had just heard.

"Where you goin'? To the city?" Mann wondered. "Yo, how long you stayin'?"

"Nah, I'm done. After this batch is done I'm leavin' Baltimore. I'm headed to Atlanta, me and Netta."

Mann couldn't understand why Tone wanted to leave. They had a good thing going in Baltimore. Together they had started laying the foundation for a major drug organization, brick by brick. So for him to just up and leave was inexplicable. He suspected Tone's new girlfriend had something to do with this.

"When did you come up wit' this? And why is you just now tellin' me?" his cousin stated, determined to make sense of it all. "So this ain't got nuttin' to do wit' that shootout we had the other night or ya girl, huh?"

This was something he'd never talked about with his cousin. He didn't want anyone else's opinions factoring into his personal decision.

"I been thinkin' about leavin'," he went on to explain. "Only thing really keepin' me here was Sonya. But now that that's over, I'm out! We had a good run. No arrests. No indictments. No nothing. How long can our luck hold out?"

"Nigga, what the fuck I'm suppose to do, huh?" Mann shot back. "I ain't got the dough you got. This shit is bread and meat right here. I ain't ready to just hand over somethin' I built up to the next nigga. I got's to ride this shit till the wheels fall off."

"Mann, I been tellin' you to save ya money. Put somethin' away fa a rainy day," Tone commented.

"Nigga that's easier said than done," Mann told him. "A nigga got bills, bitches, and a spendin' habit. C'mon my nigga, you know how that goes."

Tone knew very well what it was like to be young, dumb and getting money. He knew about the reckless spending. He knew about living for today and dealing with tomorrow when it got here. Still, that didn't justify Mann's irresponsibility with his money. However, Tone understood his plight.

"Best I can do for you Cuzzo is co-sign for some consignment for you wit' the connect. He gonna hit you off on my strength. Please, please, whatever you do, don't fuck dis up. My name ridin' on this. Nigga, it's a one shot deal if you do. If you fuck up, it's over."

"Bet, that's all I want. The opportunity to do my own thing and be my own man. I got this," Mann assured him.

Mann felt like he could do it. After all, he had been Tone's lieutenant, he had been responsible for a little bit of everything. Running his own show wasn't anything more than what he had been doing for his cousin.

"I'll see you on the block tomorrow," Tone told him as he prepared to leave. "Be out there earlier so we can move this work a lil faster."

"No doubt," Mann replied. "Catch you in the A.M."

When Tone had exited the house, Mann was still hyped at the prospect of having his own drug operation. Tone had done well in Baltimore. He hoped his cousin would do the same. He wasn't just passing off his drug connection out of sympathy. He thought his cousin could excel if given the chance. Well, here it was and as he told him, he'd better make the most of it. Tone was leaving town, any problem Mann had, he'd have to figure it out on his own.

Somewhere in the back of his mind, Tone was already beginning to imagine life in Atlanta. He wouldn't be doing anything illegal to jeopardize his freedom down there. Tone planned on leaving his illegal life behind.

CHAPTER 18

It had been three and a half days now and counting. Netta had fretted over every second, minute and hour. Finally, the big day had come. Tomorrow they would be bidding farewell to Baltimore, forever. The couple had jammed some of their worldly possessions inside a large U-Haul box truck. They hitched a car trailer to that in order to transport Tone's brand new BMW M3. Everything was set. There was nothing left to do except for Tone to collect the rest of his money off the streets and for Netta to say her goodbyes.

Netta's bucket list of things to do before she left Baltimore was short as shit. She felt like she only had to share her business with one person before she left, and that was Mimi's mother, Ms. Tina. The woman had done so much for her in the short time that she knew her. She housed Netta when she didn't have any place else to go, fed her, nurtured her and loved her like she birthed her. So Netta felt justified in her actions to go see her. She completely disregarded Tone's warning to, *stay in the house.*

Netta was glad to finally be coming from under that dark shadow that haunted her during her daily routines. It seemed to be waiting inside the apartment, ready to rear it's ugly head every time Tone hit the streets, leaving her alone. Suddenly, her fears and concerns were a thing of the past.

Netta stood face to face with Ms. Tina as the two women gushed over each other.

"Where's the baby?" Netta wondered, referring to Mimi's infant son.

"The baby ain't no baby no more," Ms. Tina replied. "That boy is in daycare now. Thank God, cause my grandson is a handful. So you mean to tell me you just up and leavin' Baltimore huh? Girl, you playin' around."

"I wish I was, Ms. Tina," she replied. "It's true, I'm leavin'."

"I wish you could take that god damn daughter of mines with you," she said in a stern tone with the happiness leaving her eyes. "That girl out here carryin' on with them drugs. I don't know what the devil got into her."

Netta felt inadequate. She wished she could help Mimi, if only for her mother's sake. However, she knew it wasn't that easy. Mimi had to hit rock bottom first. She had to want to get clean for herself. For Netta, the fact of the matter was, she couldn't save anyone until she saved her own self.

"Them drugs gone be the death of her," Ms. Tina stated, in a matter of fact tone.

Netta shook her head in agreement as the terrifying sound of a mother's pain filled her ears. In Netta's book, pain was pain, regardless of whom it came from or what it was about. No pain resonated with a mother more that the pain of losing a child to death, drugs or the streets. That went beyond agony, especially when you have to watch your child die the slow death of addiction.

How could Netta tell Mimi's mother that her and her daughter weren't connected any more? That severance of their friendship was deeper than a simple disagreement. She didn't know about Mimi any more. In the past she had viewed her as a friend, a sister and her close confidant. After Netta's brush with death, and Mimi's disappearance, she was left with an unshakable negative image of her so-called friend. Which lead her to an undeniable conclusion, they weren't friends at all, merely friendly.

"Wow." Was all Netta managed to say.

"I'm so glad you got your shit together and got your head on straight…Ain't nothing out here in Baltimore but trouble. I wish you nothing but the best in Atlanta," she said with finality, sad that she would never see Netta again.

Unable to control her emotions, Netta threw he arms around the woman and gently embraced her. "I owe you so much, Ms. Tina. Thank you for everything you've ever done for me."

Quickly the tears began flowing between the two women as they shared a very intimate moment.

"Nothin' is gonna change between us," Netta assured her. "No matter where I go or what I do, you will always be family."

All at once Netta's mind began to fixate on all the special moments that they shared in this house. The birthdays, all the holidays, Thanksgivings and Christmases. She would always cherish those wonderful times there, when she allowed herself to relive those memories. This house and these people who occupied it would always have a special place in her heart. No matter how far away she moved.

It was a good three hours before Netta emerged from the home and hopped into an awaiting cab. Her first coherent thought was she was going to spend the entire night wide awake, unable to sleep. She was happy, but she'd be even happier this time tomorrow when they were on the highway.

Netta knew that she would be too excited to sleep. She was looking forward to the move.

As the cab slowly drove off, headed back to Owings Mills to take Netta home, a few cars down a non descript late model car pulled out of a parking space and proceeded to follow her. At the wheel was Stink, Black's younger brother. He stayed a discreet distance behind the cab to avoid Netta's detection. He wasn't there to harm Netta, not yet anyway. His role was to observe and report his findings back to his brother.

On the other hand, Tone had taken all the necessary precautions to be safe, carrying a gun at all times. Being cautious, not driving straight home. Constantly looking in the mirror to make sure he wasn't being followed. But even with those safety measures in place, he still wasn't completely safe. His significant other, Netta, undid all that with a quick trip to the hood.

Netta had only herself to blame for this. Her surprise visit wasn't a surprise at all. Netta had called ahead to make sure Ms. Tina was home. She in turn got in touch with Mimi and tried to convince her to come see Netta. Her daughter declined. However, what she did do was pass the information on to Black that Netta would be dropping by. He paid her handsomely for the information with some dope.

"I just seen that bitch Netta, yo. She put some shit in a U-Haul truck parked in her parking lot. It's a big truck. I think they moving somewhere, yo. I bet it's outta town. We gotta get'em now. I'm tellin' you, yo. What you want me to do?" Stink said to his brother Black.

"What did I tell you to do?" Black asked. "It's time to take care of business and get rid of all of these whores, yo."

It took every ounce of self-restraint for Black not to get right back at Tone. He wasn't trying to go back to jail, he knew if he set another foot in a Baltimore courthouse, for anything, least of all a murder or an attempted murder charge, he may not ever see the light of day again. So instead of engaging Tone in a shootout, Black hatched a plan to kill him, Mann, Netta and Mimi simultaneously.

Black did the smart thing, just watching, waiting and bidding his time. He had people following both Netta and Tone. So he was aware of their every move. Meanwhile, Mimi was being baby-sat around the clock by a host of workers, keeping her high as hell, tucked away in a stash house.

However, now was the time to strike. There were no temporary solutions … everyone had to die.

Mann exited the stash house using the back door, under the cloak of darkness of the alleyway. Although he was visually alert for whatever he might encounter out of the ordinary. Mentally, he was elsewhere. His mind was on seizing control of Tone's drug operation. For once in his life, Mann would be the boss. He smiled at the mere thought of that.

At any minute Mann expected to reach his vehicle and head home, just like he always did at the end of the day. This time it was different, he was in a celebratory mood, he wasn't in the mood to use his brain in any sort of capacity, except for drinking, smoking and sex. As soon a he got home he was going to indulge in all three things. His girl was already home waiting on him with the liquor, weed and some good pussy. Now all Mann had to do was get there.

Mann emerged from the alleyway. His eyes quickly scanned the immediate area to the left and to his right, not a soul was in sight. He continued walking the short distance to his car, a black Toyota Cressida. He admired the freshly detailed vehicle as he approached, it seemed to sparkle underneath the street light. He clicked the remote, unlocking the car from a short distance away. Mann entered the dark tinted interior and stuck his key in the ignition. Just as he began to turn the key, he heard a voice in the back seat.

"This from Black," Stink snapped. "You whore!"

Quickly, seven gunshots in rapid succession tore through the backseat, lodging in Mann's upper and low torso. With blood gushing everywhere, he collapsed on the steering wheel, causing the car horn to blow loudly and attract unwanted attention. Stink jumped out the backseat, continuing to fire as he fled the scene on foot, running straight to a getaway car that was parked around the corner.

Mann desperately tried to move his body into an upright position and start the car to drive himself to the hospital. He could do neither. The pain was too intense. Every second he fought to stay conscious only prolonged his misery. Finally, Mann succumbed to his internal injuries, passing out and dying right in the driver's seat before any medical attention could arrive.

At nine o'clock at night, coming down from a high, nothing looked more inviting to Mimi than another bag of dope. Black showed her no mercy, he kindly obliged her with the drug.

"Here, yo," he said, passing her the beige like substance. "This some new batch I want you to try out and tell me how it is."

Up to this point Black was a trustworthy, reassuring presence around her. He wasn't like the other guys who wanted sex in exchange for some dope. He looked out for Mimi whenever she was dope sick and wanted to get the monkey off her back. Black supplied her with an endless amount of dope. That good dope that he gave her would chase away the black clouds that seemed to hover over Mimi, and make her feel good again.

"Okay," Mimi replied, her voice still slurred and her hair was a tangled mess.

Eagerly, Mimi reached up, taking possession of the dope and began snorting. Black grinned in anticipation of the drug's affect. The more Mimi snorted, the wider his smile became. A few minutes later, when every morsel of the drug was gone, Mimi began to feel funny. She fell back on the couch in an attempt to feel better. However, a feeling inside her told her something wasn't right.

Not a minute later, Mimi began sweating profusely as the battery acid mixed with heroin raced through her veins. Everything all at once seemed to cross her mind … her mother, her father, her son, even Netta. Her concern for life and the living were too little, too late.

"Help me," she cried. "Please..."

Black glanced down at her and smiled. He gave her hand a firm squeeze. "See you in hell, bitch!"

In a few moments it was over, Mimi died as a result of respiratory failure. She stopped breathing and proceeded to turn blue. Without even thinking about what he was doing, Black wrapped Mimi's body up in an area rug, placed it in the trunk of his car and drove to West Baltimore and dumped it in Druid Hill Park.

Now there were two down, with two more to go.

Late that night, Netta found herself pacing around her bedroom in nothing more than a white bathrobe. She hadn't heard from Tone all day, although he told her earlier that he had a lot of running around to do. Still, with every passing moment, doubt was seeping into her mind. She was beginning to worry, big time.

Netta paged him, and then she paged him again. She waited and waited for a phone call on the landline, but none came. She glanced outside her bedroom window to see if she saw any sign of Tone pulling up. She saw none. She began to get fidgety and overanxious as she awaited his arrival home for the night. She glanced over reassuringly at the moving truck they had parked in the parking lot. Netta told herself her escape from this personal hell was only a couple of hours away. She had never wanted anything more in her life.

It seemed too good to be true. However, it was just that simple. They would leave Baltimore in the morning after Tone had gotten a few hours of sleep. Or maybe she could convince him to sleep in the truck while she drove the first leg of the trip.

Now Netta was thinking too much. Tripping. Second guessing herself. She decided to lay her ass down. Worrying about Tone's whereabouts was about to give her an ulcer.

Netta went to the closet and grabbed the gun out the box, placing it under her pillow. She forced herself to try and get some sleep, just in case Tone agreed to her crazy plan of leaving as soon as he returned home, in the darkness of the night.

Netta hadn't been asleep all that long, two hours at best, when she was awaken by a disturbance at her front door. Her mind was still cloudy when she heard the rattling of the doorknob. The noise shattered the peace and tranquility of the night. She heard the squeaking sound of the front door that alerted her to the fact whomever it was had just entered the house.

"Tone?" she called out. However, no reply came.

Netta sensed danger. In her mind if it wasn't Tone, then who could it be? There was only one logical explanation in her mind. There wasn't anyone behind that door that was coming to make sure she was safe and secure. If they had gained entrance to her apartment, then they were coming to kill her. She was scared and her fear blocked her ability to think clearly, it blocked her ability to reason, her ability to do anything but protect herself.

To be on the safe side, Netta grabbed her gun from underneath her pillow. She wasn't going out like she had before. She wasn't going to be victimized again. This time she would be ready for whoever or whatever happened next.

Quietly, Netta got up out the bed, moving a few feet away from the door, assuming a firing stance. She bent her knees slightly, extending her arms, holding her weapon tightly with both hands. There would be no surrender or no retreat for her. She was going to make a stand. This was it. Fleeing wasn't an option.

Netta's body was numbed by fear, still somehow she got the strength to defend herself. That turned her into the strong chick she had been before her world had been turned upside down by the beating.

Bitch, you not trying to be tough. You are tough, she told herself.

Fear overrode her caution.

She could hear the sound of footsteps approaching as the person began closing the distance between them. Netta didn't say anything, she didn't want to give up her position. She just stood there, gun in hand, aiming at the door. The idea of Black coming to get her had been suddenly solidified in her head by this unidentified person in her apartment.

"Open the door yo!.... It's..." a voice said, forcefully turning the doorknob.

She didn't get a chance to hear the rest of the sentence as two loud gunshots drowned out his words. The shots tore through the door, coming to rest inside the man's chest cavity.

Netta cautiously approached the door as she tightened her grip on the gun. She steadied her hand, preparing to finish the job. A horrified look adorned her face when she opened the door and saw what damage had been done, or better yet, whom she had done it to.

Tone lay on his back, slumped on the floor, bleeding profusely.

"I'm sorry, Tone. I.... I didn't mean to hurt you. I didn't know it was you," she cried.

Not knowing exactly what to do, Netta cupped his head in her lap as Tone went into shock, bleeding out all over the rug. The muscles in his face tightened as he struggled to talk. Swallowing blood, no words came out.

In this close proximity she could smell blood mixed with the strong scent of alcohol coming off his breathe. This led Netta to jump to the conclusion that Tone had been drinking. Maybe he was drunk and that's why he didn't respond to her call. He must have spent the day celebrating, drinking with his people before his departure the next day.

"Oh my God," Netta screamed. "What the fuck have I done to you, yo?"

Drunk or not, Tone didn't deserve this. To be shot down in his own house by the woman he loved.

Precious time slipped away as Tone's condition only worsened. From time to time he seemed to want to say something. But the best he could manage was mouthing his words. He began choking on his own blood as Netta desperately tried to comfort him. However, there was nothing she could do. She was forced to watch him die.

Quickly, his eyes took on a glassy look and his bodily movements ceased. The man once known as 'New York Tone' on the streets of Baltimore was no more.

Cursing herself, Netta looked down at Tone, motionless. She was emotionally distraught, unable to deal with the consequences of her actions. Suddenly, Netta didn't want to start a new life in Atlanta without Tone, or face the possibility of life in prison for homicide. So she grabbed the gun and placed it to her temple. Without a second thought, she pulled the trigger. The automatic gun recoiled as soon as the bullet left the chamber and it logged in her brain. Netta slumped against the wall, her brains spattering everywhere.

The crime scene she left behind looked like a lover's quarrel, possibly domestic abuse, or a murder-suicide. Who would believe that she accidentally killed her boyfriend? She couldn't believe it herself.

A swirl of bright lights and police cars greeted Black and Stink as they arrived at Netta's apartment complex. Nosey neighbors stood outside in pajamas and bathrobes as the police cordoned off the crime scene with yellow tape.

"That's the building yo?" Black asked.

Stink responded, "Yeah, yo. That's it."

A muscle twitched in Black's jaw as he was overcome with anger and confusion. He didn't know what was going on, but what he did know was he couldn't do what he came to do.

"Go see what the fuck is goin' on, yo," Black ordered.

After parking the car in a discreet area away from the commotion, Stink went and blended into the crowd in an effort to find out what was going on. After going on his fact finding mission, Stink returned to the car with some very important information to tell Black.

"You ain't gone believe this, yo," Stink commented. "Both Tone and Netta dead."

"What?" Black snapped in disbelief. "Who said that?"

"A couple of broads up there, yo," he said. "And they ain't got no reason to lie to me."

Black sat in the passenger seat, stunned by the news. He wasn't mad that Tone and Netta were dead. He was mad that their death didn't come at his hands. Black wasn't prepared for this. He shifted his eyes back to the crime scene, before he allowed it to sink in.

"Let's go, yo," he told him.

They drove out the housing complex, almost undetected. Black took one last glance at the innocent bystanders and their sympathetic looks didn't soothe him. The only thing that would make him feel better was knowing that both Tone and Netta suffered a great deal before they died.

CHAPTER 19

"Ma'am?...." the cab driver said. "....Ma'am?"

Netta awoke in a panicked state, eyes wide-open, her hands placed on her chest. Her heart was beating fast. Her breathing was labored. She was alive. Curiously, she scanned her surroundings. She snapped out of that fantasy back into reality. It had all been one bad dream. For a moment she felt certain that it had been real.

So many bad thoughts were invading her mind at once. Netta was having a hard time processing it all. The dream seemed so real, all she had now was bittersweet memories along with a gang of regrets. She shook her head in disbelief. Slowly, she began to recall what really happened. Her thoughts were becoming clearer by the second. Now that she was coherent no dream could pull her mind in a different direction.

Something bad had transpired in Baltimore many years ago. Something so terrible it caused her to flee the city in fear of her life. People had been killed in real life. That surely wasn't a dream. Netta and Tone had assassinated Black on his drug block. While making their escape, his brother Stink had caught up to their vehicle on a motorcycle and shot and killed Tone at the traffic light. Mimi was killed by Netta, in retaliation for setting up Mann to be kidnapped and killed by Black. It was a deadly domino effect where all the dominoes had fallen but one. Netta was the sole survivor.

It was just a vicious circle of violence and revenge that led to multiple murders. Yet Netta was the sole survivor. She cherished every day of her life because she knew just how easily it all could have been taken away.

Netta locked eyes with the cab driver in the mirror. The lost look in her eyes was a telltale sign that she wasn't as alert as she should have been.

"Hey, what's goin' on?" Netta replied, needing clarity.

It was then and only then that Netta realized that she had been dreaming. But it had felt so real to her. For Netta, it was impossible not to recall the dream with vividness and not obsess about what she had done to trigger it all. She cringed at a couple of mental images of the various murders. She hated the fact that her imagination was running wild at the moment. She couldn't control her thoughts, so they became an unavoidable burden. Her dream had painted a very different version of herself; Netta was very vulnerable at the moment. If she couldn't handle these demons, then she wasn't any good to anyone else, including herself.

She was thankful to still be alive. There was no way, under any circumstance, that she would kill herself. Once again her past had haunted her. It was something that she had overcome, but not something she could easily forget.

"I'm driving you to Hartsfield-Jackson International Airport for a flight back to Baltimore. We were in the middle of a conversation," the cab driver admitted, "when you must have dosed off. The only reason I woke you was because we're getting close."

"Oh, wow," Netta replied. "I'm sorry. I've had some rough nights these past few days. I guess everything must have caught up with me. It's a long story. Probably would bore you to death."

The cab driver replied, "Long stories that people don't want to talk about are never boring."

You could say that again, Netta thought.

What the cab driver had shared with Netta was real helpful. She was still shaking off the suicidal thoughts from the dream. She was still having a hard time believing that her dream wasn't real. Lately, she had been wondering how life would have turned out if Tone hadn't been murdered. She wondered how life would have been had they had a chance to raise their child together. Would she even be in this predicament now?

Netta was feeling very disappointed. She wished she could turn back the hands of time and do a few things over. She wished the man upstairs would grant her a do-over. She'd gladly take it. However, as things stood, she knew that wasn't going to happen, it was all wishful thinking. In her lifetime she had learned to live with both the disappointments and the regrets.

"At least from my point of view," the man explained, "life can be physically and emotionally draining at times. But God never places a burden on us heavier than we can bear. They say God gives his hardest battles to his toughest soldiers."

There was a long stretch of silence. Netta looked out the window as the airport slowly began to come into view.

Netta didn't bother to comment. She knew that his statement was a lie. Life had beaten her down so many times, thrown her all kinds of curve balls that she wondered just how she had survived it all.

Netta sat quietly in the backseat of the cab, lost in thought. She scrunched up her forehead as if she had a lot on her mind. She looked at the small sleeping figure sitting next to her. She was more concerned with his future than she was for her own. In the darkness of the cab her son had her undivided attention. Netta took a deep breath and sighed.

Instinctively, she pulled her son close, kissing him gently on his head. He was not just her son, but also her only friend. He was Netta's reason for being. Her boy felt like a blessing, a gift God had bestowed on her for taking her man. She looked down at her love-child, remembering the baby she had carried to term. There was an indivisible connection between them, a bond that death couldn't break. She loved her son so deeply, more so than she had ever loved his father. Just the memory of Big Tone brought her back to ten years ago. To a time when she thought that she would have him in her life forever. That was ancient history now. She would do well to forget him.

Now it was all about Anthony Thompson, Jr. That is who she was living for. Not too long ago this type of love was unfathomable. The only emotional thing that life had made her experience on a consistent basis was pain.

The boy had possessed the physical features of his deceased father, Tone. It was unbelievable just how much of his father's traits had been passed on to him. Netta began to wonder had her son's disease been genetically passed down from his father. At the moment it was too soon to know. However, what she did know was, she was headed back to

Baltimore, to the world-renowned John Hopkins Medical Center, to find out.

It was ironic how her journey, which began in Baltimore, was leading her right back home. This time under totally different circumstances. Her son had been diagnosed with a rare medical ailment. He was in need of specialized medical treatment. It was a treatment that Netta could only find from a select group of doctors in Baltimore.

Netta held out the hope that her son would receive the life saving treatment that he so desperately needed. She held out hope, because hope is all she had. However, only God's mercy and modern medicine could save the boy; the thought of which had stricken Netta with grief. She felt like she was losing everything she was trying so desperately to keep.

Maybe I deserve to pay for the things I've done in the past, but my son doesn't, she thought. *I have to do everything in my power to make sure that doesn't happen.*

She couldn't understand why all this was happening to her now. After all she had gone through. Netta wasn't the person she used to be. She had evolved so much over the years since she had left Baltimore unceremoniously. She had carved out a better life for herself and her son in Atlanta. She was now a hard working single mother, and she was proud of that. She had once been a money hungry gold digger. Netta wished she could erase parts of her past. She wished she could change some things. But to change one thing might mean to change everything. Right now, she liked the person she was and the woman she had become.

Netta was sure that once she arrived back in Baltimore she would see reminders of the fateful day that forced her exodus. She couldn't avoid that if she tried. She wasn't immune to it. Netta knew once she arrived back in Baltimore, she had to be very careful not to alert the streets to her presence. Lives had been lost over her and because of her. The act of murder was a very perilous thing. There were still people alive who loved the deceased; she knew they wouldn't forgive or forget her and they might seek retribution.

That proposition didn't stop Netta from returning home. Things were what they were. Not what she wanted them to be.

As the taxicab began slowing down, signaling their arrival at her terminal, Netta placed her head in her hands and took some deep breaths. She closed her eyes and said a silent prayer to God that none of the drama that she was previously involved in returned to haunt her.

THE END

URBAN GRIOT PUBLICATIONS
PRESENTS
NORTH
35W
Kayla
a novel by
LAMONT NELSON

★ URBAN GRIOT PUBLICATION ★
&
★ SHANNON HOLMES MEDIA ★
Presents
STREET TALES
STREET TALES

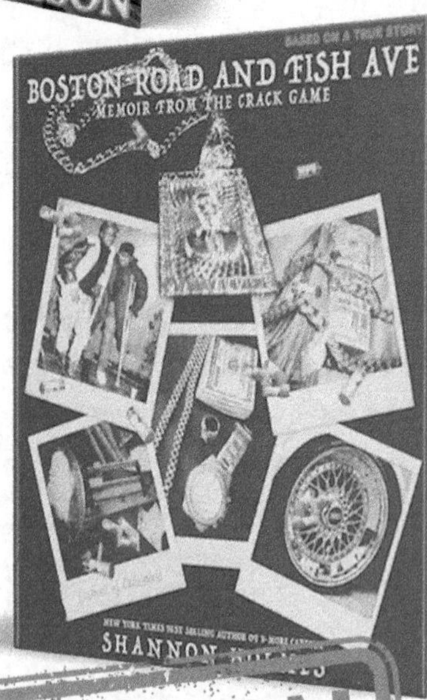
BASED ON A TRUE STORY
BOSTON ROAD AND FISH AVE
MEMOIR FROM THE CRACK GAME
SHANNON

COMING SOON